PENGUIN BOOKS

A TOUCH OF PANIC

Laurali R. Wright is the author of *A Chill Rain in January*, *Sleep While I Sing*, *Fall from Grace*, *Prized Possessions*, and the Edgar Award-winning *The Suspect* (all available in Penguin paperback). Her newest suspense novel is *Mother Love*. She lives in British Columbia.

Also by Laurali R. Wright

Laurali R. Wright

A Touch of PANIC

A KARL ALBERG MYSTERY

PENGUIN BOOKS

PENGUIN BOOKS
Published by the Penguin Group
Penguin Books USA Inc., 375 Hudson Street, New York, New York 10014, U.S.A.
Penguin Books Ltd, 27 Wrights Lane, London W8 5TZ, England
Penguin Books Australia Ltd, Ringwood, Victoria, Australia
Penguin Books Canada Ltd, 10 Alcorn Avenue,
Toronto, Ontario, Canada M4V 3B2
Penguin Books (N.Z.) Ltd, 182–190 Wairau Road, Auckland 10, New Zealand

Penguin Books Ltd, Registered Offices: Harmondsworth, Middlesex, England

First published in the United States of America by Charles Scribner's Sons, 1994
Published in Penguin Books 1995

1 3 5 7 9 10 8 6 4 2

THE LIBRARY OF CONGRESS HAS CATALOGUED THE HARDCOVER AS FOLLOWS:
Wright, Laurali, 1939–
A touch of panic: a Karl Alberg mystery/L. R. Wright.
p.   cm.
ISBN 0-684-19672-7 (hc.)
ISBN 0 14 02.3300 8 (pbk.)
1. Alberg, Karl (Fictitious character)—Fiction.
2. Police—Canada—Fiction.   I. Title.
PR9199.3.W68T68 1994   93–42386
813´.54—dc20

Printed in the United States of America
Set in Plantin

This book is for my friend
Suzanne Zwarun

Author's Note

The author wishes to acknowledge the advice and suggestions provided by Elaine Ferbey, Brian Appleby, Jim Looney, Fred Bott and Bob Halliwell ... any inaccuracies are her own. In addition, this book owes much to the continuing perceptiveness, patience and generosity of John Wright.

There is a Sunshine Coast, and its towns and villages are called by the names used here. But all the rest is fiction. The events and the characters are products of the author's imagination, and geographical and other liberties have been taken in the depiction of the town of Sechelt.

$\mathcal{W}$*hat would remain forever in memory was the chalky taste of dust in his mouth, and thunking sounds thick in his ears, and the humiliating need to pee. Underneath his terror was something telling him not to pee and not to cry, just to wait, because pretty soon it would be over. But how long was pretty soon? Could he last that long? Until pretty soon was up?*

His face was in the dust because Lester had pushed him over, and now Lester was kicking him. Instinctively, the boy curled into a ball, but when a kick landed on his back he jerked partway straight again and then Lester kicked him in the stomach.

He heard himself breathing. Every time he got kicked, his breath was shoved out of him like a gasp, and it sounded like he was crying even though he wasn't. He heard Lester breathing, too, and his breathing had the same sounds in it — gasps and panting, like he was crying. But it was just because of the hard work he was doing, kicking his brother.

The boy always remembered thinking how strange that was: that being kicked and doing the kicking could make the same sounds come out of you. And at the same time he was wondering how come he was doing any thinking at all; when you were lying in the dust with somebody kicking you, there should be nothing except hurting going on.

The hurting came later. At first, when he realized that Lester had stopped kicking him, had laughed and sauntered away, the boy was only relieved and very grateful to Lester for stopping. Then pain poured into and over him.

He opened his eyes, which he'd squeezed shut in case Lester aimed a kick at his head, and saw the grass at the edge of the path, blades of it dusty and crooked. He'd never noticed before how grass doesn't grow straight up at all but shoots off to one side or another.

Maybe something's broke, he thought, trying to sort out where the pain was coming from. It felt like it was coming from everywhere, but it couldn't be. Lester couldn't have kicked him on every single part of his body.

There was some clover growing among the blades of grass, its white flowers standing up straight and tall on sturdy stems, and the boy had never noticed this before either — that the top part of the clover flower grew upwards but the smaller bottom part of it grew downwards.

He leaned with his fists on the dirt path and pushed, scrabbling his bare knees up toward his chest. The hurting didn't get any worse, so he sat back on his haunches for a minute and then stood up.

Sunshine was poking down through the trees. The boy's heart was still going a mile a minute, and his body still felt like maybe it'd been run over by a truck, but at least he was in the normal world again. He heard some birds chirping somewhere, and saw a big fat bee hovering above the clover.

He spat dust from his mouth, wiped his hands on his shorts and picked up his lunch pail. He hadn't cried. He hadn't peed his pants.

The boy trudged along the path, which led through the woods from the schoolyard to the road that went past his family's dairy farm, three miles away. He should have taken the school bus home.

But he liked walking. It gave him time by himself, to think about stuff. And how was he supposed to know that Lester would decide to beat him up today?

Lester, who was ten, four years older than the boy, had always been pretty mean to him but he'd never knocked him over and kicked him before.

The boy wondered, as he emerged from the woods onto the shoulder of the road, if he should tell his mom. Squinting against the bright sunshine, he looked for the shimmering oasis at the end of the pavement — and there it was, straight ahead. He could walk and walk, though, and he knew he'd never get to it.

Pastures with little islands of trees spread themselves across the valley toward the mountains, which were fuzzy with heat around the edges. Everything was green or blue or purple. The sunlight was almost blinding. Any day now the strawberries would be ripe. This would be the first year he'd be picking, along with his brothers and sisters — except for Lester, who had to help out on the farm. The boy hadn't been looking forward to strawberry picking, which you had to do right out in the blazing sun, but now he did, because Lester wouldn't be there.

No, he wouldn't tell his mom, he thought, trudging along the shoulder of the road, carrying his lunch pail by its metal handle. Inside was the wax paper his sandwich had been wrapped in, neatly folded, and in the lid, an empty thermos that had held milk. By lunchtime the milk was always lukewarm, so he poured it down the sink in the boys' bathroom. The one thing in the world that could make him throw up was milk that wasn't really, really cold.

It wouldn't do any good to tell. They were always telling on Lester, all of them, and nothing ever happened. There was too much work to do. If there were marks on him where he'd gotten kicked his mom wouldn't notice, or if she did, she'd think his dad had made them.

He'd pretend nothing had happened, he thought, turning into the long, long driveway that led to the house. There were cracks in the walls, inside the house, and all the paint had worn off the outside.

And he'd try to stay out of Lester's way.

Chapter

1

$\mathcal{B}$ritish Columbia's Sunshine Coast stretches from Langdale to the village of Lund, a distance of about eighty miles. It is reached by ferry from Horseshoe Bay, a few miles northwest of Vancouver. The three largest towns on the Coast are Powell River, at the northern end; Gibsons, next door to the ferry terminal at Langdale; and Sechelt, which is roughly in the middle.

Those who live on the Sunshine Coast live with blue-edged islands tumbling across the seascape, mountains rising from dense coastal forests, and a climate that is the most congenial in Canada.

Like the rest of the world, they also live — sometimes obliviously — with a certain amount of crime.

"So are you having any fun?" said Karl Alberg. It was early morning on the last Friday of May, and he was pouring coffee into a big white mug. The telephone was wedged between his head and his shoulder so he could have both hands free.

"Fun? Fun? Hey, it's all work and no play up here," said Cassandra Mitchell.

"Do you miss me?" he said, smiling. Now he had one hand for the phone and one hand for his coffee.

"Yeah," she said. "As a matter of fact, I do."

1

"Don't sound so surprised." He noticed that he was studying the calendar, which displayed four months per sheet. He took a ballpoint pen out of his shirt pocket and printed "SAILING" through the week of July 31 to August 6.

"Do you miss me?" she asked him.

"Yeah," he said, gazing happily at the calendar.

"Good."

He hung up, still smiling, and took his coffee out to the sunporch. From here he could see down the hill into Gibsons, and the small harbour where he kept *The Sea Nymph*, his twenty-seven-foot sailboat. He almost hadn't bought her because of the damn name. He couldn't change it, either, because that would be unlucky.

It was a cloudless day, bright and summery, and Alberg had half an hour to enjoy it before he'd have to leave for work.

It was good to miss somebody. But at the same time he was actually enjoying Cassandra's absence, too. Having the place to himself again. It was, after all, a small house, and she'd brought a hell of a lot of stuff with her when she moved in with him more than eight months ago. And he had been right about the closet: it wasn't nearly big enough. They had had to buy wardrobes. They'd found a matching pair that had once belonged to an elderly couple who lived in a big old house on Garden Bay, about sixty miles up the Coast. They were nice pieces of furniture, with mirrors on the doors, big drawers in the bottom and a shelf inside, above the clothes rail. But they were colossal, and there was no room for them in the bedroom now that Cassandra's dresser and night table were in there, along with Alberg's, so one of the wardrobes was in the living room and the other took up half the sunporch.

He'd had to get a second medicine cabinet, too, which now stuck out from the bathroom wall right where a watercolor of an old Bristol Channel cutter used to hang; he had moved the watercolor to his office.

2

Carrying his coffee, he went down the steps from the sunporch into the backyard and admired his new cedar fence, which was five feet high around the back and three feet at the front. The house had new eavestroughs, too, and the front porch had been replaced, and the back one repaired. The handyman was returning next week to start constructing a small brick patio off the sunporch. The roses, cut back when the work on the fence was done, had already recovered from this trauma by sending out new shoots and a second crop of buds.

Alberg wandered over to the southwest corner of the backyard, where Cassandra had planted some vegetables before she left for her librarians' conference: tomatoes, cucumbers and two zucchini plants. Yeah, he thought, it had been an eventful spring. Lots of stuff taken care of around the house. He and Cassandra working hard at getting used to living with each other. He patted his stomach and figured he'd lost a little weight, too. He hadn't done any sailing yet, but he was going to go off up into the Gulf Islands during the first week of his holidays. By himself, because Cassandra didn't really like to sail. He complained loudly about this, but he was actually looking forward to getting out on the water alone.

Looking around the yard, he found himself wishing that it was September, because by then he and Cassandra would have been together for a year and he was hoping they'd get married, then, and buy a house together — a bigger house, spacious enough for both of them and all their things. This one was a squeeze, no question. So far they'd both been very polite and considerate, but it was hard. A sunporch was no place for an oak wardrobe.

Alberg went back into the house, rinsed out his coffee mug and drove the twenty miles from Gibsons to the Royal Canadian Mounted Police detachment in Sechelt, which was halfway between Gibsons and Earl's Cove, where ferries crossed Jervis Inlet to Powell River.

Half an hour later he was in his office, with a copy of the local paper spread on the desk in front of him. He turned to the column that dealt with court cases. It contained twenty items this week, including Robert Steven Coyne, eighteen, fined $450 for driving while disqualified; Gerald Mark Filewich, thirty-four, sentenced to three days in jail for being unlawfully at large; Cecile Edith Laliberte, thirty-one, fined $350 and given a three-month suspension of her driver's licence for driving with a blood-alcohol level over 0.08; and Paul Roger Middleton, twenty-three, who'd received a $150 fine and twelve months' probation for assault. Wow, Karl, pretty exciting stuff, thought Alberg, tossing the paper aside — and a qualm of doubt, a murky splotch of dissatisfaction, muddied the waters of his life for a moment. But it was a fleeting sensation. He told himself frequently that he preferred the Gerry Filewiches and the Paul Middletons of this world to kidnappers, rapists and killers, and he knew this to be true.

He straightened the photograph of his daughters that hung on the wall next to his desk, above the Bristol Channel cutter. It was reasonably up to date — they'd sent him a new one for Christmas. Gone to a photographer's studio, too, had it done right.

Sid Sokolowski tapped on Alberg's office door and pushed it open. "Two things. Remember the coke dealer went missing last week? Kijinski? His folks filed the report?"

"I remember."

"The boat crew's been noticing this van up on a little point where they were pretty sure no road goes. It's there one day, it's still there the next day, and on and on." The sergeant eased himself around the door and into Alberg's office. "So I sent Michaelson to check it out. There's this logging road, that's how it got in there."

"Kijinski's?"

"Yeah," said Sokolowski, nodding.

"No sign of him?"

"Uh-uh."

"Let's get an area search going," said Alberg. "And check the van real good. What's the other thing?"

Sokolowski looked blank.

"You said, 'Two things.' When you stuck your head in."

"Oh yeah. Almost forgot. We got an old fellow out there, says he wants to see the head honcho. That's what he said. 'The head honcho.'" The sergeant shook his head. "Funny old guy."

Alberg followed him into the reception area, where an elderly man sat on the bench next to the door.

"Mr. Dutton," said Isabella Harbud, the detachment's secretary-receptionist, "this is the person you want to see. Staff Sergeant Alberg, this is Reginald Dutton, Mr. Dutton, Staff Sergeant Alberg."

"Hi, Mr. Dutton," said Alberg.

"I gotta have a word with you," said Dutton, who was completely bald. He was about five feet eight, stocky, wearing grey polyester pants, a pink shirt and a dark green jacket with an old Finning Tractor emblem on the pocket, and he was leaning on a cane. Alberg figured he was in his late seventies.

"Sure," said Alberg. "Come on through into my office."

"Not on your life," said Dutton. "I want witnesses to this." He jabbed a thumb in the direction of Isabella and, looming behind her, Sid Sokolowski.

"Okay," said Alberg agreeably. "What's on your mind?"

"Rent," said Reginald Dutton. "That's what's on my mind. Rent."

Alberg looked at Isabella, who was sitting with her chin in her hand, rapt. "What's this about?" he muttered to her.

"Listen to the man," said Isabella, turning her golden eyes upon him, then back to Dutton.

"What's this about?" said Alberg again, to Reginald Dutton this time.

"You're on my land," said Dutton. His eyes, magnified by his glasses, were immense and angry. "This is my land," he said, banging his cane on the floor. "And you guys, you've never paid me a penny of rent. I'm here to evict you."

Isabella sat up with a little sigh. "Mr. Dutton lives at Shady Acres," she said, referring to Sechelt's new nursing home.

"But I used to live here," he said. "Right here." He banged the floor again. Then he looked out the window. "No. Not right here. Over there a ways, the house was. Down the hill a bit. Right here I think was the barn."

"You want a cup of coffee, Mr. Dutton?" said Alberg.

The elderly man looked at him sideways, suspicious.

"I can see we've got a lot to talk about," said Alberg. "So we might as well have a coffee. Right?"

Dutton thought about it. "I guess. Two creams, two sugars."

Alberg poured, added cream and sugar, stirred, handed it over the counter to him. "How long's it been since you lived here?"

"I lose track." Dutton sat down carefully, laid his cane along the bench next to him and held his coffee mug in both hands. "Forty years. Maybe three."

"Uh-huh."

"We're gonna need my lawyer here." Reginald Dutton drank some coffee, looking up at Alberg through his glasses, his eyes huge.

"Right," said Alberg. Through the window behind Dutton, he saw a young man wearing a white uniform moving briskly up the walk toward the detachment. Moments later the young man came through the door into the reception area. He nodded at Isabella and sat down next to Dutton.

"I've been looking all over for you, Reginald."

"Have you, now," said Reginald Dutton, sipping at his coffee.

The man in white sat back, crossing his arms. "I'll wait while you finish your coffee."

6

"And then what?"

"And then I'll take you home."

Alberg, Sokolowski and Isabella watched while Reginald Dutton raised the coffee to his mouth three more times. Then he handed the mug to the male nurse, who stood and gave it to Isabella.

Mr. Dutton struggled to his feet, leaning on his cane. "Next time I come," he said to Alberg, "I want to see a rental agreement. It's that or you're out. Definitely."

"Gotcha," said Alberg.

"Okay, Reginald," said the nurse, offering Dutton his arm, "let's go."

"I'll be back," Dutton called over his shoulder, as the nurse shepherded him through the door. "Definitely."

Gordon Murphy slapped on aftershave and looked at himself in the hotel-room mirror for reassurance — and got it. He smiled at his mirror-self. Raised an eyebrow. Made his eyes into bedroom eyes. Gave a little growl, from deep in his chest.

And then into his mind wriggled the woman he had recently buried in his rose garden. Gordon Murphy swore out loud. Quickly, he rinsed his hands, dried them and left the bathroom.

What the hell's happening to me? he said to himself, striding restlessly to the window, looking out at the mountains encircling the resort village of Whistler, which was an hour's drive north of Horseshoe Bay.

But he knew what was happening. He just didn't want to admit it. He was flirting with darkness again, with the bottomless black depths of depression. He knew why, too. And he knew what must happen to prevent his falling in and drowning there. But every time it was a little more difficult; every time the struggle was more intense, the possibility of failure more real and present.

He stared out at the mountains and the hotel courtyard below and tried to resuscitate his confidence.

Gordon Murphy believed that life had treated him, in the main, with unusual generosity. He considered himself physically, intellectually and emotionally more attractive than most people. His achievements were greater. The colors of his world were brighter and clearer. His sexual appetite was larger, and so was his satisfaction. He gripped the world in his two fists as if it were the flesh of a woman — he was capable of many kinds of ecstasy. But for this he paid a price, and the blackness of depression was part of it.

Decisiveness could stave it off. He'd learned a long time ago that it wasn't decisions in themselves that were important, but simply the making of them. Confronted with a crossroads, progress was impossible until one had decided which way to turn. The danger lay not in making a wrong turn: there was no such thing as a wrong turn. Danger lay in an inability to turn in any direction at all. Proceeding — regardless of the direction — was good. Not to proceed — that was bad.

Gordon stood at his hotel-room window and felt himself to be stalled. Hesitant. Not proceeding.

He forced himself to pick up his briefcase and the key to his room. He walked to the door, opened it and went through into the hall. He locked the door, slipped the key into his jacket pocket and headed for the elevator.

The afternoon session didn't start for another hour. He found a bar and ordered a vodka martini.

There were certain hypotheses for which no proof was needed, no corroboration sought. They were instantly, instinctively accepted — no, recognized — as truths. And one of these, Gordon believed, was the concept that the purpose of love was to draw together two incomplete people who then became a whole. Plato had said this. (Well, he had had Aristophanes say it.) Gordon Murphy had known the truth of it absolutely, the first time he heard it. He wasn't convinced that it applied to everybody on earth. Or that everyone to whom it did apply would actually find his correct other half. But he did know that it was true of him, and that his quest would eventually be triumphant.

Ever since his fortieth birthday, his whole life had been focussed on finding that individual, his true love. He knew that when he found her they would create heaven on earth, and all things would be possible. Several times — four times — he thought he had found her. Each time he'd been wrong. He'd had to live with some fairly dreadful consequences, as a result of these several misapprehensions of character.

"Shall I run a tab, sir?" said the waiter as he set down Gordon's drink on a coaster.

"No," said Gordon, pulling out his wallet.

And now, suddenly, time was running out. He'd looked up one day, just a few months ago, and found that he was fifty years old. Not that he looked it. He knew he looked good, and a lot younger than fifty. Nevertheless, that's what he was. Fifty. There was absolutely no more time to waste.

On occasion, recently, doubt and irresolution had slithered into his mind. But mostly he kept the faith and was steadfast. There would be little point in having other halves unless predestination could be counted upon to make sure that at least a selected few actually did find one another.

Gordon looked down at the table — round, shiny, dark and glowing — and his life spread itself before him there, spread itself upon the table like a hand of cards and, yes, there was order in it, and purpose, and a great deal of progress had been made. Sure, he'd made mistakes — four of them. But he had learned from every one, and that was the important thing: to learn, to use every experience as a springboard to get you closer to where you wanted to be.

He picked up his martini and drank, and over the rim of the glass he caught the eye of an acquaintance who was sitting with several other people on the other side of the room. He set down the glass, nodded at her, searching his memory for her name — Mary Lou Hildebrand, that was it.

Sometimes he wondered if all four women had in fact been wrong. What if one of them had been right? And she had tricked him into believing that she was wrong?

But the right woman wouldn't have tried to trick him, would she?

Unless it had been some kind of test.

Ah, he thought impatiently, there was no profit in this kind of thinking. He knew damn well every single one of them had been wrong for him. He'd been too eager, that was the problem. Too keen to find her. He'd let his zealousness cloud his judgment.

He had to get organized again. Get busy, get looking, mount the search again. Join things. Advertise. Christ knows, he thought, the world is full of women. Even if he restricted his pursuit to B.C.'s Lower Mainland he knew he'd find somebody.

But this time, she *had* to be the right one.

Gordon Murphy finished his martini, picked up his briefcase and slid out from behind the table. On his way to the door he passed Mary Lou Hildebrand's table and stopped to say hello. She introduced him to her friends, none of whom he knew. When she got to the last one, the woman whose back had been to him as he drank his martini, Gordon's easy poise deserted him.

"And this is Cassandra Mitchell," said Mary Lou.

Gordon Murphy stared at her, dumbfounded.

"Everybody," Mary Lou was saying, "meet Gordon Murphy. Gordon's with the School of Library Science at U.B.C."

Her short dark hair, shot through with silver, fell around her face in soft little waves. Her skin was the color of cream.

Gordon Murphy took her hand, smiling. He had recognized her instantly. He always did. "How do you do?" he asked, softly, slowly.

The look of her surprised him. She was in her forties, and adorably plump. He had expected her to be younger. He had expected her to be slender and lithe, like the others.

"How do you do?" said Cassandra Mitchell.

Ah Christ, what a beautiful name.... Of course she was different than the others. She *had* to be different; after all, *they'd* been *wrong*.

"Cassandra is the librarian in Sechelt," said Mary Lou.

He felt a gentle tugging, and realized that he was still holding her hand. He laughed, and released it.

God, the joy in his voice!

The joy in his heart!

That evening, back in Sechelt, it occurred to Helen Mitchell out of the blue, like a migraine headache or an attack of the dreaded lergy, that the room in which she now sat watching television was very likely the last room she would ever live in. Now there's a cheery observation, she thought, gazing around from her brown tweed easy chair.

Helen Mitchell was fully dressed, wearing comfortable navy slacks, a blouse with a flowered pattern and an Irish fisherman's cardigan. On her feet she wore knee-highs and a pair of sturdy slip-on walking shoes.

She was seventy-six years old. She had a shiny helmet of grey hair, a proud bearing, excellent vision, reasonably good digestion and only partial dentures. She did have a bad heart, however, which is why she had made the decision some months earlier to move out of Golden Arms, where she had been virtually on her own, and into Shady Acres.

She probably wouldn't die here, though, she thought, eyeing the bed — they'd ship her off to the hospital to do that.

Sometimes she was able to believe that it would be years before she had to worry about dying. Except for her heart, her health was excellent. And she retained a firm grip on each of her several wits; she had interests, friends.... Occasionally

11

she tried to pretend that Shady Acres was an apartment hotel somewhere in Europe, a modern-day equivalent of the place where Simone de Beauvoir and Jean-Paul Sartre had lived, on separate floors. This was a stretch, though, even for Helen Mitchell's imagination.

There was a knock on her door, and one of the night nurses peeked her head in.

Helen found this more than a little irritating. She was a woman who cherished her privacy. But she would never have moved in here if she hadn't also recognized her need for the attentiveness of a professional nursing staff: she really didn't want to be found dead on the floor one morning. So she had to put up with people tapping on her door and immediately opening it. She usually tried to respond instantly to their knocks, calling out "Come in!" before they had a chance to do so without her permission. Some of them had cottoned on to this and would wait that extra second or two, but others hadn't noticed or didn't care or couldn't distinguish sufficiently among the residents to see that if it weren't for the weakness of her heart and the disappointment that was her daughter Cassandra, Helen Mitchell wouldn't be in Shady Acres at all.

The night nurse entered wearing a smile and bearing a small tray on which sat a paper cup and a glass of juice. "Pineapple, right?" she said, advancing toward Helen, whose easy chair was positioned next to the shallow bay window.

"I hope you don't think I'm going to take that now," said Helen to the nurse, who shook her head, still smiling.

"You take it whenever you like, Mrs. Mitchell. I have to give it to you now, though, because I'm about to go off my shift."

Sleeping pills doled out at 8 p.m. for reasons bureaucratic, thought Helen bitterly. When the nurse had left she let her head sink back and admitted to weariness. It was extremely taxing, living in this place.

She had to acknowledge, though, that it could have been worse. It was a new building, there was no chipped paint yet, no scraped doorjambs, nothing was worn or broken. And she liked sitting next to her ground-floor window and looking out onto the well-tended perennial bed beneath it, and the stretch of lawn beyond that, and the other wing of Shady Acres across the way.

Her room was comfortably large. It wasn't a great deal smaller than her two-room accommodation at Golden Arms had been. She didn't have a kitchen here, but she'd been allowed a small refrigerator — she'd wanted a hotplate as well, but the management had stood firm. They didn't lock their doors, at Shady Acres, and what if somebody else should come in while she was out, she'd been told reprovingly, somebody less mentally fortunate than she, somebody who might play around with the hotplate and set the place on fire? But at least she had the fridge, where she kept juice and bottled water and fruit and an occasional bottle of white wine. She probably wasn't supposed to have wine. Perhaps they'd even said so when she first moved in. If they had, she must have decided not to hear them.

She also had her television set, with cable service, and her own telephone, and bookcases, and another armchair for visitors, and a tiny coffee table. And although the food wasn't particularly wonderful, it was adequate. Helen Mitchell had never enjoyed cooking. She was satisfied to have someone else prepare her meals. She had gathered together a small group of women to share her table in the dining room, women who while not precisely kindred spirits were at least still fully aware of what was going on around them.

She hated the fact that the bathroom was equipped for a wheelchair. But it was gratifyingly spacious, and she'd prettied it up by placing an arrangement of dried roses and strawflowers on the counter, hanging a huge bright fabric calendar on the wall, and laying a rainbow-striped carpet (rubber-backed, of course) on the floor.

And in her room there were photographs of Graham and Millie and the children, her dead husband, and Cassandra.

And her own spread covered the bed.

Helen Mitchell, her head resting in her hand, watched television for another hour, as the bright spring evening emptied itself of light. Then she closed the curtains, undressed, went into the bathroom for a few minutes, and climbed into bed. She swallowed the sleeping pill with the juice and turned out the light.

It was nine o'clock.

The thief eased along the edge of the lawn next to the west wing, keeping clear of the flower beds. Few lights shone from the windows, although the front of the building was brightly illuminated.

It was a mild, pleasant night; there was no wind, and no moon rode the cloudless sky.

The thief counted the bay windows that jutted into the night and stopped at the sixth. With precision, in silence, he removed the screen and put it carefully on the grass. Then he set to work on the window.

His silhouette against the building was ethereal; he felt himself at these moments to be invisible — this was, after all, his only real defence against discovery. He worked slowly and with infinite care, untroubled by time passing, his skilfulness no longer remarkable to him. Although young, he was an experienced thief. A journeyman thief.

He slid the window slowly open.

He glanced behind him: nothing. Nobody. So he faced the window again. This was a tricky moment. The thief couldn't see into the room through its two pairs of curtains. He had no way of knowing whether its occupant might not have awakened for some reason — having suffered a sudden attack of indigestion, maybe, or felt a cool breeze as the thief pushed open the window. It was indeed a tricky, anxious moment.

He lifted himself up onto the sill and swung himself over, through the gap in the curtains and into the room.

And he heard soft snoring coming from the bed, and knew that all was well.

He pushed the window closed and stood immobile for a couple of minutes, until his vision had adjusted to the near darkness. He saw Helen Mitchell's handbag sitting in its regular spot on top of the mini-fridge and moved soundlessly across the carpeted floor toward it. He opened it, took out her wallet and looked inside: in the dim light he saw three twenties, two tens, three fives and a two. He removed a twenty and a five, closed the wallet and put it back.

He looked at the watch, the golden wedding band and the diamond engagement ring sitting on Mrs. Mitchell's bedside table and idly passed his gloved hand through the air above them, as if his were a magician's hand. But the jewellery remained where it was.

The thief tucked Helen Mitchell's twenty-five dollars into one of the pockets in the front of his jacket.

Then he moved silently to the bookcase that stood against the wall next to the dresser. He took a small flashlight from his jacket and aimed its beam across the shelves, examining Helen's selection of reading material. He reached for a book, hesitated, scanned another shelf, and finally took a paperback novel. He thrust it into a pocket and moved the books on either side to close the gap.

The thief slid the window open and peered outside, where nothing appeared to have changed. He leapt lightly down, over the flower bed and onto the grass. Then he closed the window, replaced the screen, and smoothed as best he could the earth he had disturbed.

The night, he thought, was young.

The thief zipped closed the pocket containing his loot and considered his possibilities.

15

Reginald Dutton was lying in bed, propped up on two pillows, holding the remote and staring at the television screen. He had taken off the pajamas the damn nurse had insisted he put on and was wearing boxer shorts with a blue stripe in them, a white undershirt and a pair of black socks. He'd pressed the Mute button on the remote, because although he liked to see television he didn't often like to listen to it.

Every few minutes he got up and opened the hall door and looked intently up and down. John Forster, who lived in the room two doors away, had gone out, and Reginald was waiting for him to come home. He desperately needed somebody to talk to. People were taking advantage of him all over the place, he knew it, he was sure of it — it was the only damn thing he *was* sure of.

But after a while he forgot that he was waiting for John, he could no longer remember why he was going to the door and looking up and down the hall. So he stopped doing it.

By now it was news time on the TV, and if there was one thing Reginald Dutton did not like, it was news. He turned the television from one channel to another, but they all seemed to be giving him news: people getting shot, people getting blown up, multi-vehicle traffic accidents, big storms happening God knows where... Finally he turned off the set.

He dumped his pillows on the floor and lay flat on his back with his hands at his sides, looking up at the ceiling and pretending he was in his coffin, something he did from time to time, not knowing why. Maybe he was trying to figure how he'd feel when it was the real thing. Though that didn't make any sense unless he expected to actually be aware of himself lying there in his coffin, dead. He confronted this possibility and decided it wouldn't be a hell of a lot worse than the situation he was in here and now.

He retrieved one of the pillows, pounded it a couple of times, positioned it to his liking and arranged his body for sleep. He was stiff and aching now, from having forced himself to lie flat. Or maybe from some damn disease that was killing him only he didn't know it yet.

He'd fooled the nurse again tonight, shoving the sleeping pill under his tongue until the silly twit was out of the room (backed out, she did, like always, smiling her silly smile at him), and then he'd spat the pill into his hand and flushed it down the loo. Now he was thinking that hadn't been such a good idea. Because now he couldn't sleep. He'd have to ring the damn bell and get somebody in here to give him another pill. They got you hooked on the damn things, he thought, and then you were helpless, terrifyingly sleepless without them. He was enraged to realize this, and decided he was damned if he'd ask for another one. He'd lie here the whole damn night if need be, awake and aching, with eyes like sandpaper and a heart that occasionally quailed.

Reginald flopped over in his bed. And fell immediately asleep.

Later, he wakened, suddenly. His eyes flew open. He was staring at the curtained window. He didn't know what had wakened him — had he had a dream? Had one of the damn nurses come in to spy on him as he slept? He turned onto his back, looking toward the door that led to the hall, and saw a figure standing by his dresser: that was it, all right, some damn spy nurse was in his room.

Reginald sat bolt upright in his bed. "Get outa here," he said loudly, with a fine snarl in his voice.

The figure whirled around.

Reginald noticed several things simultaneously in the dim light: the figure was not a nurse; he had something in his hand; and the top drawer of Reginald's dresser was open.

"Hey!" Reginald squawked.

And then — he could scarcely believe this — the figure turned to him, and his right hand tucked something into his pocket while he placed the index finger of his left hand over his lips. "Shhh," said the thief, and he moved swiftly to the door and was gone in a flash.

"Hey!" said Reginald. He threw back the covers and pushed himself out of bed. He tottered unsteadily to the door, opened it and went out into the hall. He saw nobody, but he yelled "Stop thief!" anyway. Then he grinned to himself. He'd always wanted to say that. "Stop! Thief!" he yelled again.

Chapter

2

*A*t about noon on Saturday, the door of the Sechelt bus station opened and a woman came out — and as soon as she saw her, little shivers of dread started plucking at Winnifred Gartner's spine. But she ignored this, and rolled open the window. "Over here," she called out. Winnifred, who was in her sixties, was tall, large and grey-haired.

The woman came toward her, carrying a worn black suitcase. "How'd you know it was me?" she said.

"You're the only stranger." Winnifred reached behind her and opened the back door. "Hope in." She was Sechelt's only female taxi driver. She called her big square cab Grey Greta.

Winnifred lived in a neighborhood a few blocks from the centre of town. Her house was covered with something that looked like tarpaper: her husband, Henry, had been preparing to install aluminum siding when he died, five years ago, and Winnifred hadn't yet gotten around to having the job finished. She'd noticed when she left home this morning that the banister was falling off the railing on the front steps, and she had to get at the windows pretty soon, too; they hadn't been washed on the outside for — it must be close to a year.

Winnifred fully intended to fix up the place, just as soon as she had time. Maybe she'd do it herself, or maybe she'd hire somebody. Every time she began giving it serious con-

19

templation, though, she abandoned the idea in case she were to be seen as giving in to Alistair. Alistair McNeil, who lived up the street from Winnifred, was an odd-jobs man, although he called himself a gardening company or some darn thing. Still, she told herself, as her passenger climbed into the back seat, people had to give themselves these little airs. Everybody did it. Even Winnifred did it, in certain aspects of her life.

"I guess you know everybody in town, don't you," said her passenger, heaving the suitcase up onto the seat next to her and pulling the door closed.

Winnifred was busy checking her out in the rearview mirror. Winnifred had been driving cab for forty years, the last thirty on the Sunshine Coast, the first ten in Vancouver, and she checked people out automatically, man or woman, made no difference. Putting aside the ominous feeling in her spine, which might or might not be relevant, she couldn't figure this woman out. She had categories for passengers — the ones she didn't know, the strangers. She didn't get many strangers. Visitors to the Sunshine Coast usually had cars.

"Not any more I don't," she said. "There was a time when I could say yeah, probably I knew just about everybody in town. But not any more "

Her name, the woman had told Winnifred's dispatcher, was Naomi Hellyer. She was in her twenties, short and slight, with a full head of hair more red than auburn, and fair skin and freckles. Her eyes were brown. There was a dimple in her chin. She sat somewhat hunched over, with her knees together and her feet splayed out to the sides, hands clasped in her lap, her handbag on the seat next to her suitcase, and she was wearing a suit, a brown-and-white checked suit, with a white top showing between the lapels of the jacket. Her handbag and her shoes were white, and Winnifred had noticed that although these had been recently cleaned, they were worn. She'd come from the ferry on the bus.

"Where to?" said Winnifred, and the woman gave her an address.

Winnifred turned and rested her arm on the back of the seat. She said, kindly, "That's only a couple of blocks away. Do you want to change your mind and walk? Save yourself the fare?"

The woman looked stricken. "I didn't know this was such a small place," she said, and she covered her face with her hands and began to cry.

Winnifred, aghast, grabbed the box of tissues from a shelf under the glove compartment. "Here," she said. But she had to nudge the woman a couple of times. "Here. Kleenex." Finally Naomi Hellyer stretched out a hand and took the box, pulled out a handful of tissues and wiped her face.

"I'll drive around a bit, should I?" said Winnifred. She didn't wait for an answer but started the motor and proceeded slowly up the street, through the town, around the block. "You okay?" she asked a few minutes later. "Feeling any better?"

The woman laughed a little and helped herself to more tissues. "Yeah, I think," she said, dabbing at her eyes. "Whew."

Winnifred decided she liked her. Her face was a tad rabbity, her eyes were bleak and swollen, the reddish hair was probably dyed. But for the moment, anyway, Winnifred liked her.

"I had to come," said her passenger, "because my kids are here."

"Uh-huh," said Winnifred, turning the corner onto Trail Avenue. To the left, a block away, lay the still blue waters of Trail Bay and off in the distance, the long, lumbering, purplish shape that was Vancouver Island.

"He threw me out," said Naomi Hellyer. "Though it shoulda been the other way around." Winnifred glanced into the rearview mirror. Her passenger was looking straight ahead, through the windshield. "And he brought the kids over here. Because his people come from here, somewhere around here, I don't know exactly where." She sniffled and blew her

21

nose. "So here I am to say what's done is done, I'm sorry, are you sorry, let's start over again and all that shit," she said with sudden bitterness.

Winnifred looked again into the mirror, and their eyes met. She studied Naomi Hellyer for a moment, thinking about the spinal warning she'd had, and about how her spine was silent now.

"Is it the right thing to do, do you think?" said her passenger.

Winnifred shrugged, negotiated the corner and drove back down the main street toward the bus depot. "Probably worth a try, I guess."

Naomi, looking out the window, said, "It sure is a small town, all right." Winnifred heard her sigh; there was a catch in her sigh, a remnant of her weeping. "Okay. Take me there, will you?"

A couple of minutes later Winnifred pulled up in front of a small white house crouched beneath towering cedar trees. The yard was covered with a sparse lawn. A screened sunporch extended across the width of the house; behind it, drawn curtains shielded the windows.

Naomi paid the fare. She forgot about tipping, but Winnifred didn't remind her, like she usually did when that happened — which was more often than people thought.

"Thanks for the Kleenex," said Naomi. She climbed out of Grey Greta, dragging her suitcase behind her.

"Here," said Winnifred handing her a card. "This is my phone number, if you ever need another cab."

She watched Naomi as she moved along the sidewalk and turned onto the walk leading to the house. Naomi stopped there and gave Winnifred a little wave — just wiggled her fingers at her, really — and Winnifred took this to mean she should drive away now, but she found she couldn't do that, not just yet. She waved back and put the cab in gear, but stayed where she was, watching.

22

Naomi climbed the steps to the sunporch. She put the suitcase down and adjusted the shoulder strap of her purse. Then she knocked on the door. A minute or so passed, and she knocked again. She glanced back at Winnifred, behind the wheel of Grey Greta. She turned to the door again, and knocked again. Waited. Knocked. Waited.

Winnifred began to feel like she was intruding upon something painfully private. She moved the cab slowly down the street, watching Naomi in the rearview mirror. And Winnifred's last sight of Naomi, the image she took home with her, and brooded upon, and fretted about, was Naomi knocking, her head bent, shoulders bowed, while a few feet away — Winnifred was almost certain she had seen this — two small, pale faces watched, impassive, from a crack between closed curtains.

"We haven't found any sign of him yet," Alberg said gently to the elderly couple who faced him that afternoon across the table in the interview room. "Just the van."

Walter Kijinski took off his baseball cap and rubbed his bald head. "It don't make no sense. What the hell would he be doing out there on a goddamn logging road? Him and that van."

His wife, Ethel, clung to his arm. Walter Kijinski was short but massive, with a thick neck, bulky thighs and a heavily muscled torso. He wore overalls with a denim shirt underneath and workboots.

"You mentioned a partner," said Alberg.

"Yeah. This was a fairly new thing. He was pretty secretive about it. Wouldn't you say, Ethel?"

She nodded. Her grey hair was tightly permed. She reminded Alberg of a bird, bright-eyed and never completely still. "He was in business with somebody, he said. With who? we'd say. But he wouldn't tell. You'll meet him, he said. When? we said. But he never said."

"What kind of business?" said Alberg.

"Don't know," said Ethel.

"How come you're asking this stuff?" said Walter, suddenly tentative. "You don't think something funny's going on, do you?"

"I don't know what to think yet," said Alberg. He stood up and ushered them out of the interview room. "I promise I'll call you," he said, steering them through the detachment and outside, down the walk to their car, "just as soon as I've got something to tell you. Anything at all."

Back inside, he checked with Sokolowski about the missing Kijinski's telephone records, which the sergeant told him would be made available on Monday or Tuesday.

"You think they really don't know what he's up to?" said Sokolowski, putting on his jacket.

"He's their youngest. And the only one who graduated from high school. They don't know, or they don't want to know." Alberg glanced at his watch. "Okay, I'm calling it a day, too." He grabbed his jacket from the hatrack in his office and yelled at Isabella to go home, then walked out into the parking lot behind the detachment. He climbed into his car, thinking about young Kijinski and Kijinski's mysterious partner. Started the motor. And found himself unable to decide what to do.

He had nobody to go home to, he realized. This felt decidedly odd. It was amazing how quickly he had become used to having somebody to go home to again.

He should go there anyway and feed his cats. But they'd wait for him, snoozing away on the bed; wouldn't even wake up until they heard him come in the door and maybe they wouldn't even budge then, except to stretch and yawn; they might wait until they heard the automatic can opener at work before they dropped to the floor and wandered into the kitchen to rub against his legs while he put food in their dish. No point in going straight home on account of the cats.

He could go to a restaurant.

He finally decided to be virtuous. He'd pick up some salad fixings and maybe a sourdough roll.

He drove into Sechelt and parked in the middle of town, then strolled through the village. He passed the library and looked through the big windows, where ordinarily he might have caught a glimpse of Cassandra — but it wasn't for long, after all, she'd be home tomorrow. He ambled past, thinking maybe he'd get a coffee at Earl's before doing his shopping. Not that he needed more coffee, he drank the stuff all day long. Maybe he'd go home, walk down the hill to the pub and have a beer before making his salad.

He spotted Sid Sokolowski at the end of the next block, talking to a mechanic at the Shell station. Alberg knew he was not the most sociable guy in the world, and he was surprised to find himself hoping that Sid might invite him home for dinner.

As he approached he saw that Elsie was there, too. The two of them and the mechanic were huddled around a bright red Chevy S10 Blazer. "Hi," said Alberg.

Elsie turned and smiled at him. "Hi, Karl. How do you like my new vehicle?" she said.

"Elsie," he said wonderingly. "A four by four. You amaze me."

"Huh," said Sid, nudging one of the tires with his foot.

"Sid doesn't like it much," said Elsie. She was animated and energetic. Alberg was mildly surprised to see that she was wearing jeans.

"Well, Sid doesn't have to drive it, does he." Alberg circled the Blazer slowly, gazing upon it with admiration.

"She's had it only two weeks and already it needs work," said her sullen husband.

"It's nothing serious, though," said the mechanic reassuringly.

"Do you know Ronnie, Karl?" said Elsie, and she introduced them. "Ronnie's the best mechanic on the Coast," she said proudly, as if she had invented him.

25

"What's the problem with it?" said Alberg.

"It's an electronic glitch," said Ronnie. He was of medium height, and as thin as a whippet. "Something in the engine management system."

"Yeah, my Olds has one of those."

"What year?"

"Ninety-two."

"Oh yeah, it'll have one, all right."

"One what?" said Elsie.

"It's an onboard computer," Ronnie explained. "It picks up signals from various sensors in the vehicle, and controls — "

"Yeah, yeah, okay," said Sid. "When can she have it back?"

"I'll get at it first thing Tuesday," said the mechanic. "How's — noon?" he said to Elsie. "That okay?"

"That's fine," she said.

Sid was already moving off toward his station wagon, parked around the corner. Since the grocery store was in that direction, Alberg followed. Elsie was still talking to the mechanic.

"Did I tell you," said Alberg, "that Cassandra's out of town?"

"No," said Sid.

"Yeah, she is."

"You know," said Sid, stopping at the wagon, fishing in his pocket for his keys, "the guy's last name is Plankton. Can you believe that?"

"Who are you talking about?"

"Him. That mechanic. Ronnie Plankton. That's nis name." He unlocked the driver's door and pulled it open, then leaned on the roof of the wagon, looking across at Alberg standing on the sidewalk.

"What's wrong with that?" said Alberg.

"Well, what kind of name is that? I mean, you can't tell if the guy's English or Portuguese or what." Alberg had long since despaired of trying to persuade the sergeant that nationality was not on its own an entirely reliable key to understanding character.

Elsie came up beside Alberg. "How's Cassandra?" she said. Sid got in the wagon, shut his door and reached over the seat to unlock the passenger side.

"Fine," said Alberg. "She's away just now — "

"Give her my best," said Elsie. She got in, waved, and Sid drove away.

"Shit," muttered Alberg, watching the station wagon move off. He headed back toward his Oldsmobile. He'd go home, walk down to the pub and have a sandwich there, with his beer.

Cassandra Mitchell rode upstairs from the convention floor late that afternoon with Mary Lou Hildebrand, who was trying to persuade her to serve on some committee or other.

"Mary Lou," said Cassandra as the elevator stopped, "no more, okay? I said I'd think about it." She stepped out onto the third floor.

"I have to know by tomorrow, Cassandra," said Mary Lou, holding the elevator door open.

"Fine, but this is still today," said Cassandra. She gave Mary Lou a wave and headed for her room. Once inside, she dumped her convention material on the desk and dropped onto the king-size bed. She hated committees.

She reached for the phone on the night table and called Karl, but there was no answer. And he refused to have an answering machine, so she couldn't even leave him a message. Where was he, anyway? But she smiled to herself, knowing that he'd be puttering on his boat or munching a hamburger down at the pub. Or, of course, he might be at work.

Cassandra ran a bath and soaked for a while, daydreaming. She and Karl were going to spend one week of vacation time separately and two weeks together. They hadn't yet decided where to go. Maybe they'd fly to San Francisco. Maybe they'd drive up into the Okanagan Valley. Cassandra was very contented, lying in the bath and thinking about Karl and the future.

When she'd dried herself she looked critically into the mirror at her middle-aged body. It was a little heavy here and there. Somewhat loose and flabby, maybe. But she liked her short hair. She wouldn't want to say that it made her look younger, exactly; it was just more flattering. Cassandra was rapidly approaching her fiftieth birthday, and was resolved to accept this with equanimity.

She had begun dressing for dinner when the phone rang. She thought it might be Karl. Or maybe Mary Lou.

"This is Gordon Murphy. We met, yesterday."

"Oh, yes," said Cassandra, mildly flustered. She remembered looking up at him as he leaned forward to shake her head. An attractive man of about her age, tall and big, like Karl, but dark-haired, greying, lithe and muscular. His grip had been warm and firm. And his smile was dazzling; she'd never seen such perfect teeth. Good god, she'd thought, staring at his mouth, maybe they aren't real. "I remember."

"Are you free for dinner?"

"No, I'm afraid I'm not," said Cassandra, watching herself in the mirror. She was holding her hairbrush, and on her face was an expression of great concentration.

"What about tomorrow?"

"Tomorrow I won't be here for dinner. I'm leaving in the afternoon."

"Then we'll have lunch together, shall we?"

Cassandra turned from the mirror. Her clothes were laid out on the bed. She was standing there in her underwear, talking to this man. "I don't know," she stammered, "really, I'm not sure — "

"I'll pick you up at your room at noon."

"Oh no," said Cassandra quickly. "That won't be necessary."

"We'll meet in the restaurant, then?"

"Yes. Well — yes, okay. All right."

"Good. Noon tomorrow. I look forward to it."

Cassandra was a convivial person who enjoyed the company of other people, enjoyed exchanging confidences with them — with friends like Phyllis Dempter and Mary Lou. Therefore it would have been natural for her to say to Mary Lou at dinner that evening, "What's with this guy Murphy, anyway?" But she didn't.

She looked around the restaurant from time to time as she ate, but didn't see him.

She had felt slightly bullied by the insistence of his invitation and wondered why she'd accepted. She also wondered, irritably, privately, as she drank carrot soup and listened to Mary Lou, who was prattling on about her committee again, why it was that the first new man to become attracted to her in years — since Roger Galbraith, in fact — had appeared only after she'd moved in with Karl.

"So what do you say, Cassandra?"

"What's the purpose of the damn committee?" she said with a sigh, surveying the arrangement of eclectic greens that made up her salad plate.

She was back in the same restaurant shortly after noon on Sunday. Gordon Murphy was already there. He stood up as she approached the table. He was wearing a light grey suit with a white shirt and a red tie with dark grey stripes. Cassandra wondered as they greeted one another what strenuous regimen he followed in order to look so ostentatiously fit. His eyes were large and dark, his mouth full-lipped and sensuous. There was a small scar at the edge of his right eyebrow.

They ordered lunch, and Gordon consulted Cassandra before selecting the wine.

His voice was low, deep and warm. It was very nice indeed, thought Cassandra smugly, to feel attracted to someone new at her advanced age.

She was at first slightly rattled in his presence, but he talked easily about a great many things, none of which had anything to do with libraries, the one thing they knew they shared. She decided he was a deft conversationalist, and a talented one, because by the end of the lunch he had discovered, and remarked upon, many things they had in common, including the fact that neither had ever been married, their love of cities — especially Vancouver, and of travelling and dancing...

"I haven't been dancing in years!" said Cassandra, delighted, suddenly confronted with happy memories that emerged mustily from the past to beckon her.

"We must go dancing," said Gordon Murphy, laughing, and he placed his warm hand gently, briefly, over hers.

Oh-oh, thought Cassandra. Oh-oh.

"That would have been lovely," she said, smiling at him, "but I'm afraid it's not possible. I'm — I'm in a relationship with someone."

He leaned back in his chair with a quizzical smile. "Now what does that mean?"

"Well, I'm — living with someone. A man. I should have said something earlier," she added quickly.

"Not at all," said Gordon Murphy. "I invited you to lunch as a colleague, as someone whom I'd like to get to know. Whether you're in a relationship does not, I assure you, matter to me in the slightest." He looked at his watch and pulled out his wallet, and laid a credit card in the small tray upon which the waiter had delivered the bill.

"I'd better get going," said Cassandra, picking up her handbag from the floor beside her chair. "I want to catch the four-thirty ferry."

Gordon Murphy stood and pulled out her chair as she rose. "Thank you for having lunch with me," he said, smiling down at her.

Yes, he was much darker than Karl, thought Cassandra. Much — darker.

"It was a pleasure," she said. "I hope we'll meet again."

"Oh, we will," said Gordon Murphy, his broad smile broadening further. "Trust me."

Chapter

3

*A*listair, the odd-jobs man, stood on the sidewalk in front of Winnifred's gap-toothed picket fence and stared across the broad expanse of barren earth toward her house. His arms were folded, his feet truculently apart. He had a little brown beard, Alistair did, and a rectangular body that was clothed in an olive garment that reminded Winnifred, peeking out at him from behind her living-room curtain, of things she might have dressed the twins in when they were toddlers, an all-of-a-piece garment with long sleeves and a zipper up the front and a little collar that was open at the neck and showed his white undershirt. On the left breast "McNeil's Garden Services" was embroidered inside an oval that was supposed to resemble a leafy tree branch but didn't because it was done in bright red stitching. Winnifred stepped out from behind the curtain and waved at Alistair, who shook his head at her, droopy-faced and critical, and turned around to go home.

He did this maybe once a month in the wintertime and as often as a couple of times a week in spring and summer.

Winnifred didn't get any complaints from anybody else about the state of her yard. It bothered only Alistair. She was on a corner lot, so she had only one real neighbor, and she knew for a fact that he was a fellow who smoked so much dope he'd probably never taken any notice of who lived next to him. On the street side, the cedar hedge had grown so tall it was impenetrable. And across the road from Winnifred lived a nice young couple with a baby and a kid about six. They kept their place looking neat as a pin, but they didn't require that the rest of the world do the same.

Winnifred sometimes went up the street to Alistair's place and stood there, hands on her hips, staring at it, tit for tat, just to shake him up a little. She'd make her face have no expression at all, and she'd aim her strong glance across the property like a searchlight, taking in every single little thing: the rhodos and the spreading juniper and the drifts of daffodils and the climbing rose and the sparkly bits of glass or whatever the hell it was that was stuck all over the stucco, which was so ugly it made Winnifred shiver. And of course the lawn. It wouldn't surprise her to see Alistair out playing golf on that front lawn one day. Sometimes she knew he was in there, peeking out at her, just like she peeked out from her front window at him, but he never revealed himself to her.

She turned from her window, now that he'd taken off up the street for home. She picked up her big denim purse and the letter she'd written to the twins the night before, and went out of the house.

She wrote the twins at least once a week.

Out on the porch, she squinted up into the sky, which was a deep blue — the color of Winnifred's eyes.

The twins had never complained about her work, which Winnifred thought was pretty special. They'd never suggested that they found it embarrassing to have a mother who drove a cab. But then their father, Henry, had been a teacher. This was a respectable, even a dignified, career, and it made up for Winnifred's.

Once she started driving a cab she'd never wanted to do anything else. She'd begun when she was at university, because it was flexibile hours and instant money. But after three or four months she was stealing time from studying and then from classes to spend more time on the job, and shortly after the Christmas break she dropped out. Never went back to school. Drove a cab in Vancouver until she met Henry, which was just past her thirtieth birthday. They'd gotten married within months. Things were getting a bit rough in the city even then, so a couple of years later Henry got a teaching job in Sechelt and they moved to the Sunshine Coast. Winnifred had gone into business almost right away.

She'd always loved her work — and she loved it even more here than she had in Vancouver. She knew a great many people in Sechelt, and in the other towns scattered along the Coast, too.

Behind the wheel of her cab, Winnifred checked her supplies: food and drink (two small bottles of fruit juice, a roast beef sandwich wrapped in foil and a small packet of oatmeal cookies); reading material (two magazines and a paperback science fiction novel); and a notebook with a pen attached, for jotting things down that she might want to tell the twins.

She glanced into her rearview mirror in time to see Alistair McNeil's olive green van passing. What a dumb thing it was, this brittle hostility that had developed between them. Sometimes when he turned up in front of her house she was tempted to stroll outside and invite him in for a drink. But she knew he'd melt off down the street at the first sign of her front door starting to open.

It had started when Henry died and Winnifred had let the place go to the dogs. Well, what the hell. Winnifred had no interest in mowing grass and pulling weeds. So she decided to find out what nature would do if left to her own devices. And she'd turned out to like it a lot. There was a bright scattering of buttercups in the middle of the yard, a flock of dandelions over there by the drug addict's place, and along the fence some flowers that had grown unbelievably tall. Her friend Valerie Pritchard had told her they were foxglove — wild foxglove. This year they'd been five feet high. And in the back grew another kind of flower Valerie had identified as lupins. The grass grew very tall in the early spring, except in the places where there was moss, but when the hot days of summer came it shrank neatly down to a short brown carpet. Winnifred was pleased with all this, and marvelled at how many hours Henry had spent out there keeping things neat when by doing nothing at all he could have had all this riotous flowering done by nature herself.

Anyway, Winnifred recalled, Alistair had ambled down the street one day with his hands in the pockets of his overalls or whatever he called them. She was sitting out on her front porch at the time, eating cherries and spitting the pits toward the middle of the lawn, wondering if some of them might take hold and start growing into trees. She saw Alistair but paid him no mind. And then he paused, right in front of her gate, and she could see that he was about to say something to her. Winnifred had squinted at him, trying to read the writing on the left side of his chest.

"I live up the block a ways," he said. "I heard about your loss."

Winnifred nodded and spat, whanging a cherry pit what must have been seven feet. That was a good one, she thought, and took another cherry from the bag that was clasped between her knees. She saw that her fingers were stained purple. So her mouth must be purple, too. She must be altogether a sight, sprawled in her lawn chair, spitting cherry pits. What must this guy think of her? she thought. Who the hell cared.

"I was wondering," he said, leaning on her gate, "if you're planning to stay here. I mean, it's a big lot. Probably too much for one person, right?" He looked back and forth across her front yard.

Winnifred looked at him blankly. "Have we met?"

"No."

36

"Well, who the hell are you?" she said.

"I'm Alistair McNeil," he said, straightening up, "of McNeil Garden Services."

Winnifred was shaking her head. "I don't need any garden services."

They'd just gotten off on the wrong foot, she thought, starting up the cab, listening intently to the motor's reassuring purr. She knew that. She was sitting there eating cherries and discharging the pits into her front garden, which had already begun to look shoddy but hadn't had time yet to become gracefully wild, and this guy comes along, and for whatever reason she had found the sight of him intolerably irritating.

"I don't need any garden services," she had said, and while he was still blathering away there at the end of her walk, right by her front gate, she'd picked up her bag of cherries and floated inside, slamming the door behind her.

They hadn't exchanged a word since. But every so often she'd see him coming up the street, and she'd hide behind her curtain, and he'd end up in front of her house with his arms folded, looking sad or outraged or disapproving; and sometimes she stayed there behind the curtain and sometimes she waved at him, but always she could feel a small grin taking over her face when she saw him there, bearded and sorrowful.

If she spotted him in town, she always honked and waved. He never knew how to react to that, and what he did depended on whether he was alone. If he was alone, he ignored her. If he was with somebody he waved back, a weak little wave accompanied by a weak little smile.

She let Grey Greta warm up while she called in.

Winnifred's "dispatcher" was Miriam Pennyworth, a middle-aged woman who ran an answering service out of her home.

"What's up?" Winnifred said to her over the car phone.

"Got three trips for you," said Miriam. "Mrs. Lakatos at ten; she'll be at the SuperValu and she says she'll have a carload of bags because her son and his wife and the kids are coming for the weekend. Mrs. Mitchell at eleven. She's got a hair appointment with Arnold — she'll need a ride back, too. And there's a Mr. Bromberg, he wants you to pick up his wife." She gave Winnifred the Brombergs' address.

"Now?" said Winnifred. "Bromberg, he's first?"

"Yeah."

"Okay, I'm on my way."

She took her time, it was such a beautiful day, ambling along the road looking at the wildflowers, the brothers and sisters of the flowers that occupied her yard, singing to herself. Eventually, about ten minutes later, she pulled up in front of a brown-shingled house where a group of small children huddled together on the porch.

"Dad, he's here," one of them shouted, as Grey Greta slowed and stopped, and behind the children a man and a woman appeared.

Winnifred, getting out of the cab, stopped, her mouth falling open. She had never in her life seen anybody so pregnant.

"My wife's going to the hospital," said the man, a less than bright looking individual who hadn't yet combed his hair today — but who could blame him, thought Winnifred, staring in dismay at his wife.

"You should've told us this was an emergency," she said, fumbling to get the back door of the cab open.

The woman was making her way awkwardly down the stairs, the children moving out of her path, and one hand gripped the railing while the other cradled her enormous belly.

"It's not an emergency," said the man, trailing after his wife. "She's just gonna have another kid."

"Oh god," said the woman, sagging. Winnifred rushed forward and caught her. The husband looked on.

"Come on, you guys," he said, to the kids, apparently satisfied that Winnifred had things under control, and he started back up the stairs.

"Hey, wait!" said Winnifred, holding onto the woman.

"Hurry," the woman whispered. "Oh god."

"Can you walk?"

"No."

"Call an ambulance!" Winnifred yelled desperately at the retreating husband.

"Hurry," said the woman.

Winnifred looked at the open door of the cab. "Holy hell," she said, and lifted the woman in her arms.

"Oh my god," said the woman.

"Hang on," said Winnifred, staggering a step toward Grey Greta.

"Too late," said the woman.

"What? What?" Winnifred looked down — in time to see the newborn child, bloody, lying upon the grass.

Two hours later she was sitting in her living room sipping tea, looking blankly out the window, living it over and over again: laying the woman upon the grass, next to the baby; barging into the house to demand blankets; covering the woman and the child; calling the ambulance; cursing out the useless husband.

She had for several minutes been convinced the child was dead, killed when he struck the ground, until it dawned on her that anything making that much noise was almost certainly alive.

"Forty years," she kept muttering to herself. "Forty years. Never had such a thing happened. Never."

She'd eventually thought to call Miriam. She couldn't do Mrs. Lakatos and she couldn't do Helen Mitchell, she told her.

When she'd drunk enough tea and relived the episode enough times, she pulled herself together and headed back out to Grey Greta.

"Okay, I finally stopped shaking," she told Miriam. "I'm on the job again."

And Miriam told her that Naomi Hellyer needed a cab.

She was standing on the sidewalk in front of the house that contained her husband and children when Winnifred got there, and her black suitcase was sitting beside her.

She picked up the suitcase, climbed in and shut the door.

"No luck, huh?" said Winnifred.

Naomi had spent the last two nights on the porch, she said. Her husband wouldn't talk to her. He wouldn't let the kids talk to her, either.

"You going back to Vancouver?"

"Not without my kids," said Naomi, breathless. "I won't go without my kids."

Winnifred thought about her spare room, which was there for the twins. I shouldn't do this, she thought, her spine ajangle.

"You can stay at my house if you like," she said. "For a couple of days, anyway."

■ ■ ■

"Come on, Lester, stop it, please, oh shit, Lester, don't — come on, I'm gonna start yelling, somebody's gonna come — "

"Nobody's gonna come, fuckhead. You're gonna die out here."

"Why me? Why is it always me? I never do anything to you, not ever."

Lester finished the last knot and pulled the bandanna from around his neck. "Because you're there, snotface." He wrapped the bandanna around the boy's mouth and tied it at the back of his neck. Lester was twelve now, and still a lot bigger and stronger than his brother.

The boy mumbled behind his gag. Lester cupped his hand behind his left ear. "Can't hear you. Gotta go."

The boy leaned back against the tree to which he was tied. It was Saturday. He was supposed to be cleaning out the henhouse. Everybody had chores to do, and nobody would notice that he was missing until the work was all done. It'd probably be Annette who set out to look for him. And she'd find him, too. But meanwhile he'd have to sit here on the damp ground tied up to this stupid tree for hours. And when he finally did get home, he'd get in trouble for not doing the henhouse. So he'd have to do that, and he wouldn't get any dinner as a punishment, unless he asked his dad for a beating instead and he didn't know if he'd be that hungry or not.

The woods were full of sounds. Birds, insects — he could get stung by a wasp or a bee, sitting here, with no hands to flap at them and no legs to run away on.

There were slithery sounds, too, made by things rubbing against ferns and crawling along the ground. The boy wasn't afraid of snakes, but he didn't like the idea of one of them creeping across his body thinking it was a log. And he wasn't afraid of raccoons, either.

But what if there was a wolf in the woods? Or a coyote? Did wolves and coyotes eat people? Maybe they'd take a chew of him to see if they liked the taste. The boy moaned into the bandanna, which felt awful in his mouth. He shoved at it with his tongue, and luckily Lester hadn't made the knot very tight, so he managed to push it out of his mouth.

He'd just gotten used to all the small- and medium-sized noises in the woods when suddenly he heard some very loud ones; something was crashing crazily through the bush.

And that was when he got really scared. Because he knew that sometimes there were bears in the bush, and if a bear came along he'd be in big trouble — he'd be dead. And it wouldn't happen fast, either. First the bear would slash at him with its claws, rip him open, right open, probably in the stomach; and then he'd reach in and swipe up big chunks of his insides while the boy watched, in agony —

Something touched his shoulder. The boy screamed.

But it was only Annette, come to rescue him.

"You've gotta tell," she said, staring down at him. But she shook her head, because she knew he wouldn't.

He continued to think about the imaginary bear as Annette untied the ropes. Only now it was Lester the bear was after. He was running through the woods with the bear at his heels. And the bear slashed at him, and big red stripes appeared down Lester's back, like they'd been put there by a giant fork.

"Come on," said his sister, hauling him to his feet. He had to stand still for a minute, leaning on the tree, until the pins and needles were gone from his legs.

In the boy's imagination, Lester fell down, shrieking.

"I'll help you with the henhouse," said Annette, who was eleven. She was fearless. But angry all the time, which often got her into trouble. "They don't know you haven't done it yet."

And the bear started eating Lester. Bit by bit. Mouthful by mouthful. Leaving his head until last. So Lester's eyes would have to watch the rest of him getting devoured.

Chapter 4

$\mathcal{I}$n 1981, Gordon Murphy won five million tax-free dollars in the 6-49 lottery. This made it possible for him to live the way he knew he'd been intended to live.

He began by purchasing a house in Shaughnessy, Vancouver's most prestigious neighborhood and one of its oldest. It wasn't large, for a Shaughnessy house. But it was Gordon Murphy's pride and joy. It sat on an acre of land, along with a single garage, a greenhouse, two terraces and a gazebo, the whole works surrounded by a five-foot stone fence.

Gordon's house had a large, modern kitchen, a formal dining room, a living room, a sitting room, a powder room and a solarium on the main floor. Upstairs was a master bedroom with en suite bathroom and dressing room, a second bathroom and three more bedrooms. And there was a small bedroom and bath in the attic, too.

It was said by those who thought they knew him that upon moving into his house Gordon Murphy had slipped easily into the role of a man with old money, a man whose work was more hobby than career. And in this observation they were more correct than they knew.

Gordon Murphy stayed in Whistler through the weekend, and drove back to Vancouver on Monday to avoid travelling when the highway was crowded.

The weather had remained fair, which was lucky: the Squamish highway offered spectacular views of sea, sky and mountains, but in bad weather it also served up floods and falling rock, frequently resulting in road closures lasting from a couple of hours to several days.

Gordon sailed along the Sea-to-Sky Highway in his chocolate brown 1991 BMW, out of the mountains surrounding Whistler, dipping and diving through deep valleys, emerging finally on the shores of Howe Sound at the town of Squamish. It was an exhilarating drive, and Gordon, exhilarated before he set out, was close to intoxicated by the time he swept into Squamish. He stopped there for lunch, and set off more sedately for the last leg of the trip, which took him generally south into Vancouver. It was midafternoon when he pulled into his driveway and opened the gate in the stone wall with the remote control.

First he unpacked. Then he took a tour.

The house was furnished with glass-topped tables and halogen lamps, leather sofas and ten-foot potted trees, art deco ornamentation and futons in the bedrooms. It had suited Julie Garcia perfectly, but Gordon, inspecting, room by room, realized that it was completely wrong for Cassandra. She would never put up with it. He began planning the necessary redecoration — but stopped himself quickly. He was a man who learned from his mistakes. Yes. He would not try to invent something for her until he knew her a great deal better than he knew her now.

He mixed himself a gin and tonic and settled in the sitting room, whose glass wall faced north, admitting copious quantities of diffident, indirect light.

Gordon had had off-and-on relationships since he was fifteen. He'd always been physically attractive to women and

44

never had any trouble getting dates. *First* dates, that is.

He came on too strong, they told him. Relax, they said. Wait, they said. Take it easy, they said. And then, No! they said.

Gordon had given up the struggle for a while. To hell with them, he'd thought, and turned for the satisfaction of his sexual needs to the discreet addresses listed under "Escort Agencies/Body Care" in the classified ads.

This was fine, until he turned forty and became obsessed with finding his other half. The perfect companion. Somebody who would look after him. Somebody to share things with, show things to, do things with. He grimaced with embarrassment, recalling Mistake Number One, and drank, and rattled the ice in his glass. Jesus.

She had caught his eye because he thought she looked a lot like Julie Andrews. Didn't sound like her, though. Didn't have an English accent, and couldn't sing. Gordon met her at the gym. He courted her slowly and respectfully. He continued going elsewhere for sex, though, so that he would be able to control his ardor when he was with her. This turned out to be a very good idea; he gave himself full marks for foresight.

But he wasn't about to take on a life partner without trying her out in bed. So finally, *finally*, they were tumbling in the sheets together. And the same damn thing happened. He grabbed her "too hard," kissed her "too roughly," penetrated her too deeply. She was insulted. She protested. He was too much of a man for her — for all of them, he thought, sipping his drink. That was the trouble.

She dumped him.

He was furious. It wasn't as if it hadn't happened before. But this, now, was serious business. He was engaged in a profoundly earnest quest. His attentions were solemn and honorable, and not to be cavalierly dismissed. He brooded for several days over how to teach the Julie Andrews lookalike a lesson.

He mailed a small foil-lined box to her at her work — she was a secretary in a downtown engineering firm. It contained kitchen garbage: apple peel, coffee grounds, the contents of an ashtray (Gordon smoked the occasional cigar). A week later he sent another parcel, this time to her home: A Frig-O-Seal container, the smallest size, packed with some of his shit.

Each parcel had a fictitious return address, but she knew who'd sent them, all right. She called, and shrieked and squawked at him. He had held the receiver away from his ear, frowning in distaste, amazed that he'd ever thought there was any resemblance between this bitch and Julie Andrews.

Well, yes, okay, he thought, finishing off his gin and tonic, so he'd made mistakes. But he had *learned* from them. He had learned to be extremely cautious. To take things extremely slowly. Until he was absolutely sure.

But it was such a complicated process, he thought. He had to dredge up equal amounts of seduction and sincerity, patience and eagerness, courtesy and coercion... he willed himself to relax.

So complicated, ah, yes... first put out the bait — which was, of course, him...

He threw his head back and let his deep sexy laughter echo through the room. You make love like a son-of-a-bitch, Gordon, he assured himself; once you put your mind to it you can hand out climaxes like candy; suck their tits and lick their clits and knead their butts and explore their mouths with your tongue.... He closed his eyes and sighed. Irresistible. That was the word for him. When he concentrated.

And out of bed? Well, there was the money, wasn't there. And the car. And his tony manners. And nobody listened more sympathetically to their chatter.

He sprawled on the sofa with his head back, eyes closed, smiling, thinking about Cassandra Mitchell.

And if all of the above was still not quite enough, there was always the house, which he would prepare just so, make ready

46

and waiting, deftly rearrange and reorder to suit her specific requirements. Whatever he determined these to be.

But four times, he reminded himself, all this hadn't been enough to achieve success.

He got up and took his empty glass to the kitchen. Four times he'd been deceived into thinking she was someone she was not.

But this one was no trickster. He smiled to himself, looking out the kitchen window at the rose garden, remembering how she'd blushed when he put his hand on top of hers. This one was as transparent as glass.

He moved upstairs to his den. He sat down at his rolltop desk, took out paper and pen, and set to work devising a strategy for the seduction of Cassandra Mitchell.

Nathan Kijinski had been missing for almost two weeks when, on Sunday morning, May 30, his body was found washed up on a beach five miles north of Sechelt.

His van was transported to Vancouver that afternoon, and Serious Crimes reported to Karl Alberg late Monday that traces of cocaine had been found in it.

Meanwhile, telephone records revealed that young Kijinski had made frequent calls, over the past three months, to a phone number in Squamish that belonged to someone called Frank Morton. Kijinski had managed to avoid arrest during his short life as a drug dealer. Morton hadn't been so lucky. His sheet consisted of several busts for trafficking and one charge of aggravated assault. He had spent a total of fifteen months behind bars.

The Squamish RCMP had been keeping a casual eye on Morton, but when at Alberg's request they sought him out Monday evening, he was nowhere to be found. A warrant was issued and his apartment searched: he had apparently packed up his clothing and personal effects and fled, which came as a surprise to his landlord. He had left behind his furniture, such as it was, a few kitchen utensils and some dirty laundry. From the condition of the food in his refrigerator it was determined that he'd left town no more than a couple of days ago.

The medical examiner reported that Kijinski had died not by drowning but as the result of blows to the head.

By Wednesday morning, there was a Canada-wide bulletin out on Morton, and Alberg had for the moment turned his mind to other matters.

"I'll be gone about an hour," he told Isabella in the reception area; he'd parked out in front today, instead of in the lot behind the detachment. Sid Sokolowski was sitting at the table that served as his desk, lost in thought.

"If it's not rude of me," said Isabella, whose long grey hair was scooped away from her face, held back by two large tortoiseshell combs, "or forward, may I ask where you're going?"

"I'm going over to the paper, to see Lou." Louie Barber was the editor/publisher of the local newspaper.

"Constable Duggin's already been there, remember?" said Isabella. She waved something in the air. "This here's his report. I was just about to put it on your desk." Barber had called in a panic early that morning to report that somebody had heaved a large rock through his plate glass window.

"I know, Isabella," said Alberg patiently. "I'm just going to say a few soothing words to the guy. Why am I explaining myself to you?" He glanced at his watch. "Besides, I want him to run a 'Police seek this man' piece on Frank Morton. And then I've got to have a word with Winnifred." He headed for the door.

"Wait a minute."

"What is it, Isabella?" he said irritably.

"You have to delegate more."

"I've been telling him that," Sokolowski said, bestirring himself from his meditation.

"Oh for Christ's sake, you two — not now," said Alberg. But Isabella stood up quickly and stepped toward him, and he

48

knew he wasn't going to get away until he'd heard her out.

"Most of the stuff that has to be done around here," she told him, "anybody can do it. But some stuff can only be done by you. And what if there's a big pile of it still sitting on your desk when your holiday time rolls around?" She stepped back, and sat down again. "I thought I better start working on you about this early."

He gazed into her tiger's eyes for a moment. "Okay," he said with a sigh. "You're right. I'll delegate."

"Good," said Sokolowski.

"But I've got to talk to Winnifred myself."

A dream had awakened Winnifred — early and suddenly — that morning. She dreamt she was driving Grey Greta along a mountain highway and turned a corner to find herself far too close to a small white car that was right behind a bus. Winnifred braked and tried to swerve, and in doing so she swerved right off the highway and off the cliff. It was a pale blue day. The earth was so far below her it looked like the view from an airplane window. She closed her eyes. She was falling rapidly, and she knew that when she landed she would die. She wondered if it would hurt. She thought, maybe I'll only be injured — but knew that this wasn't possible, that it was much too far to fall, that she was certain to be killed. She realized that the falling itself, though swift and terrifying, was also strangely pleasant, and she wondered how much longer it would last, and opened her eyes to see how much closer the earth was now — and awoke. And her body, which had believed itself to be falling, reacted violently, as if it had abruptly landed upon the bed. Winnifred was shocked. She found it profoundly upsetting that a dream could deceive her body as thoroughly as it had deceived her mind.

It was not quite six o'clock but there was no hope she'd be able to get back to sleep.

She put on a pot of coffee, which was ready by the time she was out of the shower. She poured herself a cup and made herself two pieces of toast and slathered them with peanut butter, and while she ate she added a few lines to the current letter to the twins.

When it got to be a decent hour she put the letter aside and made another call to the hospital.

"It's Winnifred Gartner," she said to the nurse in the maternity ward.

"My heaven, Winnifred," said the nurse, sounding exasperated. "He's fine, he's just fine. We told you that yesterday."

"If he's so fine, what's he doing still in the hospital?" said Winnifred, who would never as long as she lived forget the sight of that tiny infant lying on the ground, still attached to his mother by the umbilical cord.

"It's not the baby we're keeping in here so much as his mother," said the nurse, Lucille Grettinger; Winnifred took Lucille's elderly father to the seniors' indoor bowling every Wednesday.

"What's the matter with her?" said Winnifred, alarmed.

"Nothing," said Lucille. "Except she's tired. She's got four kids at home, and now a newborn, and, well, you saw the worthless entity she calls a husband. She needs a couple of days' peace and quiet."

Winnifred hung up, mollified, and turned back to her letter. "Naomi Hellyer that I told you about," she wrote, "she's still here, asked if she could stay until the end of the week so I'm hoping she'll be gone Friday. She's no trouble — out most of the day doing god knows what, none of my business — but you know me, I like to have my house to myself otherwise I'd be living in a hotel now wouldn't I. Don't know what got into me, inviting her to stay. I guess it was the sight of that baby bouncing on the grass — one thing just led to another — there's no rhyme or reason to it but then there's no rhyme or reason to most things in my opinion."

She signed the letter, put it in an envelope and printed Rollie's name there, because the last one had been for Polly, and put the envelope in the pocket of her cardigan. Next she filled up her thermos with the rest of the coffee and put her lunch into a paper bag: a packet of cookies, a chicken sandwich from the freezer compartment of the fridge, a Golden Delicious apple.

The front-door buzzer sounded.

"Winnifred," said Karl Alberg, when she opened the door. "Hi. Can I come in for a minute?"

She let him in, of course, and they sat down in her living room, which was a room filled with things made of pine — a pine sofa and two pine chairs and a big pine coffee table. The sofa and the chairs were upholstered, with big soft cushions covered in bright flowery material, so that the room was summer-filled on the greyest, rainiest days of winter.

"You better hurry up, Karl. It's getting late."

"Alistair McNeil came to the detachment the other day, Winnifred. He wanted to lay a complaint against you. Because of your house and yard."

Winnifred sat there and listened to him, because she didn't have a choice. She could tell he wasn't enjoying himself, she could tell he was embarrassed. It was a stupid situation. Karl knew it and Winnifred knew it, too. So she sat there, listening, and after a couple of minutes a wave of heat suffused her face; she hadn't felt anything like it since going through the change. It took her a second or two to realize it was a hot flash of rage and mortification.

"What can he do?" she asked Karl.

"He can't lay any charges. We told him that. This isn't a police matter. But now he's threatening to get up a petition calling your place an eyesore. And if he does that, and if he gets enough signatures, he can take it to council and ask them to make you do something about it."

Winnifred's face was beet red — she could feel it — and her heart was racing.

51

"I don't know, Winnifred," said Karl. "Maybe you want to do something, maybe not. It's up to you."

"I thank you for coming yourself in person," she said, standing up. "I know you're a busy man, and I appreciate it."

On her porch he said, "Maybe — maybe just do the siding, Winnifred." He gestured, embarrassed again, squinting at the tarpaper on her house. "You're probably losing a lot of heat here."

"I'll consider it, Karl."

She closed the door after him and leaned against it, thinking, trying to separate out her anger and put it someplace where it wouldn't get in the way of the rest of her life. But that was apparently impossible, at least for the moment.

She heard Naomi stirring in the guest room. I've got to deal with that, too, with Naomi, she thought. Whatever had gotten into her, inviting a total stranger into her house? But she better not do anything about that now. Her decision-making was out of whack, put there by that old fool Alistair McNeil.

Winnifred picked up her thermos and her lunchbag and slammed out of the house. She fired up Grey Greta and propelled her up the street, screeching to a halt in front of Alistair's house. She glowered at his front door, simmering, and for a moment she was strongly tempted to drive across the perfect front lawn and crash her taxicab right through his living-room window.

Alberg had been back in his office for about an hour, toiling away at a stack of paperwork, when Sokolowski knocked on his half-open door. "The old guy's back, Staff. Dutton."

"Shit."

"I think he's forgotten the rent business, though. Wants to report a robbery, he says."

"Can't Michaelson look after it?" Corporal Garnet ("Mike") Michaelson had recently developed a passionate interest in theft.

"I tried. But only the head honcho's good enough for this guy, remember?"

Alberg followed him into the reception area, where Reginald Dutton stood, leaning on his cane. He was clad all in white, except for a straw hat with a brim into which was tucked a small bright green feather.

"Mr. Dutton," said Alberg. "What can I do for you today?"

"I been robbed," said the elderly man. "But the damn twits over there don't believe me. I been telling them for days to call you fellas. But they just ignored me. So here I am. The silly buggers."

Alberg came around the counter and gestured to the bench. "Why don't we sit down here."

"It wasn't much," said Reginald Dutton, slowly letting himself down onto the bench. "Just a jar of loonies. Half full, I think it was. A little jar, it used to hold those pickled onions." He placed the cane across his knees and glared up at Alberg. "But it's the principle of the thing."

"Right, I understand." Alberg sat down beside him. "When did you notice it was missing?"

"I noticed it when I noticed the damn thief putting it in his pocket," said Reginald Dutton dryly.

Alberg glanced up. Sokolowski, now sitting at his desk, must have summoned Michaelson, for the corporal was standing at Isabella's shoulder, notebook in hand.

"You're getting this, are you, Mike?" said Alberg.

"I surely am, Staff," said Michaelson.

"Okay. Tell us about it, Mr. Dutton."

"I woke up in the night." He stopped, frowned. "I think it was night. Anyway, they can tell you when it was because I came out yelling 'Stop thief,' so they'll remember that all right. Woke up, saw this thief rummaging in my dresser drawers. Hollered at him." He looked at Alberg, amazement on his face. "The man winked at me or something." He shook his head. "Then he took off with my jar of loonies."

"Can you describe him?"

"I didn't see him good. It was dark. No, can't describe him."

"Okay. We'll check it out. Corporal Michaelson will want to see your room."

"Good. Fine. Not now, though." Dutton limped to the door and opened it. Leaning heavily on his cane, he picked up an object that had been leaning against the building. "I gotta do this for a half hour first," he said. "Then you can send him over."

Alberg, Isabella, Sokolowski and Michaelson watched as the old man made his way down the walk, dragging behind him, by the handle affixed to it, a piece of thick cardboard about a foot deep and two feet long. When he reached the street he held it aloft and began slowly parading back and forth in front of the detachment.

"Jesus Christ," said Alberg, staring at Reginald Dutton's sign, which read: The Mounties Owe Me Forty Years Rent.

Chapter

5

*W*innifred slept in until ten o'clock Saturday, as was her habit on weekends. She got up and wrapped herself in a robe and opened her bedroom door a crack, to see if Naomi was up yet; she wasn't.

Winnifred moved around the kitchen as quietly as possible, putting on the coffee, drinking a glass of juice.

The smell of coffee drew Naomi from the spare room.

"Here, sit down," said Winnifred. "I'm going to make you some breakfast."

"Oh, I couldn't eat anything. Not first thing in the morning."

But Winnifred went ahead and cooked her scrambled eggs and bacon and whole wheat toast, and sat down across the table from her while Naomi picked at her food.

"Now, Naomi," she said firmly, "you've got to get yourself a plan."

Naomi gave her a quick look and brushed her hair behind her ear. "I know." She'd been spending her days walking up and down the street in front of the house occupied by her husband and children, hoping for a glimpse of the kids. The only time she got one was when she saw the grandparents arrive to pick them up. The old folks would whisk the kids into a car, an old yellow Dodge Duster, ignoring Naomi, and they wouldn't let the kids talk to her, either.

"It's not fruitful, what you're doing," said Winnifred, her hands clasped on the tabletop.

"I know."

"You should see a lawyer is what you should do."

"Oh yeah," said Naomi bitterly, "and pay him with what?"

"You can get one free if you don't have any money. Legal Aid. Anyway, I'm going to call Social Services and get you an appointment."

Naomi put her elbow on the table and propped up her head with her hand.

"You need advice from somewhere," said Winnifred, "and that's what the Social Services people are there for."

Naomi dragged her fork through the scrambled eggs and speared a piece of bacon, then changed her mind and shook it back onto the plate.

"Would you please eat?" said Winnifred. "You're no good to your kids, starving yourself to death."

Naomi took a bite of eggs.

Winnifred watched her for another moment. "What happened between you two, anyhow?" she said suddenly. "Why did he throw you out?"

Naomi slipped her a stony glance.

"When you first got into my cab," said Winnifred, "you said you were going to apologize to him. Tell him you wanted to start over."

"Yeah? So?" Naomi put her fork down, tines clutching the edge of the plate, handle resting on the tabletop.

"Apologize for what?"

"Since when is this any of your business?"

Winnifred considered. Then she said, "Since you started occupying my guest room."

"I didn't ask to occupy your damn guest room," said Naomi sullenly. "It was your idea, not mine."

Winnifred sat there thinking. "And if he threw you out," she said, "then why did he turn around and move out himself?"

"I'm not responsible for the workings of Keith Hellyer's diseased mind," said Naomi. "And I really resent your tone of voice, Winnifred." Her voice quivered. "I really do. I thought — I thought you liked me."

Winnifred watched the tears fall down her face. "We'll go to Social Services," she said. "Get you some help." She put her hand on Naomi's shoulder and gave it a little squeeze. But Naomi, weeping into her paper napkin, jerked away.

Winnifred got up from the table and went into the living room, to open the drapes. As she turned to head off toward her bedroom, she glanced casually outside, and saw Alistair McNeil. He was wearing his coveralls and walking slowly up and down the sidewalk in front of her house, carrying a sign. Winnifred stared in disbelief. The sign read THIS HOUSE IS A BLIGHT on one side and ON THE LANDSCAPE OF SECHELT on the other. And there was an arrow on each side, pointing at Winnifred's house.

She rushed to her front door and threw it open. She stood on her front porch, in her dressing gown and slippers, red-faced and furious, glaring at Alistair McNeil. "You toad!" she shouted. "You worm! You hairy-faced, snarly-souled viper!"

"Sticks and stones, Mrs. Gartner," Alistair called out airily. "Sticks and stones might break my bones, but names will never hurt me."

"Right, fine, okay, you got it, sticks and stones is next!" said Winnifred, and she slammed the door. She leaned against it, a hot lump in her throat, breathing heavily.

Naomi emerged from the kitchen, her face bright with curiosity. She peered out the living-room window. "My goodness," she said, and she turned to grin at Winnifred, her good humour apparently restored.

Saturday, June 5, 1993.
Reginald Dutton is an elderly gentleman of small stature who nevertheless carries himself with a soldierly

bearing and a confidence surprising in one who can no longer claim complete possession of his mental faculties. (This is not to say that his statement should be held to be suspect. But it does somewhat cloud the issue of whether he did in fact see what he purports to have seen.)

He confirms that on the night of Friday, May 28, he was awakened from sleep by he does not know what. He immediately sat upright in his bed, from which vantage point he observed a shadowy figure busying itself with something in one of Mr. Dutton's dresser drawers.

Mr. Dutton called out. He cannot recall what he said, except that it was something in the way of an exclamation. The figure straightened quickly, and turned to face him, but since the room was in shadow, except for a small amount of moonlight leaking in, a slender frame around the window, Mr. Dutton could not distinguish facial features. He is reasonably sure that the figure was a male person. He says that this person was tall, but in comparison with Mr. Dutton himself most males would appear to him to be tall. He says the person was wearing dark pants and a dark jacket.

The person made a gesture of some sort — Mr. Dutton cannot remember what it was. The gesture was not unfriendly, he thinks; in fact, Mr. Dutton's impression was that it was meant to be conspiratorial. The person then made a swift exit into the hall. As he moved, Mr. Dutton noted a squeaking sound that he said might have been made by rubber-soled shoes on the tile floor, or was perhaps the noise that is made by leather rubbing against itself.

Mr. Dutton followed the intruder into the hall as quickly as he was able, but his advanced age, and particularly the arthritis that afflicts him, impaired his movement. By the time he had opened the door, the person had vanished.

Mr. Dutton called out, and in due course someone came to his room. He was, however, unable to convince the aide (whose name is Norma Ratcliffe, and who is approximately thirty-five years of age, stocky of build, with braided hair pinned on top of her head, a rosy complexion, and blue-green eyes) that there had been an uninvited guest in his room. Not even when Mr. Dutton searched his drawers and discovered that his jar of dollar coins was missing could Ms. Ratcliffe be persuaded that he had been robbed.

Mr. Dutton tried, unsuccessfully, many times over the next several days to convince any number of persons at Shady Acres to summon police. He finally then came in person to the detachment to make a report.

I have weighed the matter carefully and am of the opinion that the elderly gentleman did in fact see an intruder and that this intruder did in fact abscond with Mr. Dutton's loonies.

Signed, Constable Garnet (Mike) Michaelson.

The apartment above the Sniders' fish-and-chip shop was occupied by Mary Jefferson, who worked as a cashier in the SuperValu. The Sniders didn't charge much rent because the odors of fish and chips seeped through the ceiling of the shop into the apartment. But that was okay with Mary, who loved fish and chips and had them often because she was a person who stayed thin no matter what she ate.

Mary had two consuming passions. One was to own a house. She had grown up in a big family — eight kids, there were; she was somewhere in the middle. Mary had lived in a crowd all her life, until she left home. She liked living on her own so much that she doubted she would ever get married. She liked sex well enough, but figured she could have her share of that without loading herself down with a husband and kids. But with or without a husband, with or without kids, Mary Jefferson was going to have a house of her own someday, a place she could fix up just the way she wanted it. That's why she lived in a cheap apartment, so she'd have more money left over at the end of every month to stash away in her savings account. She was twenty-five now and she reckoned that by the time she was twenty-eight she ought to have saved enough for a down payment on a modest one-bedroom place, just a small place, but with special accommodation for her hobby — which was her other consuming passion. Then maybe after a while she'd fix up the house, sell it and buy something a little bit bigger, a little bit better. Every night Mary spent the time between wakefulness and sleep fortifying and embellishing assorted elements of this dream.

On Saturdays, she worked three to eleven.

She left her apartment a few minutes before three on this Saturday afternoon; the SuperValu was just up the street from the fish-and-chip shop.

The apartment was uncomfortably warm, even with the curtains closed against the sun, even with the window open, and the smell of fish and chips and the oil in which they were cooked hung in the air, almost visible.

As the hours passed, the sun moved away from the window and the temperature in the apartment became more comfortable.

By evening it was cool there, and even the odors from the shop seemed less intense.

Daylight faded, and the streetlights came on. It was dark before nine o'clock, except for the lingering glow on the western horizon, a golden streak between sea and sky.

Shortly after ten, the lock on Mary's apartment door shuddered delicately.

The apartment opened into a hallway, which had a flight of stairs at each end, one leading to the street, the other to the lane behind the building.

Inside the apartment, Mary had left no light burning. This wasn't necessary, because there was a streetlamp almost directly outside. Even the bedroom in the back of the apartment wasn't dark because of the bright lights installed out there by stores that backed onto the lane.

The living-room curtains moved slightly, dreamily, in the breeze that came through the partially open window.

The lock shuddered again, then — reluctantly, unwillingly — capitulated. The door was pushed open, slowly, softly, and the thief slid into Mary Jefferson's apartment, covert and quiet; like a shadow, or a phantom. He closed the door behind him and stood motionless for a moment. Then he carried his duffle bag swiftly to a small room between the bathroom and the bedroom.

Here a small washer and dryer sat next to one another, and in one corner was a jumble of cleaning instruments: mop, broom, window scrubber, vacuum cleaner. The thief pulled a stool from its place in another corner and stepped up on it in order to reach the top shelf of the cupboards above the washer and dryer. He carefully slid toward him a large cardboard carton and with an effort lifted it down. He stepped off the stool and put the box on top of the washer and opened the flaps. Inside, nestled in shredded newspaper, were the various parts of a brand-new telescope. It was a superior instrument — the thief had checked it out. He emptied his duffle bag onto the floor — it contained soft rags, large and small — and proceeded to quickly, deftly wrap each piece of the telescope and pack it in the bag. Then he picked up the shreds of newspaper that had fallen onto the floor and put them back in the cardboard box, refolded the flaps on the box and put it back on the shelf, replaced the stool and pulled tight the drawstrings on the duffle bag, which he slung over his shoulder.

In the living room he set the bag down for a moment while he checked Mary Jefferson's bookshelves, which sat next to her television set. Several paperback true crime books were piled neatly alongside some hardcover volumes, including *The Joy of Cooking*, *Family Medical Guide*, a dictionary, a thesaurus, *Modern English Usage* and telephone directories for Vancouver, Edmonton and Regina. The thief opted for true crime. He plucked from the middle of the pile *The Boy Next Door*, by Chris Loken, and slipped it into one of his zippered jacket pockets.

Then he glided to the door, opened it, set the lock and slipped into the hall. The door closed and locked behind him.

Chapter 6

A week later, Frank Morton turned up in Calgary.
Alberg flew out of the Vancouver airport Friday morning and was at Calgary police headquarters by midafternoon.

When Alberg told him the estimated date and time of Nathan Kijinski's death, Frank Morton thought hard and then his face brightened wonderfully. "I was at my dentist! In North Van!" he said, triumphant.

Alberg, staring at him moodily, had a feeling he was telling the truth. And sure enough, he was. Alberg called Vancouver and spoke to the dentist. Morton had spent a couple of hours there, getting a broken tooth fixed.

"I know you want to help us get the guy who did this, Frank," Alberg said. "So tell me what you know."

"I don't know nothin'." Morton was in his early thirties and looked like he hadn't shaved in a week. He hauled a package of Craven "A" and some matches out of his shirt pocket and lit up.

"I didn't tell you you could smoke."

"What, I need your permission?"

Alberg took the cigarette from him. "You were partners. Is that right?"

Morton hesitated. Then, "Yeah. Partners."

"Partners in what?"

"Just — partners. Odd jobs 'n stuff. Washin' windows." He squirmed a little on the metal chair. "Plus we were gonna start a delivery business."

"I heard you already had one." Alberg looked critically at the cigarette in his hand. He didn't have the slightest desire to smoke it. "Making deliveries to all the cokeheads from School Road to Garden Bay."

"What?" said Morton, dismayed. "Where'd ya hear that, for chrissake? What kind of person'd tell you a thing like that?"

"Frank. Don't bullshit me."

"Them days is behind me," said Morton, sounding wounded. "I put them days behind me." He shifted in his chair. He clasped his hands on the table in front of him. He was thin and pale, and his skin was freckled. His ginger hair grew in tufts, like scrub grass.

Alberg stared at him, frustrated. "Why'd you leave town, Frank?"

"Oh, I dunno. . . . ." He stared intently at the wall behind Alberg. "I got restless. I guess that's it."

"Tell me about the last time you saw your pal Nathan." Alberg tapped cigarette ash into a tin ashtray on the table.

"Can I at least have my smoke?" said Morton plaintively.

"Talk first."

Morton heaved a huge sigh. "I went over there on the ferry, I don't remember exactly what day it was. A couple of weeks ago. We were gonna, you know, discuss it, like, the partnership — "

"The delivery business."

"Yeah. And so we did, and we went for a ride in the van, and had a hamburger and a beer somewheres, I don't know where the hell we were, I wasn't driving, and I crashed on his floor overnight because he didn't tell me the last fucking ferry left at eight-thirty, and in the morning I went home. Lookit that. Lookit that smoke, it's practically burned away."

Alberg stared at him, then handed him the cigarette. "Okay, Frank. That's all for now. I think you should seriously consider your situation, though," he said, standing. "Somebody's offed your partner. Who knows?" He shrugged. "Maybe you're next."

"Yeah, well," Morton blurted, "but here I am in Calgary, and not about to go home anytime soon, you better believe that."

Alberg told the Calgary police to let Morton go. Then he pushed Morton and his dead partner Nathan out of his mind, and set off to find accommodation for the night.

He had called his daughters the previous evening and arranged to see them while he was in town. But his talk with Janey had worried him — she seemed restless, and evasive — and when he was settled in at a motel on Sixteenth Avenue, he called his ex-wife in Kelowna, wanting to discuss their elder daughter.

"For heaven's sake, Karl," said Maura, about ten minutes into the conversation. Her voice was sharp with exasperation. "What do you want of her, anyway?"

"I want her to get herself a career. I want her to have some purpose in her life. An aim."

"What makes you think she doesn't have aims and purposes?"

"I see no sign of them, Maura," he said with dignity. "Do you?"

"Of course I do. She wanted to travel, remember? So she got a job, worked for six months, saved every penny and went travelling. She's a young woman with energy, determination, many skills — you should be proud of her."

"I *am* proud of her," Alberg protested. "But that's exactly the kind of thing I'm talking about. The girl's rootless. She's almost twenty-eight years old and she hasn't decided on a goddamn career."

There was a brief silence at the other end of the line. Then, "Good-bye, Karl." And a dial tone.

Alberg stared in amazement at the receiver. "Hello? Hello?" But she was gone. He sat down on the edge of his motel-room bed, demoralized.

A few minutes later he wanted to call her back, but he was afraid he'd get the accountant on the phone, the one she'd gotten married to. He decided to call her the next morning, when she was at work.

Alberg sighed. At least he didn't have to worry about Diana, who as a junior reporter with the Calgary *Star* had apparently found her vocation.

He'd better get himself into a better frame of mind quick, he thought, because in an hour he was meeting his daughters for dinner.

He sang to himself in the shower, and that helped, and then he called Cassandra.

"What're you doing?" he said. It was six o'clock in Sechelt. "What're you having for dinner?"

"Oh god, Karl, it's Friday. Bernie was here."

Alberg laughed. "Wait. Let me guess. Chili."

"Close. Stew. And it's over eighty degrees outside."

"Freeze it," Alberg suggested.

After a moment, Cassandra laughed. "I knew there was a good reason I moved in with you."

Alberg was smiling when he hung up.

He was to meet Janey and Diana at a restaurant in southeast Calgary. Diana had given him directions. The first thing he noticed when he stepped inside was a 1951 Fiat sitting in the middle of the floor. It was overflowing with net bags full of garlic.

He was there on time, as usual, and looked around hopefully, but he was the first to arrive. Once seated, he ordered a scotch and water, put on his reading glasses and studied the menu. He decided what he'd have to eat. He decided what wine he'd order, too. Then he took off his glasses and sipped at his scotch.

There were red-and-white checked cloths on the tables, and bottles of olive oil and cans of plum tomatoes were arrayed everywhere he looked. The place was full of people having a good time. Alberg noticed that there was a patio, hung with strings of lights and baskets of flowers. He half stood and surveyed the outdoor tables, but his daughters weren't there.

Ten minutes later, he looked at his watch.

Fifteen more minutes passed.

Diana came bustling in twenty-five minutes late. She kissed his cheek, apologized profusely and sat down, smiling. She wore a sundress, her skin was golden, her newly short taffy-colored hair sprang every which way in soft curls. Alberg felt very happy, looking at her, and smiled back — and if Janey had arrived at exactly that moment, everything would have been okay. He was certain of this, mulling over the evening later, in his hotel room.

But she didn't.

Another ten bloody minutes passed. Alberg was on his second scotch, and Diana was telling him about her new job as education reporter, and he'd decided that as soon as she'd finished they were going to go ahead and order.

"Where the hell is your sister, anyway?" he said when Diana stopped to take a breath. And immediately could have kicked himself.

"You haven't even been listening," said Diana.

"I have, I was," Alberg protested, and then he saw Janey, hurrying through the restaurant door.

In she came. She looked around quickly, saw them and made her way through the tables. "Oh I'm so sorry we're late, Daniel had a rehearsal, I completely forgot." She turned and grabbed a scruffy young man who had trailed after her into the restaurant. For a second Alberg was going to protest — what on earth was she doing, manhandling a total stranger like that — but she hugged this guy's arm and thrust him

67

toward Alberg. "Dad, I'd like you to meet Daniel. Daniel, this is my dad."

"Hi," said Daniel, sticking out his hand.

Alberg got swiftly but awkwardly to his feet, his napkin falling to the floor, and shook hands with the kid, which was like taking hold of an empty glove. And they all sat down.

Alberg glanced at Diana, who studiously avoided his eye.

Daniel wore a black leather jacket, but it wasn't the thick, squeaky kind of leather favored by motorcycle enthusiasts. It was supple, and fell in soft folds from padded shoulders. The kid hadn't shaved in a couple of days. There was a gold earring in his right year. Alberg wondered hopefully if this meant he was gay — he could never remember which ear was supposed to indicate which sexual preference. The kid was wearing jeans and a yellow shirt and sat slumped back in his chair, reading the menu. "Apple juice," he said, when the waiter arrived to take drink orders from the newcomers.

"Soda water, please," said Janey. She turned to Alberg. "Daniel's a musician."

"Uh-huh," said Alberg. Great, he thought. Terrific. "What kind of a musician?"

"A good one, I hope," said Daniel.

Jesus Christ, thought Alberg.

The kid was about Janey's age. Maybe a little younger. Who the hell could tell.

It was now almost nine o'clock and Alberg was very hungry. He signalled to the waiter. "We'd like to order, please."

"Dad," said Janey reproachfully. "We just got here."

"I didn't just get here," said Alberg. "Go ahead, Diana. Order." He saw Janey reach for Daniel's hand under the table. At least he assumed it was his hand she was after. He ordered a green salad and a T-bone steak, rare. Diana said she'd have lasagna. Janey and Daniel asked for the vegetarian special. Alberg felt dispossessed.

"So tell me about your new beat," said Janey to Diana, one

hand on the tabletop, the other one Christ only knew where.

For the next several minutes Diana chattered, Janey listened and exclaimed, Daniel daydreamed, and Alberg brooded.

Eventually his salad came, and he ate it.

"How're things in Sechelt, Dad?" said Janey after a while.

"The same as ever." The waiter whisked away his salad plate and replaced it with a platter of steak, baked potato and broccoli. He saw Daniel eyeing it and looked up quickly, feeling hostile and aggressive, but the boy was looking away now, through the window at the people walking by.

Janey was wearing denim shorts and a short-sleeved checked shirt, and she was deeply tanned. Skin cancer flitted through Alberg's mind as he looked at her. "I'm sorry we aren't going to get out there this summer," she said.

What "we" did she have in mind, Alberg wondered sullenly. He had a vision of Daniel sneering at his house, scoffing at his sailboat.

"Maybe at Christmas," said Diana.

"What's the name of your band?" said Alberg then, addressing his remark to Daniel, inexplicably unable to speak his name.

The kid just looked at him.

Janey moved uneasily in her chair. "Daniel's a violinist, Dad," she said. "With the Calgary Philharmonic Orchestra."

Chapter

7

*A*lberg took the earliest possible flight home the next day and was in his office by three o'clock, staring glumly at the photograph of his daughters that hung on the wall: he wasn't quite ready to admit that his own behavior at dinner last night had left a lot to be desired.

He started looking through the pile of reports that had collected on his desk. After a while he picked up his phone. "Sid," he said wearily. "Michaelson's at it again. For Christ's sake, Sid, talk to him. If I talk to him, I may kill him."

He was still there when Norah Gibbons took a call from a man, almost incoherent with excitement, who wanted to report that a bear had bitten his toe while he was asleep on his back lawn.

"It ran away into the woods," Norah told Alberg and Sokolowski, "when the guy kicked it."

"I suppose he wants us to find it and throw it in the slammer," said Sokolowski gloomily.

"No, he lives on his own, I think he just wanted to tell somebody about it," said Norah.

Alberg left, shaking his head.

He'd planned to stop and pick up something for dinner, or maybe buy Cassandra some flowers, but once he was in the car he couldn't think of anything except getting home to her.

As soon as he walked through the door, he dropped his overnight bag on the floor. She hurried from the kitchen and he grabbed her and hugged her tight, kissed the top of her head, and realized that his foul temper had disappeared and he was smiling. He took her face gently in his hands. "Anything exciting happen while I was gone?"

"The most exciting thing that's happened since you've been gone," she said, and pulled his head toward her to kiss him, "is that you've come home."

On Monday, Mary Lou Hildebrand called Cassandra to remind her that she had agreed to serve on the librarians' association's literacy committee.

"Our first meeting is this Wednesday," said Mary Lou, and Cassandra groaned.

"Oh, come on," said Mary Lou. "Give me a break. I'm asking you to go to a few meetings, for god's sake. It'll all be over in less than three weeks. Until the fall."

Cassandra was startled to discover at the meeting on Wednesday that Gordon Murphy was on the committee.

Grace and Henry Melnick lived a couple of miles up Sechelt Inlet Road, in a house that had been designed and built for them by an architect who liked glass and a contractor fond of cedar. The Melnicks had not had anything in particular in mind and so were happy enough with the result.

A rock garden tumbled down the hillside toward the water, and rhododendrons proliferated where the grass met the woods on the other side of the house.

Inside, the most daring thing Grace had done was to hang artwork in the bathroom.

Late one sunny Friday afternoon the Melnicks were at work, as usual; they owned and operated a furniture store that somewhat to their surprise had developed into an extremely successful enterprise.

Light filtered through wooden blinds, half-open, in the master bedroom, and poured into the living room, where two walls, two storeys high, were made of glass. Henry and Grace had seen a lot of birds, involuntary kamikaze artists, strike various spots on this vast expanse of glass and plummet to the earth, where the lucky ones lay motionless only temporarily. The Melnicks didn't have a cat.

They didn't have a security system, either, and as it turned out they didn't even have very good locks on their doors. The thief got in with no trouble at all and went straight for the safe in Henry's den, which took him somewhat longer to open.

The safe was stuffed full. Henry kept meaning to either get a bigger one or move the contents to a safety deposit box in his bank. He hadn't yet decided which would be the wiser thing to do.

The thief removed things carefully, one by one, and stacked them on Henry's massive mahogany desk: a stamp collection, stock certificates, Canada Savings Bonds. Finally everything was out except a medium-sized felt bag. This the thief put into one of his capacious pockets and pulled the zipper closed. Then he refilled the safe, closed the door and spun the dial.

He moved into the living room and browsed through the modest collection of books the Mortons kept on shelves flanking the fireplace. Most of the space was taken up by a collection of Hummel figurines. The thief took a hardcover volume from a shelf near the floor. It was one of half a dozen that matched. They were dark blue, with faded fake gold lettering on the spines. The thief took *The Hunchback of Notre Dame*.

He left the house the way he'd entered it, and made sure the door locked behind him.

Cassandra had been wary of Gordon Murphy at that first meeting. She kept her distance from him and avoided meeting his eye.

But after the second meeting she decided that he'd lost whatever interest he might have had in her. He didn't stick around to go out for dinner or a drink with the others. He just busied himself with the task at hand. And although he was courteous, he was also aloof.

On the Monday afternoon after Father's Day, Winnifred pulled over to the side of the street, rolled down her window and hollered, "Naomi! Are you crazy? What the hell's gotten into you?"

Naomi Hellyer, wearing the suit in which she'd arrived in town, and the same worn white shoes, with the worn white handbag slung over her shoulder, her reddish hair glinting in the sun, looked across the street at Winnifred but didn't reply. She was walking up and down the sidewalk in front of the house where her husband and children were staying, carrying a sign that read: KEITH HELLYER IS AN UNFIT FATHER.

It had turned into some bizarre kind of fad, thought Winnifred, watching her houseguest. Soon everybody in town would be out picketing, in complaint against one person or another.

Winnifred pulled her head back inside the cab and switched off the motor, studying the house.

The curtains of the front windows were closed, as always. There was no sign of life in there. Probably he was at work, she thought, and the grandparents had come for the kids.

Winnifred glanced up and down the block. Nobody was paying any attention to Naomi — not the young woman washing her truck in the driveway, not the little kid whizzing around in an electric car, not the guy operating a weed-eater across the street. These activities were being conducted with a singular lack of energy; it had turned into a paralyzingly hot day.

Naomi had another whole week to wait before her appointment with the Social Services people. She'd have to be a lot more forthcoming with Social Services, Winnifred thought, digging a can of Diet Coke out of the bag that also contained her lunch, than she'd been with Winnifred. The Coke was warm, but at least it was wet. There had to be a reason Naomi's husband had thrown her out, thought Winnifred, mulling Naomi over in her mind. She drank her Coke, keeping an eye on Naomi, wondering about her kids. And thinking about the twins.

Naomi was limping a little bit, she noticed, in those ill-fitting shoes.

"When are you going to be done?" Winnifred yelled across the street, when she'd drained the can of Coke.

"Five o'clock," she heard Naomi say.

It was now just after two.

"I'll come by and give you a lift," Winnifred called out.

"Fine," said Naomi. She turned at the edge of the property and trudged back in the opposite direction. "'Preciate it."

The third meeting of the literacy committee was held on the campus of the University of B.C. Afterwards, Cassandra and Mary Lou went to the Varsity Grill on Tenth Avenue for a bowl of won ton soup.

"Does Gordon have a wife?" asked Cassandra casually.

"No wife," Mary Lou told her. "He was pretty serious about somebody last year, though. Or at least, so I heard. She was a lawyer, I think."

"So what happened?"

"I don't know. One of them got dumped, I guess — I don't know which one. Then I heard she moved away." She looked curiously at Cassandra. "Are you interested in Gordon? I thought you already had a fella."

"I do. No, I'm not interested. I just wondered."

"He's a millionaire, you know," said Mary Lou, bending back to her soup.

"No, I didn't. Really. Huh."

"Won a lottery. Can you believe that? He's the only person I ever met who won a lottery."

"Me, too." Cassandra scooped up some broccoli and resumed eating.

"He's good-looking," said Mary Lou. "But you know what? I actually don't like him much."

"Yes, he is good-looking," Cassandra agreed. "I don't know whether I like him or not."

Cassandra was disproportionately pleased when, at the next committee meeting, a wry observation she made to the group at large got an appreciative chuckle from Gordon.

As they filed out of the conference room he held the door open, exiting last, and smiled warmly, looking into her eyes, as she slipped past him. She wondered if he would join them for a drink. But he didn't.

At the start of what was to be their final meeting, Mary Lou insisted that everybody go out for dinner together afterwards. "And that means you too, Gordon," she said sternly.

He shrugged and smiled. "I'm all yours, Madam Chairperson," he said.

He was charming and attentive to both Mary Lou and Cassandra, and courteous and friendly to the two male members of the committee, and Cassandra realized, watching him, that she had come to like him and was going to miss seeing him.

On the last Saturday in June, Winnifred was sitting at the end of the day on her porch, drinking iced tea and watching Alistair McNeil, who was once more parading back and forth in front of her property. She was wondering what would be her punishment if she were to smash into him with her taxicab, or blow up his house while he slept, or run him through with one of the crossed swords that hung above her fireplace. The relentless heat, which persisted, was fraying her already intolerably frazzled temper and melting what was left of her goodwill, and she was seriously considering doing some heavy-duty law-breaking when her neighbor, the dope addict, burst through his front door waving his arms in the air. He was a thin, tense young man, wearing shorts that revealed white legs and bony knees and an alarmingly thin torso that looked almost collapsed in upon itself. Winnifred watched with great interest as the young man hurtled down his steps and across the grass and up to Alistair, who quickly lowered his sign, holding it in front of him as a shield.

"What's with you, man?" shouted the young fellow. "You got no life or what?"

Alistair muttered something that Winnifred couldn't hear.

"*You're* the eyesore, asshole, *you're* the eyesore on this block, the only one on the whole damn block. Go away, get outa here." He started making violent shooing gestures, jumping excitedly up and down as he did so, and his voice got higher and louder. "Fucking persecution," he yelled, "that's what it is!" He tore the sign from Alistair's hand and crashed it down upon Alistair's head.

"Huh!" said Alistair, amazed, falling to his knees and grabbing at his head.

The young man sped back into his house.

Winnifred was up and moving toward the gate. She opened it and hurried through. "Are you all right?" she said anxiously to Alistair McNeil, who was still on his knees, bowed over, clutching his head.

He didn't answer. She knelt near him. Cautiously, he prodded the top of his head with his fingertips, and looked at them. "No blood," he mumbled.

"Thank goodness," said Winnifred with relief.

He looked at her then, and blinked several times, as if trying to clear his vision — which might very well be the case, thought Winnifred, alarmed.

"Maybe you've got a concussion," she said. "How many of me can you see?"

Alistair McNeil climbed clumsily to his feet. "One too many," he said. Slowly, he reached down to pick up the sign.

Then he walked carefully away, toward his house.

Winnifred watched him for a while. Which way had he meant that? she wondered.

Inside, she poured herself some more iced tea. Then she returned to the lawn chair on the porch. Eventually she took her drink for a walk around the house and yard. Karl Alberg was probably right, she decided. Her heating bills were much higher in the winter than they ought to be. Maybe the siding — yes, maybe she ought to do herself a favor and get the siding done. But not the yard, she thought, looking at the dead grass and the weeds; the wildflowers had long since faded and died. And not the fence, either, she thought, making her way around the house and back onto the porch.

Just then Naomi arrived, truculent and resentful. "Nobody gives a shit," she said, tossing down her sign. "Nobody gives a damn shit about a guy who treats his wife and kids so bad."

Keith's neighbors had not banded together on Naomi's behalf. Keith's neighbors continued to ignore her altogether.

Winnifred went inside and washed her hands, then took things out of the fridge to make dinner.

"A cop car cruised past me today," Naomi told her indignantly, sitting at the kitchen table with her chin in her hand.

Winnifred sliced tomatoes and cucumbers, and placed them on two dinner plates alongside pieces of cold barbecued chicken she'd picked up at the SuperValu after work.

"Slowed right down, deliberately," said Naomi, "so they could stare me in the face."

This was ridiculous, thought Winnifred. The twins had called yesterday, wanting to know if Naomi was still here, and had been shocked to learn that yes, she was. Never mind, she'd told them, Monday she goes to Social Services, they'll set her up somewhere.

"Damn cops," said Naomi.

Winnifred put the plates on the table, got cutlery from the drawer and fetched the salt and pepper. "Sit down. Eat."

They pulled out chairs and sat.

"I got so fed up," said Naomi sullenly, pushing a cold chicken leg around on her plate with her fingers, "just before I came home, I broke into the damn place."

Home, thought Winnifred. She calls this home.

"You did what?" she said, dismayed.

"You heard me. I broke in. Went around the back, smashed a window, unlocked the door, went in."

"You're looking for trouble, Naomi. That's just plain stupid."

"They're gone." She looked bleakly into Winnifred's face. "Gone. There's not a sign of them. See, I been traipsing up and down there all those days for nothing."

Winnifred gazed at her for a moment. "Why don't you go home, Naomi," she said quietly. "You must have friends in Vancouver — family — people who can help you find your kids. Who can help you do it properly."

Naomi sat back and put her hands in her lap. "I'm not budging," she said, her head bent. "Not until I find my kids. And that asshole Keith. Who's got no right to have them. They shouldn't be with him. They *shouldn't*."

"Well," said Winnifred with a sigh, "I'm afraid you're going to have to find someplace else to stay. No, don't cry, Naomi," she said quickly, "it's not going to do you any good. My twins want to come to see me, I must have the room free for my twins."

A scene wrote itself quickly in Naomi's head. She rejected it with embarrassment. But nothing else presented itself, and Winnifred was preparing to get up, to leave the kitchen, to divest herself of her responsibility. So Naomi gritted her teeth, took a deep breath and fell to the floor, clasping Winnifred around the knees.

"Oh, please, please," she sobbed. "Let me stay just a few more days, oh, please, Winnifred, please, I'll sleep on the couch, or the floor, I'll be such a help to you you wouldn't believe it, please, Winnifred, please please . . ."

Winnifred reached down to pat her shoulder. Naomi lifted her face, cheeks shiny with tears, lips trembling. "Oh, Naomi," said Winnifred. "Whatever am I going to do with you?"

■ ■ ■

It was a beating like all the others. There was nothing special about it, nothing different. It wasn't any worse than any of the others, stretching back over eight years. But as it was happening, something occurred in his brain. Something firmed up in there. Something clicked on.

He was fourteen, and had not yet experienced the growth surge he was so eagerly anticipating. Lester had, of course. At almost eighteen, Lester was six feet tall, and he weighed a hundred and eighty-five pounds. He could fling his younger brother from one hand to another, and frequently did.

The important beating occurred out behind the barns. The boy was raking up manure and Lester was supposed to be helping him. He was in a real bad mood, and the boy said something to him — asked him a question, that was all: "Are you taking Karen to the prom?" Lester was about to graduate from high school.

"Who the hell else would be taking her to the prom?" said Lester. He looked sharply at his brother, and the boy's heart sank. He stopped raking and bowed his head. He listened to Lester's ranting but didn't hear what he was saying. It didn't matter what he was saying. He listened, and waited, and sure enough, Lester threw aside his rake, and then his brother's, and grabbed his brother by the shoulder and he punched him in the belly. Then he threw him to the ground and kicked at him as the boy tried to crawl out of reach of his feet, which at least were clad in sneakers instead of workboots.

The boy, crawling, acknowledged to himself that Lester was especially fond of kicking him. Which meant that in addition to

80

hating him — for whatever unknown reasons — Lester must also have contempt for him.

This was when the thing happened in his head. He stored it away, whatever it was, to think about later.

He kept trying to get to his feet, but couldn't until Lester had tired of kicking him, which took a few minutes. Then Lester stalked off, leaving his brother with the whole job of raking up the manure. But the boy didn't mind that. He pulled himself up, brushed off as much shit as he could from his jeans and T-shirt and his arms and face, and checked for injuries.

He picked up his rake and got back to work. And while he worked, he realized that he'd had a change in his attitude. But he didn't know what this signified.

After dinner, he heard Lester on the phone to Karen, talking about when he was going to pick her up: they were going to a movie in Chilliwack. His parents and Annette were out doing the milking. Rosamund and Tracy were clearing away the dinner dishes. Philip was weeding the vegetable garden and that's where the boy was supposed to be, too — he'd been on his way out the door when he heard Lester on the phone.

The boy turned and walked silently through the living room, up the stairs and into the bedroom that Lester shared with Philip. He saw Lester's car keys on top of his dresser. He picked them up, slid them into his pocket and glided back downstairs and out the front door. He went around the house, grabbed a shovel from the jumble of gardening tools lying next to the porch and headed for the henhouse.

The hens scattered when he entered, then surged around his feet; but when they realized that he hadn't brought more feed, they lost interest.

The boy dug a hole in the middle of the dirt floor of the henhouse. He dropped Lester's keys in the hole and filled it in, then joined Philip in the vegetable garden. Philip was pulling weeds among the cabbage plants. The boy started on the peas, which were growing on netting that had been strung up like a tent.

About fifteen minutes later, just as their parents and Annette were coming back to the house from the barns, Lester erupted from the house, shouting, "Where are my keys? Who took my car keys?"

Rosamund and Tracy appeared, big-eyed, in the doorway behind him.

Blank stares greeted Lester's outburst.

"Somebody took my keys!"

"Nobody took your keys," said the mother. "Who'd want your keys? You put them somewhere. That's where you'll find them."

Ronnie Plankton gazed across at his brother from the pea patch.

"Did you take them?" Lester roared, staring at him.

Ronnie shrugged.

"Have you got them?" Lester yelled at Philip.

"No," said Philip, barely glancing at him.

"Mom? Dad?" said Lester accusingly.

His father backhanded him across the side of his head. "Keep a civil tongue in your head. You're never too old to get a beating." He brushed past Lester and went into the house.

Ronnie watched, from a distance, as Lester tore apart his vehicle, and his bedroom, and his closet, in a fruitless search. Ronnie Plankton had never been so happy.

Lester eventually hot-wired his vehicle. Ronnie watched this, too, with great interest.

From then until Lester left home, one year later, Ronnie stole from him. He took cigarettes. A single sock. His watch. And then, maybe a week later, he'd replace the watch, put it back exactly where he'd found it.

He stole magazines, the ones Lester hid under his mattress. He took a love letter from Karen. Lester's favorite belt. A road map of B.C.

Lester never caught him.

Oh, he suspected him, all right. But no more than he suspected the others.

And he never caught him.

Lester didn't stop beating him up. But Ronnie found that getting beaten up didn't bother him as much. He didn't like the physical pain, of course; but the other hurt never happened again.

He never again felt the pain of powerlessness.

Chapter

8

*C*assandra Mitchell answered the phone at the library and heard, "It's Gordon Murphy, Cassandra. I'm passing through Sechelt today — may I stop in and get a tour?"

It was Monday, July 5.

Cassandra found herself scurrying around the library with a feather duster, wielding it wildly upon shelves, tables, windowsills. When it became clear that she was irritating the group of senior citizens who met every morning to read the newspapers, she came to her senses. She flung the duster upon the floor behind the counter and put on a pot of coffee.

Cassandra Mitchell was overqualified and underpaid for the job she held — but that was on paper. In real life she and the Sechelt library were an almost perfect match. When she had arrived, almost twenty years ago, it was supposed to have been a temporary move. Neither Cassandra nor her brother Graham had expected that their mother would live much longer, and Cassandra had accepted the responsibility of being the offspring who stayed nearby: their widowed mother lived in Sechelt. Now, all these years later, Cassandra was still here. Fortunately, Karl Alberg had appeared. She frequently told herself that if he hadn't, she would have been long gone by now.

She glanced at the coffee pot, which was still dripping, and checked her watch. He wouldn't be here for another hour. She took a walk through the stacks, looking for left-behind sweaters and umbrellas.

She had become extremely fond of her job, even though it was one she had never imagined for herself. Eons ago, her master's degree in library science newly hung upon the wall of her West End apartment, Cassandra had begun work as a first-level librarian at one of the larger branches of the Vancouver Public Library. Three years later she had become head of adult services. Then a summer in Europe persuaded her that there wasn't enough adventure in her life, and she decided to take a year off to live in a foreign place.

But her mother's heart condition had at that point revealed itself, and Cassandra found herself in Sechelt, B.C. instead of in Florence or Athens, in charge of a library operated by volunteers because it was too small to have any claim on tax revenues. She and her brother each had income from small trust funds set up by their maternal grandparents. Graham diverted his to Cassandra for the first several years she was in Sechelt, until the library board was finally in a position to employ a professional. Even then, though, it was officially a part-time position, and Cassandra was paid far less than if she'd still been working in Vancouver.

She found a hairbrush on the long reading table at the back of the library, and a leaky milkshake container that the janitor had managed to miss. The smell of coffee wafted toward her through the open door to her office.

She could have refused to live in Sechelt. But she didn't. She could have attached a time limit to her agreement with Graham, and in retrospect, she realized that that was what she ought to have done. Now it was probably too late to go and live in Greece or Italy because now there was also Karl.

These were not matters that preoccupied her often any more, and she was surprised to be mulling them over today. It had something to do with Gordon Murphy, she thought, lifting the hinged section in the U-shaped counter.

She looked over her shoulder toward the stacks, and then out the window, looking for his car, although it was still too soon. Winnifred Gartner's cab passed by, and two kids who should have been in school ran along the sidewalk.

Cassandra filled the watering can and tended the three Ficus benjaminas, which along with a couple of schefflera created a pleasant screen between the library and the six wide windows that stretched from the floor to the ceiling. Then she struggled to put her mind to the day's work. She had to find two more volunteers. Paula Reynolds had given her a list of possibilities, but Cassandra decided she'd better wait until she'd had her first cup of coffee before getting on the phone. Her telephone persona tended to be brisk, verging on impatient, and tact and persuasiveness were called for when attempting to recruit people to do a lot of work for no money and little appreciation.

She poured coffee into the Mountie mug Paula had given her and sat at her desk, determined not to waste any more time. She had to make up a list of agenda items for the library board meeting; work out, with Paula, a summertime reading schedule for preschool and elementary school children; find somebody vaguely artistic to do a poster promoting library activities for distribution throughout the village; organize the book sale — donations and discards; and arrange for a suggestion box, which had been Karl's idea. She would get help with some of this from today's volunteer, a woman whose intelligence and good sense Cassandra had come to rely upon.

The sun slanted through the skylight, glinting off the small metal box with a sign — FINES — taped to the lid. Cassandra looked at it curiously, as if waiting for it to reveal something. Then she frowned. What was it doing over there on the coffee machine table? She got up and picked up the box, shook it, opened it. Silver. Loonies. No paper money.

Cassandra knew Paula hadn't robbed the fines box. Paula often borrowed from it — so did Cassandra — but the money was always promptly replaced.

She got her assistant on the phone and said, "Wasn't there some paper money in the fines box?"

"Yeah," said Paula. "A twenty, a couple of tens, I think. At least one five. Yeah, sure. Why?"

"It's gone."

"Gone."

"Gone." Cassandra thought for a moment. "Maybe we're wrong. Maybe we deposited it."

"I think we'd remember, Cassandra. But have a look."

"I will." Cassandra heard the door open and looked up. Stella Boynton, the day's volunteer, had just arrived. Cassandra gave her a wave while fumbling in the desk drawer. She flipped through the pages of the deposit book. "Nope."

"Somebody's robbed us," said Paula indignantly.

"It looks like it."

The door opened again. "Gotta go," said Cassandra. It was Gordon Murphy.

He was wearing an open-necked shirt and jeans. Cassandra was slightly shocked to see him casually dressed. He had seemed so utterly at home in a suit and tie each time they'd met that she had been unable to imagine him in anything else.

Not that she'd been trying. He'd been in her mind very little, really.

She could see a tuft of greying hair on his chest. He was indeed a large man — big across the shoulders and chest — but not flabby. His waist had thickened, but there was no roll of fat there. She wondered about his legs. Cassandra liked strong, muscular legs.

"Hello, Cassandra," he said, smiling. His voice was soft, almost caressing. Two things bothered her about this. First, it was presumptuous. Second, she felt herself reacting to it in a manner she considered inappropriate. She was, after all, not a free woman.

She introduced him to Stella, who responded with a warmth Cassandra decided Gordon Murphy must be used to.

"Now," he said, still smiling, "the tour."

She showed him around; a pointless endeavor, because it was a very small library — what was to tour? And she began feeling guilty, because she was attracted to this man, there was no denying it — and she was not free to be attracted to him. It didn't matter that she and Karl weren't married, or even engaged, they were *living* together for god's sake, they had an *understanding*.

"The trouble is," she said a bit later, lifting the counter and inviting him into the staff room, "people expect just as much from a small library as they would from a big one."

"They probably get it, too, don't they?" He gestured to the computer set up on a long, cluttered table in the corner.

"Yes, almost." The computer connected the Sechelt library to more than four million books; finding any book on the data base was quick and easy. "But actually physically getting something to us takes time," she told him. "And people tend to become impatient."

The staff room, windowless and small, sunlight pouring down through the skylight, felt as cramped as a cell with Gordon Murphy filling it up. Cassandra backed toward the door. "And that's it. You've seen it all now." She had begun to doubt that Gordon Murphy really was "passing through"; how the hell do you casually "pass through" Sechelt when you had to go out of your way to get there?

As that question formed in her head, he answered it.

"It's time I left, anyway," he said. "I'm on my way up to Powell River. Meetings there tonight, and then tomorrow it's over to the Island."

Cassandra felt a surge of relief — he wouldn't be coming back this way, then — and cursed herself for her foolishness.

"It's been very good to see you," she said warmly — because she did feel warmly toward him again, now that he was leaving.

"Where's a good place to have lunch?" he said, smiling. "And would you like to join me?"

She should have said no, of course.

It was Naomi's tears that had done it. Winnifred had never been able to handle people's tears. This was probably because she didn't cry herself. Oh, tears of pain had squirted out from between her eyelashes now and again but only because of physical pain, the kind that happens when you stub your toe or bang your elbow. She'd had bad menstrual cramps in her teens but hadn't wept over them, either. It was only a certain kind of pain — sudden, intense and unexpected — that brought tears to Winnifred's eyes. And nothing else had ever made her cry. Not even losing Henry.

This was not for lack of caring, or feeling. Winnifred cared just as much as anybody, more than some, and she felt things just as deeply. The connection between emotion and weeping, however, so real and obvious in others, apparently didn't exist in Winnifred. She was as a result particularly vulnerable to other people's tears.

It bothered her, now, that this vulnerability might be preventing her from making good decisions.

Winnifred finished work at noon on Monday and as soon as she'd arrived home, and made sure Naomi wasn't on the premises, she called Della Stewart at the Ministry of Human Resources.

"I won't ask you to tell me anything you shouldn't," she began, "but I really need to know more about her, Della, what with her staying in my house and all."

"She didn't show up," said Della.

"What?"

"She never showed up, Winnifred."

"Damn."

"I was going to call you. I can give you another appointment for her but not until the week after next."

"Damn."

When she'd hung up, Winnifred sat down at her kitchen table and drummed her fingers on its Arborite surface, thinking. Then she pulled the telephone book toward her and leafed through it. Three Hellyers were listed. The middle one turned out to be Naomi's parents-in-law, who lived over by Porpoise Bay; it was the mother-in-law who answered.

"May I speak to Keith Hellyer, please," said Winnifred.

"Who wants him?" The woman spoke with some kind of English accent.

"My name wouldn't mean anything to you," said Winnifred. "Unless you use cabs, from time to time?" she added, hopefully.

"Don't do that, no."

"Oh. Well, I'm Winnifred Gartner. I live in Sechelt — "

"What do you want with our Keith?"

"The thing is — I don't know how to put this — somehow or other his wife's ended up staying here in my house, and— Hello? Hello?"

She dialled again. The line was busy. She tried again several times throughout the afternoon. Each time the line was busy or else as soon as the woman heard Winnifred's voice, she hung up.

She'd have to go out there, talk to him in person. This thought made Winnifred profoundly uneasy. She tried to think of some reason for consulting the police. Maybe if she just went to see Karl Alberg, talked it over with him, he'd have a suggestion or two.

They picked up sandwiches and bottles of juice and drove to a place on the beach. They sat side by side on a piece of driftwood and ate, and looked out at the sea, and talked again about many things.

Soon Cassandra found herself giving Gordon Murphy her history, quite literally the story of her life. He was half turned toward her, listening intently.

"And then I went to Europe for three months," she said. "That was in 1975, I guess. I loved it so much I came home determined to sell everything I owned and go off to live in a strange, exotic foreign place somewhere." She laughed. "But then my mother became ill — " She shrugged. "Oh, well."

He put a hand on her back and began massaging, gently. Cassandra let this go on for a minute, while she kept talking, and thought about his body. He was closer to her on the log than she'd realized. She smelled his aftershave and was conscious of his thigh, just inches away from hers. He reached for her now, pulled her close to him, and lifted her chin.

"No," said Cassandra, and his mouth came down upon hers.

For a second she accepted his kiss, and for perhaps a few seconds after that, she responded. He touched her breasts, gently, while he continued to kiss her, and she thought about his tongue, and touched it with her tongue. Then he removed one of his hands and she heard him undo his belt buckle and pull down the zipper of his jeans.

"No," said Cassandra, pulling her mouth away, putting her hands flat on his chest. He looked into her eyes, took hold of her head with both hands and pulled her toward him hard. Her mouth was flattened against his. She pushed at him, making sounds in her throat, but her head was held firmly. Christ, she thought — was it a bad dream? Surely — any minute now — he would stop, and she would give him holy hell.

He let go of her head and pulled her roughly off the log, onto the pebbly beach. Cassandra couldn't believe this was happening, couldn't believe that it would go on — finally did believe, and shouted something as loudly as she could. She didn't know what she'd shouted: "No!" or "Help!" or "Stop!" But something, anyway — loudly, too. But the sea was also loud, and there was nobody to hear her but Gordon Murphy.

She punched at him, desperate. He was pulling up her dress, and pulling down his jeans.

"No no no!" Tears spilled down her face. "Damn you! Damn you!"

And suddenly, he stopped.

Cassandra, her eyes tightly closed, didn't at first dare to open them. He straightened her dress. She heard his zipper close, heard him buckle his belt. She lay on the beach, becoming aware of the sharp edges of the stones under her back.

"Give me your hand," he said.

Cassandra opened her eyes. She couldn't see him clearly; the sun was behind him, his face was shadowed and featureless. His yellow shirt glared in the blinding light from the sun. She turned away, onto her hands and knees, and pulled herself upright, leaning on the driftwood. With one hand over her mouth she staggered up the slight incline to the highway, and began walking unsteadily north, toward Sechelt.

A minute or two later the chocolate brown BMW passed her, and parked. Gordon Murphy got out and came toward her. She refused to look at him. He took her face in his hands. She knocked his hands away.

"Oh, Cassandra," he said sorrowfully. "I only want to assure you — it will be so much better the next time."

Cassandra shuddered. "There will never be a next time," she said, "you son-of-a-bitch." She strode along the shoulder of the highway. Eventually the BMW passed her again, and this time it kept on going.

Winnifred heard Naomi come in.

"I got a job," said Naomi loudly, before the door was closed. "At Earl's Café & Catering. Starting next week." She joined Winnifred in the kitchen. "I used to waitress in Vancouver. I'm pretty good at it, when I want to be."

"How come you didn't keep your appointment with the Social Services people?"

Naomi shrugged. "It's better to work, isn't it? Then being on welfare?" She was leaning against the doorjamb, hugging her shoulderbag with one hand, winding her shiny hair around the fingers of the other.

"Yeah, but — your kids. They'd help you get your kids back."

"They'll be a damn sight more likely to do that if I've got a job." Naomi spoke with grim authority.

Winnifred sighed. "When do you start?"

"Next week."

"Then you can use the time between now and then," said Winnifred firmly, "to find a place of your own."

Naomi nodded, smiling a little.

"Let's go out for supper," said Winnifred, surprising herself. "To celebrate your new job."

"Sure," said Naomi, shrugging again. "If you want."

Winnifred didn't know what to think about all this. She was very glad the twins were coming soon; she needed to discuss Naomi and her situation with somebody close to her. On the surface Naomi's plan appeared to be a good, thoughtful, intelligent one: she would stay near her kids, support herself and work quietly and concentratedly to put her family back together, or at least to regain custody of her children.

What is wrong with this picture? Winnifred thought, looking intently at Naomi, who was wearing jeans and a short-sleeved blouse and sandals; her face was smooth and pale, and Winnifred thought she was a little skinnier than when she'd arrived in Sechelt.

What's wrong with it, she concluded, is that Naomi is not a thoughtful or intelligent person.

"What's going on here, Naomi?"

Naomi's eyes grew wide, and her mouth opened in surprise. She pushed her body away from the doorjamb. "Gee, Winnifred. I thought you'd be glad." Her voice was wrapped lovingly around a small tremble.

"I don't know whether to be glad or not," said Winnifred, "because I don't know what's going on."

Naomi's shoulders sagged. She looked at the floor.

"Have you got parents?" said Winnifred.

"Naturally I've got parents."

"Where are they?"

Noami glanced up. "Why do you want to know?"

"I think you should tell me about the scrape you're in."

"I'm not in any scrape." Naomi's face flushed, and her body tensed. "It's that asshole Keith's in the scrape. Not me." She whirled around and flounced off to the spare room.

Winnifred watched her go.

After a few minutes she got up. "Naomi," she said at the guest-room door. "Naomi?" She tapped lightly on the door. "There's a place just past Davis Bay, it tries to look Spanish or something. Let's go there." She waited. "The food's not Spanish. It's plain old Canadian. Okay?" She waited another minute, then pushed the door open. "How about it?" she looked in — and stood stock still, staring.

"Oh great, who taught you your manners, anyway?" said Naomi. She was in a half crouch, peering at herself in the vanity table mirror — only now she was looking angrily at Winnifred in that mirror, and Winnifred saw herself, stupefied, and Naomi, furious, bald and furious, holding her hair in her hand.

"You're not supposed to barge in on people," said Naomi. "A closed door means don't come in unless you're invited, didn't anybody ever teach you that?" She put her hair back on, and brushed it. "What are you staring at? Haven't you ever seen a wig before?"

That evening Karl, preoccupied, began complaining to Cassandra about his elder daughter, who had apparently fallen in love. Cassandra listened, making sympathetic noises.

She didn't tell him about Gordon Murphy.

It had been an experience more humiliating than frightening, she had decided. She would have been mortified to discuss it with him.

And besides, with whom would she have been discussing it, anyway: the man who loved her, or a cop? Cassandra didn't much enjoy getting involved with Alberg the cop. She couldn't get around him, or through him, to find Karl. It was as though they were too completely separate people. But she knew that they shared the same memories, the same data base, as it were — and that she was contained therein.

So she didn't tell him. She listened to him, and eventually offered the opinion that Janey was old enough to choose her own boyfriends.

And that night she clung to him, and made love to him with a tender passion, and knew that there was nothing temporary about their living arrangements.

Chapter

9

$\mathcal{W}$ednesday, July 7, 1993.

There is in the Sechelt Public Library a small metal box, kept behind the counter, from which change is dispensed to persons wishing to pay their library fines, or needing to make use of the copy machine. From this box on or about Sunday, July 4, approximately $45 was stolen.

Ms. Cassandra Mitchell, chief librarian, and her assistant Paula Reynolds, report that during the hours the library is open it would be virtually impossible for the box to be robbed. I was, with respect, doubtful about this until I was shown where the box is kept. In order for a patron to plunder the box he/she would have to lean so far over the counter as to fall on his/her face behind it, or else he/she would have to lift the hinged counter up and go in there. Since the counter is manned at all times by Ms. Mitchell, Ms. Reynolds, or one of the several volunteers who work there, this is obviously unlikely.

Ms. Mitchell assured me with asperity that the volunteers were above suspicion, as was her assistant. 'And as it was I who reported the theft,' she added, 'it's unlikely that I did the deed myself.'

As discreetly as possible, I insisted on interviewing all concerned.

The theft occurred between 3 p.m. on Saturday, July 3, at which time Ms. Reynolds opened the box to ascertain whether it contained enough money to warrant making a bank deposit (her decision was in the negative) and 11 a.m. on Monday, July 5, when Ms. Mitchell opened the box and discovered that funds were missing. Her reason for opening it at that particular moment is significant: it had been moved from its customary place behind the counter to a table in the staff room.

During most of the hours separating these two events, the library was closed.

My interviews with the staff and the volunteers succeeded only in eliminating them as suspects.

Close examination of the premises yielded no clues as to how this robbery might have been carried out.

Signed, Constable Garnet (Mike) Michaelson.

"It's for you," said Paula the following Monday morning, and Cassandra picked up the phone.

"Cassandra," he said, "it's Gordon." Warmth issued from the telephone like something wet and sticky. Cassandra couldn't believe she had ever found this warmth sexy or thought it unstudied.

She was sitting at her desk in the skylighted staff room. As she listened, incredulous, to Gordon Murphy, she was looking through the open top of the Dutch door into the library, where sunlight flooded through the windows, dappling the floor with the shadows of the fig trees.

"We made a wrong turn," he was saying, "as we headed into the next phase of our friendship. I suggest we back up and try again." He laughed, pillowy and confident. "And get things right this time."

"Your behavior was inexcusable," said Cassandra, keeping her voice low, watching the Delsey brothers, seven and ten, who were sitting in the children's section at a table loaded with books.

There was a pause, and then Gordon Murphy said, "As I said, I suggest we back up and try again."

"Not on your life," said Cassandra promptly.

The Delsey brothers, Freddie and Frank, always had a lot of difficulty deciding which books to read at the library and which to take home.

"You want to be coaxed," said Gordon, indulgent.

"I want to be left alone," said Cassandra, and hung up the phone.

She was still at her desk when he called again, an hour later. Paula was checking out Frank and Freddie Delsey's books. The boys were completely absorbed in watching her do this. Finally they lifted their eyes from the books and thanked her, took hold of the bags into which Paula had slid the books, and ambled out of the library.

"I will of course leave you alone," Gordon Murphy was saying, "if that's what you wish."

"It is," said Cassandra. "It most certainly is what I wish."

"I do think, however," he added, and she was amazed and furious to detect reproach in his voice, "that I deserve an explanation."

"You tried to rape me," Cassandra hissed furiously into the phone.

"Oh, surely not," he said, wearily. "What occurred was a misunderstanding. I misunderstood you. I admit that readily. I misunderstood your needs, your desires — the way in which you like to be possessed."

"Possessed? *Possessed?*"

"All right, then," he said good-humoredly, "the way you like to have sex. Is that better?"

"Listen," said Cassandra. "I live with a man I love. I have no time for you. Go away." And she hung up again.

"Well you are right," Winnifred wrote. "I *am* disappointed. I am *very* disappointed. Not only have I not seen you two for weeks, there was a particular reason why I was so looking forward to this visit and that was because I need to discuss this girl Naomi with somebody. I realize how busy you are, of course I do. But I think you should have made time to come over here just for a couple of hours, for a meal and a visit. I need to know what your reaction is to this girl.

She wears a wig, I found out. Underneath it she's bald as a bowling ball.

Don't you worry about me. I've got no intention of letting her clutter up my life.

Well I don't feel like writing any more today so I'm going to sign off now. You take care of yourself, and tell Rollie to do the same, and I hope to see you real soon. (I know you said next weekend for sure but I'm going to try not to count on that.)"

Earl's Café & Catering was a small place — nothing to brag about — but it was clean, at least, and properly run. And Earl seemed to be okay. Naomi liked it that he couldn't look down on her. She was a short person, and hated this. A short person in a world made for tall people. It was like she always had a crick in her neck, caused by having to look up at people. But Earl was just her height, and most of the time people in the café were sitting down, so all in all Naomi was feeling okay, late this Monday afternoon.

She'd been a bit tense and ditzy at the start of the day, especially since the first thing that happened was Earl finding out that stuff was missing from his storeroom. Of course he didn't suspect Naomi, but she felt guilty anyway, the way you do, like when you go across the border and you aren't smuggling a thing back into Canada but you feel just as guilty as if you were.

The café was such a small damn place it took her like maybe twenty minutes to sort out what was what, and by noon she'd hit her stride. By the end of the day she felt like she'd worked there all her life.

Well, no. (Naomi was trying to stop exaggerating, since a weakness for extravagance was what had screwed her up so totally.) Not all her life. A month or so.

She looked around the café at her customers to see if there were coffee cups that needed refilling or plates waiting to be taken away. A couple of women were talking at a table by the window, a mechanic was finishing up a hamburger at the counter, some type of salesman was reading a newspaper and drinking ginger ale. Naomi approached the mechanic, who'd taken her fancy. She liked the way he was put together, sleek and neat. And that he was friendly without coming on to her. "More coffee?" she asked him.

"Yeah, great, thanks." He pushed his mug toward her. "I haven't seen you here before. Do you mind if I ask what your name is?"

"It's Naomi. What's yours?" She was keeping an eye on the whole place, passing the time of day but not neglecting her work. It gave her a satisfying feeling of competence.

"Ronnie. I work across the street, over at the Shell station."

"Pleased to meet you." Naomi glanced at her watch, then out the window. And there — she could have predicted it — into a parking place in front of the café slid the great jeezly cab with Winnifred the Worrywort behind the wheel. And she climbed out of the thing and came into the café and plunked herself down on a stool next to the mechanic. "Hi, Ronnie, Earl," she said.

"Hi, Winnifred," said Earl. "Get her a coffee, Naomi. I heard about that baby," he said to Winnifred, who shuddered. Earl shook his head in sympathy. "He's okay, though, I heard."

"That's what they tell me," said Winnifred doubtfully.

"What baby?" said Ronnie, so Naomi had to stand there listening to the story about the damn baby all over again.

A blonde, middle-aged woman with long red fake finger-nails came into the café, accompanied by a large man whose face looked sunburned. The clothes they were wearing must have cost a mint, thought Naomi, eyeing them. She couldn't imagine that such people would choose to live in a small town, and decided they were tourists.

"It's five o'clock," she said abruptly, taking off her red-and-white striped apron.

"Right." Earl folded his arms across his chest and smiled at her. "You're a good worker."

"I know it," said Naomi. "So do I get the job or what?"

"You got it if you want it."

"Okay. I want it."

"I thought you already had the job," said Winnifred in a low voice, when Earl had turned away to serve the newcomers.

"I had a kind of a try-out for it. I knew I'd get it." She grabbed her purse from a shelf behind the counter. "I told you, I'm a good waitress. Let's go."

She hadn't spent any time at all looking for a place to live, once Winnifred had told her the damn twins weren't coming after all. She'd had enough on her plate. Laundry, for instance. She'd had to wash and iron her clothes, ready for work, and her wig, too, and clean her white shoes and check everything for rips and tears...

It wasn't that Naomi wasn't grateful for Winnifred's kindness. But she figured that Winnifred was no martyr, so if she'd invited Naomi to stay she must want to have her there. She was probably lonely, living in that house with not so much as a budgie for company. Probably I'm a stand-in for her kids, Naomi thought. Really, she was doing Winnifred a favor by staying with her, helping out with the dishes and whatnot.

On the way home Winnifred got a call from her dispatcher, who wanted her to take some old lady to the senior citizens' hall. Naomi was starting to feel confident again, with a day's work under her belt and a steady job in her life, so she said, "You drop me off and I'll make the supper. Have it ready when you get home."

Winnifred gave her such a soft look that Naomi twitched uncomfortably in her seat. As soon as she got her first pay-cheque, she thought, she'd start looking around for a room to rent.

"I'd only need a sleeping room," she said to Winnifred later. "I could get my meals at the café. Probably for free." She dished herself up some more mashed potatoes.

"That sounds like a good plan," said Winnifred. Naomi had made patties with a pound of lean ground beef she'd found in the freezer and defrosted in the microwave, and the mashed potatoes, and she'd heated up a jar of baby carrots, too. And made a pot of coffee. Everything was ready and the table had been set when Winnifred got home.

"Be good to have some cash again," said Naomi, talking with her mouth full of potatoes. "Get me some new stuff to wear. Maybe a new wig."

"Naomi — why did you dye your hair purple and then cut it off?"

"I was, like, acting out, you know? I read a book about it later." She speared another hamburger pattie, dropped it onto her plate and shook HP Sauce all over it.

Winnifred watched her eat, her own dinner cooling on her plate. "But why?"

"I don't know," said Naomi irritably. "Got sick of the kids. Truly pissed off with that asshole Keith. Thought purple hair would change my life. *I* don't know, for godsake." She filled her mouth with carrots and chewed energetically.

Winnifred took a bite of potatoes. They were very lumpy, and she decided she would show Naomi how to use the ricer.

Naomi sat back in her chair. Winnifred wondered what her real hair would look like when it grew back. "I started hanging out on Granville Street," said Naomi, sounding suddenly detached. "Doing some dope. Went on the job for a while." She turned to look at Winnifred. "So you know what that means?"

"I think so."

"I don't know how come I did it, and I don't know how come I got out of it, either. After a while one day I just looked around and holy shit I was in a place I did not want to be. And so I left." She pushed her plate away. "I ate like a pig. Jesus."

Winnifred fetched the coffee pot. She refilled Naomi's cup and then her own.

"So I bought me a wig, shaved off my hair and went home. But the asshole Keith wouldn't let me in."

Winnifred sat down and sipped her coffee.

"I've had a change of heart," said Naomi. "You know, when I first came, I wanted him back?"

Winnifred nodded.

"Don't want him back any more," said Naomi. "Only my kids. I don't need that asshole Keith in my life," she said, looking restlessly around the kitchen. "I might have to start smoking again, though."

The following day, a dozen red roses were delivered to Cassandra at the library, boxed, the end of each stem enclosed in a water-filled green plastic vial. The box was wrapped in wide red ribbon tied on top in a large bow. Cassandra undid the bow, while Paula watched and marvelled, and looked inside for a card. There was none. Cassandra called the florist and learned that they'd been ordered in Vancouver. She put the lid back on the box, tied the ribbon around it and thrust it at Paula. "Here. You take them."

Paula took the box, with a little gasp. "What — me?" She was in her early forties, black-haired, attractive, and of sunny disposition.

"You can enjoy them," said Cassandra. "You've never met the guy."

That afternoon, a courier delivered a letter. Cassandra ripped it open and read:

"I think you will agree that you have encouraged my interest. I am not easily dissuaded.

You deprive yourself of unimaginable joy. Please abandon this quixotic behavior."

It was handwritten, and signed. Cassandra read it several times, bewildered, trying to comprehend the person behind it. Finally she tore it in half and chucked the pieces in the wastebasket.

A few minutes later she returned to her office, retrieved the letter, taped it together and put it in her purse. She would keep the damn thing. To make sure she didn't forget Gordon Murphy, and her own appalling lapse in judgment.

"Unimaginable joy." "Quixotic behavior." She shook her head, feeling a certain amount of pity.

He called once more, the next morning. As soon as she recognized his voice, she hung up.

Several days passed with no phone calls, no floral offerings, no letters.

"Thank god," she muttered when a week had gone by.

Chapter

10

Ronnie Plankton, who was almost as good a mechanic as he was a thief, was very ordinary-looking, with a deferential demeanor. His face was young and smooth, his expression guileless. His fair hair was kept neatly short. His eyes were brown. He was an extremely polite person, warm and self-effacing, respectful of his elders and betters.

And Ronnie Plankton gathered facts, like a driftnet gathers fish: greedily and indiscriminately.

He harvested information about the community adroitly and with a tender diligence, filing away specks and grains and particles of data for future consideration. He would lie on his sofa, hands behind his head, and let his thoughts wander among the people he'd encountered that day, adding new information to old, encouraging associations and compilations. Every so often pieces of intelligence would clang together, as if magnetized. And when all the necessary elements were there, a thievery would begin to flower in Ronnie Plankton's mind.

He saw his parallel career as the way in which his own personal creativity asserted itself. Everybody had some creativity, and Ronnie couldn't help but be somewhat grateful to Lester, without whom he might never have found his.

It was midafternoon, Monday, and Ronnie's day off. He parked his nondescript grey Toyota a block up from the Arts Centre and strolled through the neighborhood for a while, then turned right and sauntered for several blocks, until the sidewalks disappeared and the distance between houses became greater. Ronnie, who read a lot, imagined that this part of the thing was for him like standing in the wings before his first entrance must be for an actor. Or — no, it would be like walking to the theatre. Nothing on the actor's mind but the role, the play, the job. Going over in his head all his lines, his blocking, his motivation. For Ronnie, though, every night was a first night.

He plodded along what had become a country road, up a hill with forest on either side, trees and bush crowding right up to the pavement. Ronnie was wearing grey sneakers, grey pants and a steel grey leather jacket with several zippered pockets. He got to the top of the hill and rounded a corner.

Here the forest had been cleared back for a hundred feet or so and modest acreages were scattered on both sides of the road. Ronnie slipped into the edge of the woods and made his way perpendicular to the road until he got to the forest at the back of the cleared land. Then he pushed through the brush, trying to avoid stinging nettles and blackberry vines, until he was directly opposite the first farmhouse, which was owned by Howard and Patricia Berkson, both of whom he knew would be at work at this time of day. Between the forest and the back door of the house were several outbuildings, a large vegetable garden and a tire hanging by a rotting rope from the branch of a big old tree.

Ronnie continued along the edge of the woods until he got to the acreage next door. The house was bigger and newer than the Berksons', and the property surrounding it had been subjected to some halfhearted attempts at landscaping. Here lived Jan and Sonja De Groot, who were in Vancouver celebrating the birth of their first grandchild. Ronnie inspected the house for several minutes, making sure of this, or at least making sure that their house was empty. The Buick was gone. Only the Ford pickup was there, parked under the breezeway.

Ronnie retraced his steps until he was once again opposite the Berksons' back door. Then he took a deep breath, stood tall and straight, and emerged from the woods — from the wings — to stride confidently toward the house. Just as if he owned it. And as he approached, he felt like he did own it. He walked toward it eagerly, with love stirring in his heart. He walked between the rows of raspberry canes and past the strawberry plot, along the plywood path that divided the vegetable garden, past the henhouse, from which gurglings and chucklings emerged, and the shed, padlocked, that probably held garden tools, and the tire hanging forlornly from the tree, and finally across the wide patch of sunburned grass that flanked the house. He took the steps to the porch two at a time, landing exuberantly, and banged lustily at the back door. He waited, calming his pounding heart, looking out toward the woods, and the De Groots' property. He saw nothing untoward, everything was still and slumberous in the midsummer afternoon. Smoke from a wood fire idled into the air from somewhere down the wooded hillside, somebody burning what they'd cleared.

Ronnie turned back to the silent house. He took a pair of grey skin-tight kid gloves from his jacket pocket and pulled them on.

He loved this moment. The whole thing was a rush, a succession of thrills, but the moment that the house capitulated, surrendered to him, opened itself to him, that was a special moment, the best moment, and he squeezed his eyes shut for a few seconds, letting the fulsomeness of it happen. Then he slipped inside and closed the door behind him.

He was standing in a small room off the kitchen. He heard the refrigerator sigh into silence, and then the faint ticking of a clock.

109

There were several hooks on the wall, from which hung coats and jackets of various thicknesses: denim jackets and lightweight poplin ones; a red-and-white plaid number, old and dirty; and a big fleece-lined suede coat that had also seen better days. Lined up on the floor were several pairs of boots, mostly men's but some women's: gumboots, winter boots, hiking boots. Also two pairs of sneakers, one much bigger than the other. To his right Ronnie saw a washer and dryer, with a cupboard above. A big green watering can sat on top of the dryer. The brown linoleum floor needed sweeping — and washing, too.

Ronnie stepped through into the kitchen. He'd do a general prowl-through first, just looking for places to look, and checking door and window closures, memorizing the furniture layout in each room.

This was only a reconnaissance mission. He knew he more than doubled the risk by visiting each of his houses twice. But he reduced this risk to a manageable size by taking the time necessary to do things right. Sweet and slow. Smart and safe.

Ronnie wasn't looking for the obvious. He had no interest in televisions or VCRs, computers or their printers, CD players or credit cards. Ronnie stole things that weren't immediately missed. This way it took a long time for a community to realize that it was being delicately but systematically plundered. And when this finally did happen, Ronnie was long gone.

The Berksons' house was small: Ronnie couldn't imagine anybody raising kids here, so either they had never had any or else they'd moved once the kids were on their own. Ronnie knew that there was money in Mrs. B's family. She had married "down," he'd been told. He wondered if she'd ever regretted that.

The furniture was old — not "good" old, but "wearing out" old. The place was a two-bedroom bungalow, and they were using the second bedroom as a guest room, Ronnie decided, peering in there at a high dresser and what looked to him like an old army cot; no mirror... no, Christ, he thought, this must be where Mr. B slept. There was men's clothing in the closet, whose door hung open, and a little clock sat on the table next to the cot. Ronnie was pretty sure he'd find nothing of interest here, but he took a swift glance around just in case and looked through the closet and the dresser. He found a gold pocket watch in the shallow top drawer, along with some handkerchiefs that looked like they'd never been used. He picked up the watch, which was a Walthem that must have been over a hundred years old. "JRB" was engraved on the lid. Ronnie pressed the catch and the lid opened. Inside was inscribed, "Thy sweet love remember'd." Ronnie closed the lid. He couldn't take it. He knew it was something Mr. B would miss instantly. He'd probably know the minute he walked through the damn door that his pocket watch was gone. Too bad, thought Ronnie, putting it back exactly as he'd found it.

His own watch made a brief beeping sound, which meant that he'd been in the house fifteen minutes. He set it for another fifteen and moved swiftly down the hall to the other bedroom, the larger one. Quickly and efficiently he went through the dresser and vanity drawers, finding nothing of interest. One of the drawers held a cheap jewel box, but the only thing in it that was remotely valuable was a jade ring that stood out conspicuously from the rest of the stuff. He opened the closet and rummaged through Mrs. B's clothes — blouses, sweaters and slacks, mostly, in a variety of colors and, he noticed, a variety of sizes as well; the larger sizes were closer to hand. He pulled over the chair from the vanity and stood on it to inspect the high closet shelf. Several handbags were lined up there, and behind them, at the very back, another jewel box, leather, worn, dusty. Ronnie dragged it toward him, took hold of it and stepped off the chair to open it.

Inside were a three-strand pearl necklace with matching earrings, a cameo and an amethyst ring surrounded by dia-

111

monds. Ronnie smiled and gave a happy little sigh. He was tempted to thrust the jewellery into his jacket pocket then and there. If it turned out this was all there was, he probably would. For the moment, though, he closed the lid and put the box back where he'd found it. If he returned, he thought, carefully replacing the chair, he'd have to do so in daylight; he couldn't see himself opening the closet, dragging the chair over and all that with her sleeping just feet away.

Ronnie went next into the dining room, where in the bottom of a china cabinet, underneath a pile of mismatched plates, he found a wooden box containing silverware, place settings for twelve plus sugar spoon, butter knife, gravy ladle, four serving spoons and a serving fork. The silver was so tarnished, he noticed disapprovingly, that it was almost black. It has been a very long time since Mrs. B had had occasion to look inside this box. Ronnie would bring felts to wrap the silver in, and a small burlap bag, and he'd leave the box behind.

There were hardly any books in the house. A set of World Books published in the sixties, a few cookbooks on the kitchen counter and some Louis L'Amour novels in Mr. B's room. Ronnie decided he would take one of these, when he returned.

His watch told him it was time to go. He didn't want to, though.

He looked around him, exasperated. This had just started happening, this not wanting to leave. He'd find himself filling with curiosity about the place he'd infiltrated, about the belongings scattered throughout the rooms and the lives that were lived here.

He stood, uncertain, in the Berksons' kitchen and finally had to force himself to head for the door.

Gordon Murphy strolled through his house Thursday morning with a notebook and a pencil. He had learned enough to begin the redecoration of his house. Workmen were arriving the next day, and the job would be completed, he had been assured, within two weeks.

He studied the rooms of his house carefully, thinking about Cassandra Mitchell. She was a woman who wore dresses. She was sexually coy — flirtatious... worse than flirtatious. She was, he reluctantly admitted, a cockteaser. This was disappointing. But even his soulmate, even Gordon Murphy's other half, couldn't be expected to be fully perfect.

What else did he know about her? he considered, tapping the eraser end of his pencil against his teeth. She was articulate and decisive in committee meetings and also, apparently, in operating her library. Less so in her private life. And it was this private uncertainty, this personal vulnerability, that brought him a rush of exultation.

He moved happily into the sitting room. He loved this stage of things, when all things were possible. He sat on a white wicker sofa and gazed at the wall of glass, small-paned, mullioned, incorporating a set of French doors at each end. Light spilled into the room from the patio, which was crowded with outdoor furniture and pots and hanging baskets filled with flowers. She'd probably appreciate the patio, he thought, and the gardens. But no glass-topped tables and pewter and leather sofas and futons.

In each room, he made a list of what had to go and what could stay. He whistled to himself, planning for his brand-new future, and was only marginally concerned about the anger with which she had rejected his phone calls, and probably his flowers and his letter as well.

Woman Number Two floated into his memory. She was a sessional instructor in the philosophy department at U.B.C. She had very dark eyes and very light hair, a combination that had intrigued him — it struck him as romantic and mysterious.

Something good, something lasting, had come out of their relationship. He had become interested in philosophy again, gone back to Plato (the sessional preferred Aristotle), whose sternness he admired, and his distrust of artists, too. And it was through conversations with the sessional that he was led to read Jean Genet's books. He'd never liked the plays much, but the books, the books...

The sessional, of course, hated Genet, in all his forms. But by the time they'd gotten that far, Gordon already knew she wouldn't do.

She was all over him, from the first time they went out together. He was revolted. Nothing turned him off faster than this kind of salacious behavior. She was lewd, wanton, and the sight of her wet, open mouth and her rolled-back eyes made him sick to his stomach.

She pestered him, wouldn't accept his decision that they go their separate ways, and finally he had several persuasive words with the head of her department, and she was not rehired.

Cassandra Mitchell's spurring of him was, he had decided, a stage in the process; a small, insignificant blip in the progress of their developing relationship. A boring stage, certainly. And irritatingly time-wasting. But he was prepared — for a limited period, of course — to be patient.

Gordon Murphy moved on, into the hallway and up the stairs, tapping his notebook lightly against the banister, planning the activities of the next two weeks.

Thursday, July 15, 1993.

Earl Chan is the proprietor of Earl's Café & Catering. He has only one employee, a young woman named Naomi Hellyer, who started working at the café on the day Mr. Chan discovered that he had been robbed. Since she had never been in the café before that day, Mr. Chan and I agreed that she was not a likely suspect.

There are no former employees whom he might have suspected of this crime. That is, there are no former employees at all. Of any kind.

114

Mr. Chan had occasion to enter his storeroom at about 11 a.m. on Monday, July 12, and although it was the third or fourth time he had visited the room that morning, it was not until this particular visit that he noticed that something was wrong. He was in search of cans of tomatoes, very large cans of plum tomatoes, which he informed me are the only kind of tomatoes that he will use in his Earl's Special Spaghetti Sauce. I was curious about how a Chinese gentleman settled on an Italian dish as his specialty, but refrained from introducing this topic into our conversation because Mr. Chan was in an agitated and preoccupied frame of mind.

Mr. Chan buys these cans of tomatoes in bulk, and arranges them on shelves in four orderly rows, one behind another. He had used up all of the cans in the front row, and several in the next. On Monday morning, July 12, he reached for a can, and then another, and was astonished to find that the entire two back rows of cans of tomatoes were missing. He judged the total number of cans of tomatoes that had been stolen to be fifty.

Mr. Chan had been divested of his usual calm and self-possession by the robbery. He hurried frantically throughout his storeroom, moving articles around, peering behind them, squinting into cupboards, standing on a stepladder to examine every nook and cranny of his storage facility.

Unhappily, he discovered the theft — in addition to the fifty cans of tomatoes — of seven giant-sized containers of ketchup, four of mustard, a ten-pound bag of salt and, from the freezer, six plump chickens.

The hapless Mr. Chan has no idea who could have stolen these items, or how he/she could have entered his café.

Close examination of the premises yielded no clues as to how — or when — this robbery might have been carried out.

Signed, Constable Garnet (Mike) Michaelson.

Chapter
11

Ronnie, working in his kitchen on Friday afternoon, was thinking about a dog he knew, named Kelly, and wondering if he ought to get one of his own. If he had a dog, he would have something to talk to. But was a dog a thing for a thief to have? That was the question.

He got the ground beef from the fridge and dumped it into a bowl, added lemon pepper, salt, a beaten egg. He went outside and cut a few stems of the parsley that grew in a pot and chopped it up. Now he got an onion and peeled it and cut it in four pieces and put it in his new food processor. He loved this thing. It was a piece of loot he'd decided to keep for himself. He turned it on — wham! just like that, chopped onion for his hamburgers. He added it to the bowl, along with the parsley, combined everything well, using his hands, and formed the mixture into four patties, which he put on a plate. He covered the plate with food wrap and put it in the fridge. He often got very hungry, and maybe she did, too. Anyway, he'd made two for each of them and if she ate only one he could freeze the other one.

Yeah, he thought, it would be good to have a dog. Now, for instance, he had nothing to do for a while, he could take it out for a walk, throw a stick for it or something.

117

He started cleaning up the kitchen, thinking about what else he was going to make for dinner. He'd cook the burgers on the hibachi. He'd make a green salad with his special honey-mustard dressing, and there was a potato salad already made, in the fridge. And for dessert they'd have pears and cheese.

He wiped the counters, rinsed the dishcloth and hung it over the dish drainer next to the sink and stood thinking for a moment, staring out the kitchen window at his back lawn and the bush behind it. It was tough, being a thief. It was hard to get a relationship going, because you always had your parallel career in the back of your mind, you were always thinking, how would she react if I told her? You were afraid you'd give yourself away. Like maybe she'd say, "Wherever did you get this leatherbound notebook?" Or, "Tell me more about your friend Alf." Or, "How come I can't sleep over tonight?" Oh, he could think of answers — he *had* thought of them — but every time it happened with a new girl he got a little more nervous than the time before.

This one might be different, though, he thought, checking in the fridge, but yeah, the wine was in there, and some beer, too, because he hadn't known her long enough to know what she liked to drink. There was a can of iced tea mix and some ginger ale, too. That oughta cover the bases, he thought.

An hour later, there was a knock on his front door. He hadn't heard a car. A dog would've heard, he thought, hurrying to answer it. He opened the door wide and smiled at her. "Hi."

"Hi," said Naomi. She was wearing a pair of white shorts and a pink top that had a high neck and no sleeves. Her skin was very fair. Her red hair shone in the sunlight. He could see himself in her mirrored sunglasses.

"Come in," said Ronnie, and he stepped back, feeling awkward. If he had a dog there'd be something else to do, something to talk about. Except maybe it would jump all over her, he thought, closing the door. But I could train it not to, he thought. "Do you want to sit outside?"

She shrugged. "I don't care."

Ronnie found her self-possession intimidating — but then all of a sudden he saw himself in the leather jacket and the jeans, gloved hands deft on each and every kind of lock, a lean silent spectre slipping unseen into someone's house.

Into someone's life.

He turned and walked through the house and out the back door, assuming that she would follow, and she did. He pulled two lawn chairs into the shade of the house. "Sit," he said, indicating the chairs. "What'll you have to drink?" And he recited what he had to offer.

Naomi said she'd have a beer.

They ate outside. Ronnie was pleased with the size of her appetite. She had only one burger, but went back for second helpings of the salads, and she had a total of three beers. But when he brought out the pears and cheese she held up her hands and said she had no more room.

Ronnie, smiling, sat on the grass at her feet. "Where'd you come from, anyway?" He began to stroke her bare ankle. He could smell, faintly, her feet, which hadn't been washed today. There was red polish on her toenails.

"What do you mean, where do I come from?"

"You just showed up here one day."

"Yeah, so?"

"So where'd you come from?"

"Vancouver."

"Why?"

"I came to get my damn kids. Quit that," she said, moving her foot away from him. "From that asshole Keith."

"Who's Keith?" His hand moved to her thigh, his fingers inching under her shorts.

"Quit that," she said, giving his hand a little slap. "Keith's an asshole. He's their father."

"You're married, then."

119

"No. What's it to you, anyhow? You're not getting that hand into my pants whether I'm married or not." She giggled.

"Oh yeah?" Ronnie got onto his knees. He nuzzled her neck. "I'm not getting it into your pants unless you want me to. Do you want me to?" Naomi turned her head. He removed her sunglasses and dropped them onto the grass. He couldn't take his eyes off her lips, and the dimple in her chin.

"You can kiss me," said Naomi, "but that's all."

So they kissed for a while, Naomi in the lawn chair and Ronnie on his knees beside her. She allowed his hands to roam her body, and she kissed him deeply and with enthusiasm, but whenever he tried to get her out of the chair onto the grass she said, sharply, "No."

Finally he sat back on his haunches. He was flushed and sweaty and unbearably horny.

"You can just forget it," she said, picking up her sunglasses. "I'm not having sex again until my hair grows back in. This," she said, pointing to her head, "is a wig."

Ronnie looked at her as if from a great distance. He saw himself watching her undress and remove her wig. Was she bald as a rock underneath it? Was her head smooth or bumpy? Was there maybe a little frizz of hair? What color was it? How come she didn't have any hair, anyway? He was intensely curious about these things.

Slipping into someone's life.

He would go visit Kelly, he thought. He would go back there not as a thief but as a visitor.

"That little kid turned up that went missing," said Sokolowski, from the black leather chair in Alberg's office.

"Thank Christ." Alberg took off his reading glasses and dropped them on his desk. "Where?"

"In the neighbors' yard. Decided he wanted to feed their chickens. Fell asleep in there. In among the hay and the eggs and the chicken shit and all."

Alberg grinned and stretched. He'd spent the afternoon doing paperwork. Two weeks until his holidays.

Sokolowski consulted his notebook. "Well, you know about the B and E over at Flynn's Electronics. It's time you did another talk to the businesspeople, Staff. They gotta get themselves alarmed, for chrissake. Guys come over from the mainland, lurk around till night, do their break-ins and get the first ferry back before anybody even knows stuff's missing."

"I know, I know," said Alberg. He put his glasses back on and peered down at the diminished stack of paper. "I'll call Felix over at the Chamber and see if I can get invited to talk to one of their lunches."

"They meet the first Thursday of every month. You could do the one in August."

"No, I couldn't do the one in August, Sid. On the first Thursday in August, I'll be in my boat, out on the briny."

Sokolowski closed his notebook. "It must be nice," he said lugubriously, "to have something to look forward to."

"I'm going out on the boat tomorrow. Just for the day. You want to come?"

"No," said Sid. "I got stuff to do around the house. Elsie's got a list."

Alberg looked at him more closely. "What's the matter?"

Sokolowski shrugged his enormous shoulders. "Nothing."

"No, I mean it, Sid. Something's wrong. You're not yourself these days."

"Who am I, then?" said Sokolowski wryly. "No, I'm me, all right. That's the trouble."

Alberg's phone rang, and Sokolowski got to his feet. "What is it, Isabella?" said Alberg, gesturing for the sergeant to stay. But Sid shook his head.

"I forgot to tell you," said Isabella. "Your ex called. While you were out for lunch."

Alberg placed the call, but the line was busy.

He spent another hour on the paperwork and then went home.

It wasn't until Saturday morning that he remembered the message from Maura. This time he got through. But he had to exchange pleasantries with the accountant, which put him in a foul mood, and the conversation with Maura put him in an even fouler one. He ended up snarling at her, and she at him. Maura, he thought, putting down the phone, had become decidedly less good-humored — altogether less nice, in fact — since she married the accountant.

"I don't need this," he muttered. He glanced across the kitchen to see that Cassandra was making sandwiches. "Is that for me?"

"It is," she said.

"You don't have to do that," he protested. They had very strict rules about divvying up the household chores.

"It's because I feel guilty about not going with you," said Cassandra.

"In that case," said Alberg, "if it eases your conscience, go ahead." He picked up the phone again, then put it down and crossed the kitchen to embrace her from behind, nuzzling the side of her neck, moving his hands up to cup her breasts. "You sure you won't change your mind?"

Cassandra leaned against him, a piece of bread in one hand and a knife, dripping mayonnaise, in the other. "I'm sure."

Alberg sighed, kissed her cheek and returned to the phone, and called Diana.

"Now what the hell is this about your sister getting married?" he said, as soon as she'd answered.

"Hello-and-how-are-you to you, too, Dad."

"Don't get sarcastic," Alberg snapped. "Oh shit," he said wearily. "I'm sorry, honey." He sat down on the kitchen stool. "I just yelled at your mother, and now I'm yelling at you. sorry. But what's going on with Janey?"

"You know what's going on. She and Daniel have decided to get married."

"But why, for god's sake?"

"Well, I imagine they love each other, Dad. But Janey's right here. Why don't you ask her?"

"Wait a minute," said Alberg hurriedly. "You mean she's at your place? Now?"

"Yeah."

"Is he there, too?"

He heard her sigh. "I guess you mean Daniel, do you? No, he's not here, Dad. Only Janey."

"Okay. Let me speak to her." Cassandra was looking at him, and he saw that she wanted to warn him. "It's okay," he said to her, trying to sound confident and reassuring. "Janey," he said, when his elder daughter got on the line. "I just spoke to your mother." He was trying to sound loving and sympathetic — and it was working; he could hear it in his voice. Then, "She tells me you want to get married," he said — and that wasn't so good. He heard a little bit of incredulity, a little bit of outrage. He took a breath and attempted to lighten his tone. "Is that right?" he said, failing utterly. "Can you actually be planning to *marry* this guy?"

"This," said Janey grimly, "is why I haven't called to tell you."

"'This'?" said Alberg. "This what?"

"This attitude you've got."

"Of course I've got an attitude. You're my daughter. I love you."

"You sure have a funny way of showing it. Why couldn't you at least have tried to be polite to him, Dad? I mean, if you can't like him, fine, but — Do you remember how you used to tell us, Diana and me, that you didn't want to hear about how we hated each other, you didn't even *care* if we hated each other?"

"I never said such a thing," Alberg protested.

"Yes, you did. All that mattered, you said, was that we had to *pretend* we loved one another."

"Never," said Alberg, beleaguered.

"Yeah," said Janey. "And now I'm asking you to do the same thing. If you can't like Daniel, Dad, at least pretend you do. Because whether you like him or not, he's going to be your son-in-law."

Alberg shuddered. "I cannot believe you're going to do this. I simply cannot believe it. You're going to *marry* him? My god, Janey, he's got no manners, he's a goddamn snob — and you want to *marry* him?"

"Yes, Dad, and I'm going to do it right, too, I'm going to *stay* damn married and I'm *not* gonna abandon my damn kids and then I'm *not* gonna shack up with some — some person other than my wife!"

Alberg listened to the dial tone. Gently he put the receiver back on the cradle. He folded his hands in his lap and stared at the telephone.

Cassandra came over and laid her cheek against his. Then she massaged the muscles in his neck, shoulders and back, not speaking to him, loving him with her hands. After a while she gave him a hug and returned to the kitchen counter. "When do you have to be down at the boat?" she said.

"Pretty soon, if I'm going to catch the tide."

"Are you all ready to go?"

"Yeah," said Alberg.

"Call her again tonight," said Cassandra, "when you get back."

"Yeah," he said, gazing at the phone. "I could do that. I guess I better." He looked over at Cassandra. "Well," he said heavily, "I guess it wouldn't be the end of the world. If she got married."

Chapter
12

*I*t was very hot when Ronnie Plankton drove home from work on Saturday, and he was sweaty and uncomfortable. There was no air conditioning in the garage, of course, but Ronnie didn't really mind that. Keeping the big door wide open cooled the place off a little, and he got to see the town passing by, too. This was occasionally useful for his parallel career. People sauntering down the street when they were supposed to be somewhere else. A Closed sign in the bakery window. Someone dressed up who's usually in jeans. Strangers, hanging about with locals, or with other strangers. These observations could come in handy. But it was still darned hot, on a day like today, with the temperature way up almost to thirty, and as Ronnie drove home in his bright green Volvo he had all the windows open and the radio turned to a rock station, volume up almost as high as it would go.

His was a small rented house, on an acreage. He wasn't an outdoors person so he didn't do much with the yard. Kept the lawn cut, that was all. He had measured a distance of seventy-five feet out from each of the house's four walls and within that square, he cut the lawn. Beyond it, weeds and brush were permitted to encroach.

He turned off the road into his driveway, which wound almost a quarter of a mile through masses of buttercups, wild roses, some weeds that had both light and dark purple flowers on them, and plenty of tall grass. And then, abruptly, there was the lawn.

Ronnie's rented house was made of stucco. There was a tiny porch on the front, reached by three stairs. The porch wasn't in the middle of the house but to one side of it, and there were two windows, identical, with identical narrow stained-glass panels along the tops. The driveway went along the side of the house and disappeared into a modest double garage.

Ronnie got out to open the garage door. Then he parked the Volvo next to the grey Toyota.

He was not thinking about the expedition ahead. He didn't allow it into his consciousness yet. But he felt it floating around in the back of his brain.

He had a shower and then, whistling, made himself something to eat and drink: a TV dinner and some strong coffee. While this was getting ready he drank a can of ginger ale, and then another. He was preparing himself as though he was going to rob, even though he wasn't. He never allowed himself to think about upcoming thievery until after he'd had dinner, until about an hour before he had to leave. In summer this wait could last several hours, and it was these hours that were the hardest part of the whole business. But the wait was absolutely necessary. He was readying himself, even though it didn't feel like it. Body was getting ready, brain was getting ready.

The thievery itself was a completely different experience than the reconnaissance. If somebody walked in on him while he was doing an inspection (that was how he thought of it), well, of course it would be embarrassing, and he might even get beaten up if it was a big guy, maybe even he'd get arrested. But he was actually pretty confident that none of these things would happen. Ronnie was fairly sure he could come up with a story that would mollify the homeowners. For instance: "My car broke down," he'd say with a sunny smile. "Your door was

open — I hoped you wouldn't mind if I used your phone."
Since he didn't actually *break* into people's houses — he
looked upon what he did as *tinkering* his way in — they'd have
to believe that they indeed had left their place unlocked.

But if somebody should walk in on him while he was in the
act of committing a robbery, that was a whole different matter. A serious matter. It would be the end of his career. Since
it would be ostensibly a first offence, he might not have to
serve any time, and if he did get a sentence, it would be light.
But it would be personally humiliating, and he knew he'd
never be able to bring himself to thieve again. So the thing
was never to get caught. This took elaborate organization and
planning, a high degree of skill, considerable courage and a
great deal of discipline.

Ronnie ate his TV dinner without noticing what it was
(noodles and meatballs with a tomato sauce) and drank two
mugs of strong coffee, black. He sat in front of the television
with the news on, but his concentration was fixed on keeping
the expedition out of his mind, and it was so intense that he
had no idea what the news and sports and weather people
were saying to him. It was like music in his head; he created
sound in his head to keep from thinking about the robbery.
The similarity with the sex act didn't escape him; delaying cli-
max by thinking hard about something else, trying not to hear
the sounds of your partner, trying not to feel her body, just for
a minute, two minutes, and then, finally, you can let it go, let
it happen.

And eventually, as news segued into situation comedies,
which disappeared into a movie of the week, the sky was dark,
and it was time.

Ronnie washed his fork and mug and the coffee pot, dried
them, put them away. Rinsed the two ginger ale cans and put
them in the receptacle for recyclable items that he kept next
to the kitchen door. Then he went down into the basement,
into Alf's room.

127

He thought of Alf's room as his office.

Ronnie couldn't afford the elaborate security stuff required to keep his parallel career safely hidden from the rest of the world, so he had decided long ago not even to try to hide anything. He told people that he had a friend who occasionally stayed with him. And this was his friend's room. The wardrobe for Ronnie the thief belonged to Ronnie's friend, whom he called Alf.

As to his loot: well, the edible stuff he ate, and things like the food processor — and of course the books — he kept. A lot of stuff he took to Salvation Army drop-off places in Vancouver. Really valuable objects — there weren't many of these — he buried in a hole in his backyard until enough time had passed so that it was safe to sell them. He wasn't into thievery for the money.

Ronnie went into Alf's room and changed into Alf's clothes — grey jeans, socks and sneakers and the grey leather jacket with the many zippered pockets. Then he took his own clothes upstairs and put them in his room. Left the TV on, and a few lights. Turned off his telephone answering machine.

And went into the garage. Set off in the grey Toyota for the house where Kelly lived.

Ronnie had made it his business long ago to learn about dogs and to befriend them at every opportunity, because of the possibility of meeting up with one while doing a reconnaissance. A dog that was deaf, maybe, or just a sound sleeper. He had built up a large internal library of dog information. But he'd never had a real relationship with one before.

Kelly was left alone every day, all day, and many nights as well. Her owners, Ferdinand and Becky Hollister, ran a restaurant-bar a few miles up the Coast. They had installed a dog door for Kelly, which was big enough for Ronnie to crawl through.

He had met the dog by accident. He was driving down the road on which the Hollisters lived, checking out burglary possibilities, when his fan belt broke. He had pulled off the road and while he was replacing the belt with his spare, Kelly wandered over, tail wagging, and made his acquaintance. When he was ready to leave, she wanted to get in the car with him. Ronnie told her to go home, but she didn't start moving until he did, and she wouldn't keep on moving unless he did, and she ended up taking him home with her.

She went in the dog door and pretty soon she was looking out at him through the kitchen window. Then she came out and barked at him, disappeared through the dog door, and again waited in the kitchen window. Ronnie by this time had concluded that the house was empty. So after a minute he followed her through the dog door. She was excited to see him in the kitchen, proud of him for having learned the dog-door trick so quickly.

Now this was a dumb thing for Ronnie to do, with his Volvo parked right over there on the shoulder of the road not a hundred feet from where he was now peering out the kitchen window. But he was, after all, returning the dog to her home, checking to make sure she had water. Which she did.

He poked around for a while, to determine who lived there, and then for a little longer, sussing the place out. But there was nothing that he wanted to steal, so he left. Kelly (he learned her name later) watched him go, apparently content, apparently confident that he would visit again.

It was about eleven o'clock when he pulled into the parking lot of a noisy restaurant two miles away from the Hollisters' place. He left the Toyota there and walked back to the house, around to the backyard and in through the dog door. Kelly loved this. She had heard him approach and was waiting for him, and swiped his face with her long wet tongue several times before he was able to get to his feet.

Ronnie wasn't worried about somebody interrupting him. The Hollisters' restaurant-bar stayed open until two in the morning. Besides, Kelly would react if anyone was approaching.

She soon got over her excitement at his arrival and followed him around as he prowled from room to room, flashlight in hand, checking things out.

It was clear that Becky was no housekeeper. The house was a mess; not untidy — dirty. The walls hadn't been washed in years. Neither she nor Ferdinand was much of a cook either; Ronnie could tell that from the contents of the fridge (meagre) and the cupboards (minimal). The dog was no more neglected than anything else in their lives. He'd been to their restaurant-bar, and it was in no better shape than the house. At least Kelly was well fed, her coat was kept brushed, she had a licence tag on her collar, her temperament was calm — obviously she wasn't an ill-used creature. The Hollisters could be criticized for lots of things, Ronnie thought, shining the flashlight into the bathroom, but not dog abuse.

He gazed down at her. She was looking up at him expectantly, panting slightly, her tail wagging. He liked this dog. He liked the way she padded through the house after him, keeping him company.

Coming as visitor rather than thief made a big difference, Ronnie was discovering. His perspective was broader. He was tinglingly aware of the whole house. It had come alive; Ronnie felt summoned. Was it the dog who had summoned him? He got down on his haunches and held her head between his hands. She looked back at him affectionately, big brown eyes, face fur blonder than the rest of her reddish coat, long tail swishing back and forth. He planted a kiss on the top of her head, stood up, and without considering what he was doing, or why, he went into the Hollisters' bedroom.

There were two chests of drawers, one tall and narrow, the other short and squat. Ronnie opened the top drawer of the short one and carefully lifted up a pile of women's underpants. He pulled out the diary he had remembered from his

130

first visit and sat in the rocking chair by the window. The dog, observing this, lay down with a sigh. Ronnie opened the diary, shone the flashlight upon it, and read.

He was absolutely fascinated, though it was not fascinating material. There was nothing in the diary that Becky Hollister's husband wouldn't mind finding out. Nothing interesting at all, really. Yet Ronnie was enthralled. He consumed the whole year, up to yesterday, by one o'clock, which was when he thought to look at his watch again.

He carefully replaced the diary and left the bedroom, and his heart was pounding with excitement, the way it used to pound while he was thieving particularly well.

He scratched Kelly's chest and gave her a quick massage right behind her ears, and went out through the dog door, swift and quiet like a shadow.

Kelly stuck her head out, watching him go, but she didn't try to follow him.

He thought about himself and his thieving as he drove home. The rush had gotten less, over time, and other things had begun to absorb him more. The deft mastery of detail. The putting on of another persona: he had to stand to one side of himself in order to thieve — it was like the actor's suspension of disbelief. He didn't completely understand why this was so, but he accepted it as part of what his artistry had come to require. It was a kind of growth, as he saw it.

And maybe another kind of growth was happening now, he thought, turning into his driveway, heading for his house, where lighted rooms and the voices of the television set awaited him. But no dog. Maybe he was leaving Alf behind. Maybe he was leaving thieving behind.

Ronnie was troubled, as he put Alf's clothes in Alf's room, and climbed the basement stairs to get ready for bed.

He thought, if he wasn't a thief but he continued to prowl through other people's houses, then what *was* he?

On Monday morning, Mary Jefferson drove her 1985 Valiant pell-mell up the hill to the RCMP detachment, parked on the street and ran inside.

She had never been in a police station before, not in her entire life. There were posters on the wall, pictures of missing people, some of them children and some of them adults. And information about Neighbourhood Watch and Block Watch and Crimestoppers. Mary wondered if inside somewhere there were other posters that showed dangerous criminals out on the loose. Murderers and rapists. And robbers.

There was a bench near the door, and a counter, and behind the counter a woman with very long, thick, greying hair was typing furiously at a computer keyboard.

"Excuse me, but I have to talk to someone," said Mary, hanging on to the strap of her shoulderbag with both hands.

The woman looked up. "Who do you want to talk to?" Her name, according to a small sign on the counter, was Isabella Harbud.

"I've been robbed," said Mary, and she sounded astonished even to herself.

"Oh dear," said Isabella Harbud. She picked up the phone. "Corporal Michaelson, will you come out here, please?" She turned to Mary. "Why don't you sit down."

"I don't think I can."

A minute later an officer emerged from a hallway. "Can I help you, ma'am?" He was in his early thirties, Mary figured. Nice enough looking. Tall, and not thin. He looked fit, but she thought they were probably forced to keep fit, policemen. She wondered if there were any women RCMP people and considered asking for one; but then it wasn't as if she'd been raped.

A surge of nausea embarrassed and dismayed her; she clapped a hand over her mouth. It was the thought of somebody in her place, poking around in her things; it was a violation, maybe not a physical one but a violation just the same.

"Miss?" The officer opened a gate and beckoned her through. "Come in. Sit down here and tell me about it."

"He stole my telescope!" said Mary, and burst into tears.

Hank Ketcham and his wife, Lillian, lived in one of the new subdivisions that had been hacked out of the side of the forested hills facing the sea. Lillian worked as a substitute teacher, and often didn't know until eight in the morning whether she'd be working that day.

Ronnie Plankton had Sundays and Mondays off. Five Monday mornings in a row he stationed himself behind a big clump of wild broom near the corner where the road into the subdivision joined the highway. On the fifth Monday he saw Lillian Ketcham's turquoise Geo wend its way up the hill, stop at the stop sign on the corner and turn left toward Sechelt. He waited for another hour, until Hank Ketcham and everybody else had left for work. It was nice there, in dappled sunlight, behind the fragrant broom.

Ronnie was there because of an inconsequential event that had occurred almost six weeks ago. It was late afternoon, and he was finishing up at work. The big garage door was open and he was lying on a creeper under a bright red Hyundai — the worst car in the world, in Ronnie's opinion — toiling away under there, when he saw a pair of legs in grey trousers and a pair of feet in black shoes, laced up, slightly dusty; probably they'd shone like glass when the guy left home this morning.

"Five minutes, Mr. Ketcham," he said to the legs.

"The clock on the wall says ten after five," said Ketcham.

Ronnie, under the car, grimaced with impatience. Most people didn't mind when he was a little bit late with a job, because they knew he did quality work. They'd hang around, chew the fat with Jonas, jingle the change in their pockets and watch Ronnie admiringly. Not this guy. Ronnie groped for the proper word to describe him and came up with *supercilious*.

"Jonas told me I could pick it up on the dot of five."

"Sorry, Mr. Ketcham. Give me five minutes and she'll be ready to go."

"Maybe if you'd forgone your coffee break this afternoon I wouldn't be having to stand around here."

Forgone, thought Ronnie. Listen to the man. Forgone. "Didn't have a coffee break, Mr. Ketcham," he said cheerfully.

"Low expectations, you know what they lead to?"

"Not sure, Mr. Ketcham. I could make a guess, though."

"Poor results. That's what they get you. Poor results."

Ronnie slid the creeper out from under the car. He got to his feet, smiled, and gestured expansively to the Hyundai. "She's all yours, Mr. Ketcham."

He had watched the man climb into the car and back out of the garage. Then Ronnie had gone into the office to check the address on the work order.

He had intended to thieve at the Ketchams' house. But things had changed in the weeks that had passed since he'd made that decision. And now he didn't know what he wanted to do there.

Ronnie slipped out from behind the broom and walked in the summer sunshine down the hill into the subdivision, which had a low decorative wall around it. He went through the wide-open gates and checked the street signs. Three streets led off from the gate: Nightingale, Sparrow and Eagle. What he wanted was Plover.

Ronnie was continually amazed at how little curiosity most people exhibited about things going on around them. Maybe they thought if something was happening right in front of their eyes it couldn't be significant, it must be okay or something. There he was strolling through this subdivision looking for the Ketchams' place, finding Plover, finding number 15, going up the walk and knock-knocking on the door — and nobody was paying any attention whatsoever. He passed mothers pushing kids in strollers to a playground area at the end of the block. He greeted the mailman. A delivery truck from The Bay rumbled into a driveway. Some guy ran out the front door of his house while putting on his jacket and bolted for the cherry Cavalier that was waiting at the curb. Ronnie moved through this neighborhood activity as if he were invisible, or else one of the family.

The front door of number 15 Plover Lane was recessed, and shrubbery lined the walk that led to it, so once Ronnie was there he knew he couldn't be seen from the street.

It took him less than a minute to get inside.

The house was full of melancholy. Even in the hallway he could feel it, a dissonant sadness that penetrated the walls. Ronnie shivered, struggling with an attack of déjà vu, a strong, suffocating conviction that he'd been here before, that whatever was about to happen had happened before. He didn't know why he was feeling this, but then the mind was a funny thing, it had all kinds of dips and hollows, all kinds of stuff was stored in it, hidden away in niches and clefts and craters and holes. Ronnie tried to shake off the déjà vu, but it clung to him like cobwebs.

He made his way slowly through the Ketchams' house, which was furnished in suites — a bedroom suite, a kitchen suite, a dining-room suite, a living-room suite. If it hadn't been for the mess they'd left behind them, the Ketchams might have been described as living in a furniture store. Ronnie was truly appalled by the disorder he found everywhere, but especially in the bedroom and the kitchen. Clothes lying all over the place, bed unmade, curtains not even raised to let the daylight in. Breakfast dishes cluttered the sink and flies buzzed around contentedly: the milk and butter had been left out on the table, and the lid was off a jar of jam. Because the rest of the house was also littered with newspapers and magazines, vases full of dying flowers, bits and pieces of the Ketchams' disorderly lives scattered everywhere, Ronnie knew the mess wasn't because they'd slept in that morning. They actually lived like this. Every day. Ronnie was disgusted.

135

The paltry selection of books the Ketchams offered him had to do exclusively with the clever investment of money. Ronnie sighed, and tucked into his pocket a small volume comprised entirely of monthly mortgage payment tables, 3 to 30 per cent.

He stood there in the Ketchams' house, looking around, deeply dissatisfied. And then a wonderful idea presented itself to him. Ronnie began to smile.

He rummaged in the kitchen cupboards until he found a pair of rubber gloves, and he set to work. He washed the Ketchams' dishes, dried them and stashed them away. He wiped the countertops, the stove and the kitchen table. And then he went into the bedroom, to restore a little order there.

When he left the house half an hour later, Ronnie was feeling excellent. Lighthearted. Happy, even. He wondered what else he was going to find himself doing, in his future as not-exactly-thief.

Chapter
13

$\mathcal{G}$ordon Murphy made his call and lay on the motel bed
to wait.

Things were going well at the house. He had decided to
leave the workmen on their own for the next week: he would
spend that time meticulously putting in place the plan that
would bring everything together — that would bring him and
Cassandra together.

He daydreamed about her while waiting, wondering what
she'd be like in bed. He knew from their session on the beach
that she wouldn't be like Woman Number Three.

Number Three was undersexed. This had been in comforting contrast to the rapacious charms of the philosopher; it
became, however, a problem.

With this woman, his skills were utterly wasted. He didn't
think she felt a damn thing. She didn't complain; she had
apparently decided that this was an area of human experience
in which she was destined to remain an outcast. She would
accept anything that he wanted to do to her. After a while he
didn't want to do anything at all.

Their last night together (although they didn't know it was
their last night) was a Wednesday, and Gordon had to teach
an eight-o'clock class the next morning. He liked to get to
sleep early on Wednesday. Good sex was an acceptable alter-

native — but he hadn't *had* any good sex. She was lying next to him having given him no sex at all, and she was relieved that he had lost his erection, he could *feel* her relief.

Oh, he knew what was in her devious brain. He'd known all along. She had decided that she would put up with having sex in order to get a husband with money, and tenure, and manners, and looks. She'd put up with *any* amount of sex for that kind of a good deal. But she was happier when she didn't have to. And now she was thinking to herself that she could put the sex stuff behind her for another day. It wouldn't occur to her to offer to try again. Any second now she was going to change the subject to something more to her liking.

"Aren't you about due for a sabbatical, Gordon?" she said. Just as he had predicted.

"That's right — 1993."

She turned onto her side and propped her head up on her hand. She'd do the warm thing now, he thought, the affectionate thing, and come back to the sabbatical later. He could see her simple mind working. She reached out a finger and stroked the lines that stretched from his nose to the corners of his mouth. Gordon took that hand in his and squeezed. After a few seconds, he let go.

"How about if I make you a sandwich?" she said.

Why not? thought Gordon, who was hungry. Among other things.

She put on one of his robes, a blue-and-white striped number made of silk, and they went downstairs. He was wearing white terrycloth that showed off his tanning salon brownness.

He sprawled in a kitchen chair and watched her work. She pulled bread from the cupboard, got lettuce and tomatoes from the fridge and went to the pantry for a tin of tuna. How the hell had she come to know where everything was? She was buttering bread, mashing up the tuna in a bowl, dancing around his kitchen like she owned it, chattering the whole time. There's too damn much going on, here in my kitchen, thought Gordon, staring at her sullenly. And far too little in my bed.

The knife she was using fell to the floor.

"Shit," she said. "Get me a clean one, will you, hon?"

Gordon rose slowly from his chair, opened a drawer in the butcher block island and handed a knife to her.

"Thanks. So where are you going, on your sabbatical?"

"I don't know." He slouched against the refrigerator. She was a small woman. He felt very big, broad and strong. "Probably nowhere."

"I've always wanted to go to the Greek Islands," she said. She had a funny concept of what a sabbatical was, thought Gordon as she looked up at him, giving him what he knew she thought to be a delectable little grin.

"Have you ever considered therapy?" he asked her.

Her smile dwindled away. "For what?"

"For your sexual hangups."

"I haven't got any sexual hangups."

He laughed tolerantly.

"I haven't."

"My dear, forgive me, but you lie there like a dead fucking fish. Except for the fucking part."

She flushed, then became pale. "It's you who needs the therapy, Gord. Not me."

It was the "Gord" that did it. He hated it when people shortened his name.

He struck her, slapped the side of her head. He had forgotten for an instant the difference in size between them. He really smacked her. She went ass over teakettle, thwacked down hard upon the floor. There was a look of immense surprise on her face. Gordon wanted to pick her up and throw her into the next room, and then through the windows into the garden.

"I think you'd better get out of here," he managed to say, and he stayed where he was while she scrabbled to her feet and ran out of the kitchen.

He waited. After a while he heard the front door slam. He'd calmed down by then, so he finished making the sandwiches and ate them, standing in the kitchen.

There was a knock on his motel-room door. Gordon swung himself off the bed and opened it.

"Winston Douglas?" She was a big, worried-looking woman with grey hair.

"That's me," said Gordon. He stepped outside, closed the door and tried the handle, making sure it was locked.

"Where to?" said the woman, opening the back door of her cab.

"Gibsons, if you don't mind." Gordon climbed in.

"I don't mind," she said. "It's twenty miles, though. Going to cost you a buck or two."

"That's fine." He shut the door and put on the seatbelt. "I'm looking for a house to rent." He pulled a piece of paper from his shirt pocket. "There are three places on my shortlist. I'd like to check them all out. Starting with the one in Gibsons."

"Okey-doke," said the driver. "My name's Winnifred, by the way. What's the address there?"

"I don't have an actual address," said Gordon. "They told me it's called the directors' house."

Winnifred, turning south, said, "Yeah, I know the place. Are you sure, though? That it's for rent?"

"Yup."

"That surprises me," she said. After a while she said, "Where are the other two places you're interested in?" and he told her. "Out near Redrooffs," she said, nodding. "They'll be on the water. Not the directors' house, though. It's smack on top of the hill, with the Gibsons harbor at the bottom."

She pulled up in front of it fifteen minutes later. Gordon inspected the house carefully from the front, and walked around to the side, and then returned to the taxi.

"Didn't they give you a key? Aren't you going inside?" said the driver, when he opened the door and got in.

"No need," said Gordon cheerfully. He smiled at her. "All in good time. All in good time."

It was two o'clock on Friday afternoon, and Ronnie Plankton was walking to the library. It was his lunchtime, but before he ate he needed to get some books. Suddenly he heard a toot, and turned to see Elsie Sokolowski waving at him from her new cherry red Chevy Blazer. Ronnie grinned and waved back, then walked on, thrusting his hands into the pockets of his jeans. He always changed out of his coveralls at lunchtime if he was going out to eat. He would have felt uncomfortable wearing them outside the garage. It would be like a doctor parading around the streets in his white coat, or an actor wearing his costume offstage. Not fitting; not in good taste. He rounded the corner and approached the library.

Ronnie had discovered libraries years ago, when he was a schoolkid in Chilliwack. At first he just went there for stories. Eventually he realized that libraries were full of facts, too. Everything he knew about almost everything, he'd learned thanks to libraries. You read, and you think, and then you do. Sometimes you have to practise a lot, and read more, and think harder. But in Ronnie's experience, if you persevered, you could do pretty well anything. If you wanted to do it badly enough.

He pushed open the door and stepped inside, nodded to the volunteer at the check-out desk and went straight to the shelves housing books about dogs. He needed to reread a few that talked about differences among the breeds and told you how to decide which one was right for your particular personality and circumstances. He selected three, checked them out and dropped them off at the garage before heading up the street to Earl's.

He slid onto a stool. The place wasn't busy — this was why Ronnie preferred a late lunch hour. Naomi was taking an order from a young couple over by the window, and there was a woman reading a paperback and smoking at a table in the corner, and a guy at the end of the counter was looking over one of the Vancouver papers and drinking coffee. Ronnie was acquainted with all of them.

The couple by the window was Warren and Wanda Kettleman. Warren was a mechanic, too, at a competing garage, and he'd taken a dim view of Ronnie's arrival in town. But Ronnie had treated him respectfully every time they met, and eventually they'd started talking about cars and now he figured they were, if not friends, then at least — well, put it this way, they'd have been good neighbors if they'd lived next to each other.

The weary-looking woman reading the book (which Ronnie craned his head to see, and which revealed itself to be something by Robertson Davies) he knew because he'd fixed her Pontiac. And later he'd robbed her. He hadn't taken much, though. Something inconsequential, he couldn't remember what. Plus the books. And that was a real hard choice. Bookcases lined the walls of one whole room in her house, except for where the window was. He'd never seen so many books in his life outside a library. Ronnie was going to have a room like that for himself one day, for he expected that his collection would continue to grow. From her house he'd taken a tiny book called *The Discoveries and Opinions of Galileo*, and two paperbacks: *King Lear* and *Couples* by John Updike.

"So what can I get you?" said Naomi. Her tone was brisk and impatient, but there was a glint in her eye that said she was glad to see him.

"A burger and fries, please," said Ronnie, smiling, "and a large Diet coke." He watched her bustle to the pass-through and give his order to Earl in the kitchen. He didn't think she'd come back to talk to him and she didn't, she marched out from behind the counter with a dishcloth and started wiping down the table the woman with the book had just vacated.

Ronnie watched admiringly. She took her job seriously, Naomi did.

"Hey, Ron," said the man at the end of the counter. "Didn't see you there." He was digging change out of his pocket. "You musta sneaked up on me."

"Quiet as a shadow, Mr. Granger," said Ronnie with another grin, "that's me." Buck Granger had a stationery store in the mall, and brought his Chrysler to Jonas's shop for maintenance work, though he took it to someplace in Gibsons whenever something went wrong with it, which Ronnie couldn't figure. He gave Ronnie a half salute and left the café.

Ronnie, his back to the counter, surveying the café and the sidewalk, had a funny sensation settle upon him. He was suddenly despondent. But energized, too. He thought about this mixed-up feeling, shifting it around in his mind like he might judge the weight of a thing by passing it from hand to hand. He was trying not to dispel it, but recognize it. And finally he understood that in one short sharp instant he had acknowledged that Sechelt had become home, and that therefore it was time to leave.

"Eat up," said Naomi.

Ronnie turned on his stool. She had the most direct gaze of anybody he'd ever met. He didn't think she saw much, though.

"Come on, don't let it get cold," she said, so Ronnie began to eat.

He felt dismayed, because he didn't want to leave Sechelt. But he always listened attentively to his instincts. So he considered his situation while he ate, and thought to himself that a change of venue might bring the spark back, the rush. Maybe he could be a thief again, instead of whatever he'd been turning into. Was there any doubt, he wondered, about whether he wanted this to happen?

Just as Ronnie was finishing up his fries, Earl came out of the kitchen carrying two large platters, one with tiny sandwiches on it and the other with little cakes and cookies, both covered in several layers of food wrap. "Can you take these over to Mrs. Wetherford?" Earl said to Naomi. He was wrapped in a huge white apron.

Ronnie put money on the counter and slid off the stool. "I'll help," he said, and took the plate that held the cakes and cookies.

"Where to?" he said, out on the street.

"Shady Acres," said Naomi.

"Is it close enough to walk?" said Ronnie, as if he didn't know where it was. Because you couldn't be too careful.

"Sure," said Naomi.

It was a grey day, but a warm one. The world seemed impossibly lush. The trees were heavy with leaves, and the breeze made sighing sounds in them. Ronnie saw flowers everywhere he turned, hanging from baskets along the main street, crowding people's yards, pushing against fences, spilling out of those garden spaces they had been allotted. He didn't know the names of many of them. This was another thing he could learn about in the library. He wondered what the next library would be like, and in what town he would find himself, and how soon.

Naomi dug him in the ribs with her elbow. "Pay attention, for god's sake. I hate it when people don't listen when you're talking to them."

"Sorry, Naomi." Ronnie lifted the plate he was carrying close to his nose and sniffed — and smelled chocolate. "What did you say?"

"Oh god," said Naomi, exasperated. "I was just prattling, it wasn't anything important — it's the principle of the thing."

"I'm sorry," said Ronnie again, and he was genuinely contrite.

They were only a couple of blocks away from Shady Acres now, crossing a vacant lot, following a trail that skidded diagonally across the lot, a narrow, reluctant opening in the wildly luxuriant grass and wildflowers that grew waist-high. Ronnie laughed out loud as he pushed through the blue and purple and white blossoms.

"Watch out for the damn bees," said Naomi, ducking, holding the plate protectively against her midriff.

"So how're your kids?" said Ronnie. They stopped on the sidewalk and brushed little bits of grass and sticky stuff from the legs of their jeans before continuing on their way.

"I don't know how my kids are," Naomi snapped. "I haven't seen my kids."

"Do you know where they are?"

"I've got a pretty good idea."

"Then why don't you just go there and see them?"

"Because that asshole Keith's mother'd shoot me dead, probably, before she'd let me see them." She slowed down a little as they approached the eastern wing of Shady Acres. "It is not fair," she said furiously, "just because I shaved my damn head, I mean, at least I gave it up, that life, at least when I came home, or tried to come home, at least I was clean, and out of it."

"What do you mean?" said Ronnie, following her up the walk to the entrance.

"I mean he's still a druggie, Keith is," said Naomi, keeping her voice low. The automatic door opened as they approached, and they went through into the lobby.

"There's no way he should have those kids, then," said Ronnie, horrified.

Naomi threw him a peevish glance. "Of course he shouldn't have them." She marched up to the reception desk. "We've got this stuff for Mrs. Wetherford. What do we do with it?"

"Oh, that's right, she's having a tea," said the receptionist, looking up at them through eyeglasses with rhinestones embedded in the frames. "Aren't we hoity-toity, though. The food here's not good enough, oh no." She waved down a nurses' aide. "Tell Mrs. Wetherford her goodies are here."

Naomi turned back to Ronnie, rolling her eyes.

He leaned close and said, very softly, "I think you should just take them."

"What?"

"Steal them. Your kids."

Naomi stared at him.

Marsha Wetherford came bustling toward them, passed them and kept on walking toward the dining room, beckoning. "Bring them in here, dear, will you?" Naomi and Ronnie followed and deposited the plates on one of the tables, each of which had a small vase with a flower in it, which Ronnie thought was a nice touch.

"Now," said Mrs. Wetherford, "help me push a few of these tables together, will you, dear?"

"Certainly not," said Naomi promptly. But Ronnie poked her in the shoulder.

"Sure we will," he said.

Ten minutes later, Mrs. Wetherford released them. But in the hall, their way was blocked by a sullen-faced woman leaning heavily upon a walker. She was a large person, tall and wide, and Naomi and Ronnie had to stand with their backs pressed against the wall until she'd made her way past them.

"Did you see that?" said Naomi indignantly. "Some people! They think they can get away with being rude just because they're old."

"Shhh," said Ronnie. And he placed the index finger of his left hand over his lips.

"Hey!" said Reginald Dutton, who had just tottered through the doorway, dragging his picket sign behind him. He came to a dead stop, staring at Ronnie.

"'Shhh' yourself," said Naomi, striding to the door.

"Hey!" said Reginald Dutton again. "You're him! You're the thief! Arrest this man!" he said to the receptionist.

"My goodness," said one of the aides, hurrying over.

Naomi stopped and looked back over her shoulder. "What's going on?"

Ronnie shrugged, and stepped toward her.

"Stop him!" said Reginald.

The aide reached Reginald and took away his sign. "I've told you and told you, the police don't like being picketed," she scolded him. "You're going to find yourownself arrested, if you keep that up."

"Don't be an idiot, woman," said Reginald excitedly. "That fella took my jar of loonies, and I want them back!"

But Ronnie and Naomi were gone.

Chapter
14

Naomi settled quickly and easily into her job, Winnifred gave her that, and apparently remained intent on getting her life together. Except for finding her own place: she seemed to have forgotten about that. When Winnifred reminded her, Naomi said oh yeah, she'd get at it. But she never did.

Then Winnifred got a phone call from Polly, who said this was a ridiculous situation and Winnifred should do something about it without delay.

And Winnifred had promised to follow Polly's advice — right away quick — so the guest room would be freed up for the twins.

Maybe if she talked to Keith, she'd thought, lying awake at night, worried and uncertain, maybe she could persuade him to get back together with Naomi. She was his responsibility, anyway. Certainly more his than Winnifred's.

She woke up Friday morning and almost as soon as her eyes were open she knew this was the day for it. The sun was shining into her bedroom through the small, high, uncurtained window, and outside she knew the trees were abundantly green and the sea was powerfully blue; it was the perfect day to do a difficult thing.

Winnifred swiftly washed herself, and dressed rather more carefully than usual in navy blue slacks and a yellow short-sleeved blouse. Furtively listening for early morning sounds from Naomi, she checked the phone book again and wrote down the Hellyers' address. She tucked her notebook into her handbag.

As she prepared and ate her breakfast and made sandwiches for lunch, she tried to rehearse the conversation she'd be having with Naomi's disapproving husband, but found this to be impossible. It all depended on how the two of them would react to each other, and what kind of disposition Keith Hellyer had, and what values and beliefs he'd been taught to hold.

Quietly, Winnifred left the house, wondering how Naomi would spend her day off. She thought about things in her house that were private. They were well hidden, of course. Naomi wouldn't find them even if she did start rummaging around.

She spoke to Miriam on the car phone and spent the morning working. She trundled Frances Cox to work and Frances' three-year-old to playschool; Herbert Kingsley to the podiatrist; and Eleanor Sullivan to the SuperValu. While Eleanor did her shopping, Winnifred drove young Angela Johnston for a job interview at the post office; then she took Eleanor home and picked up Don Yablonski, who had another appointment with the Workers' Compensation Board people. Her last fare of the morning was Poppy Maxwell, who had missed the bus to the ferry, so Winnifred took her all the way to Langdale.

On the way back to Sechelt she checked in with Miriam once more, who said, "You want to take a lunch break, Winnifred? You've got nothing until two — Tom Entwhistle wants you to take him to the bank then."

So Winnifred did. She drove to the park and found a bench among some flowering bushes. Here she ate her sandwiches and drank the bottle of lukewarm Red Raspberry fruit juice and mineral water she'd brought along. Then she climbed back into her taxi and headed north, toward Porpoise Bay and Keith Hellyer.

His parents lived in a neat two-storey house, a white one that looked like it had been recently painted. It sat on a corner, like Winnifred's house. The lot was maybe half an acre, and it had been relentlessly cultivated. There were so many flower beds in the front yard that there was hardly any room for lawn. It was a cheerless display, though, in Winnifred's opinion. Every bed was geometric, hard-edged and definite, appearing to have been laid out according to mathematical calculations, the flowers lined up like rows of troops with the tallest ones in the back and the shortest ones in front. Winnifred wondered if the three alder trees shunted up against the fence were permitted to drop their leaves in the fall. She wondered if Naomi's kids were ever allowed to play on the grass, or pick the flowers.

She opened the gate in the chain-link fence that surrounded the property and closed it carefully after her, then advanced along the sidewalk to the stairs that led to the front porch; a rubber tread had been affixed to the centre of each step. She opened the screen door and was about to knock on the inner door went it opened. A small woman in her early fifties looked up at her suspiciously.

"Mrs. Hellyer?"

"Clara Hellyer, that's me, yes."

Winnifred stepped closer, feeling overlarge, and as if she was looming. She smiled to show that she meant no harm. "My name is Winnifred Gartner."

"What do you want?"

Winnifred placed her right foot on the threshold. In doing so, she realized the extent of her determination, and her awkwardness vanished. "I want to talk to your son, about your daughter-in-law." Swiftly her hand reached out, and her hand and her foot prevented the door from closing. "He's got a duty," she said sternly.

"Yes, and he's carrying it out, too."

"But the children, they ought to have a mother as well as a father. Don't you think?"

"But not that one," said Clara Hellyer with vigor.

Winnifred gazed at her. "I really do need to talk to Keith."

After a moment the other woman said, "What's your interest in Naomi, then?"

"I offered her a room for the night. That was almost two month ago. But she's still in my house." Winnifred thought she saw a subtle relaxation in Mrs. Hellyer's mouth. It couldn't quite be called a smile.

"She likes it there, I guess," the woman said.

"I'm in the dark, Mrs. Hellyer. And I need some clarification. So I can figure out what's the right and proper thing to do."

"Chuck her out on her tush, that's the right and proper thing to do." But she stepped back and flung open the door. "Keith's not here. But I'll have a word with you."

The kitchen was what Winnifred would have expected from the outside of the place. Sparkling clean. Extremely tidy. Even the odds and ends on the little desk in one corner had been stacked into neat piles according to size.

"Sit down over there," Clara instructed. She removed a small covered saucepan from the stove and turned off the burner. She poured two cups of tea from a brown china pot and took them to the table, which sat in the corner under two windows. Winnifred, her handbag in her lap, was looking out into the backyard, where an enormous vegetable garden grew in full sun. "That's an awfully big garden," she said.

"How'd you get mixed up with our Keith's Naomi?" She crossed one thin leg over the other. Her short brown hair was shot through with grey, but she had a youthful face. Winnifred felt pain in her heart, looking at her; a pain of envy.

She explained how she'd met Naomi, and how she'd come to offer her a bed.

Clara Hellyer listened and drank her tea.

"I want my privacy back," Winnifred concluded, "but I don't feel like I can just desert her, since it was my idea in the first place that she should stay in my guest room."

"I've warned Keith, I have," said Mrs. Hellyer grimly, "she'll turn up here eventually. But I'm ready for her."

"What were they doing at that house? The one I took her to, when she got to town?" Winnifred felt herself being scrutinized. Clara Hellyer's eyes were small and dark and cold. Winnifred experienced their gaze as a penetration of at least the first couple of layers of her brain. Fortunately, she didn't keep anything there that she didn't want anybody else to know.

"It's my brother's place," Clara said finally. "He's over in Vancouver looking for work. They couldn't stay there, though, could they? Not with her parading herself back and forth on the front sidewalk, calling attention to herself like the tart she is. Keith was scared to hire somebody to look after the kids during the day so he could work — not with her making a spectacle of herself." She sat back, picked up her cup and realized that it was empty. She refilled Winnifred's cup and then her own.

There was nothing lying around in this house. Nothing waiting to be put on or put away. Winnifred saw no books face down, no folded-over newspapers, no elastic bands or paper clips or twist ties lying on the countertops, no jacket slung over the back of a chair or laid upon the kitchen stool. No children's toys. There were magnets on the fridge door, but nothing beneath them. Outdoors, the same order prevailed. The vegetable garden grew in neat rows. The paved driveway didn't have a single wayward leaf or stone or spot of oil upon its immaculate surface. And the side of the garage was almost blindingly white.

Mrs. Hellyer glanced across the table at Winnifred. "She's taking advantage of you, Naomi."

Winnifred heard a noise and looked out to see somebody opening the gate across the end of the driveway.

"And she'll go right on doing it, too," said Clara, "just as long as you let her. She's bone selfish, that girl, as well as being a tramp."

A black pickup pulled into the driveway, and a bulky young man with long hair got out and closed the gate.

"Is that Keith?" said Winnifred.

Mrs. Hellyer leaned forward to peer through the window. "That's our Keith," she said with satisfaction, and got up to fetch another cup and saucer.

He bounded across the grass and past the window and in the back door. And froze, holding the door open, at the sight of a stranger in his mother's kitchen.

"Keith," said Mrs. Hellyer, "this here's the woman Naomi's staying with. What's your name again?"

"Winnifred Gartner."

Keith Hellyer was tall and bulky, wearing jeans and a black T-shirt that revealed considerable excess flesh around his middle. His hair was cut short at the front and the sides, but fell in the back almost to his shoulderblades.

"That bitch," said Keith, expressionless, staring at Winnifred. He let the door bang shut.

"She's unhappy, very unhappy," Winnifred stammered, "to be without her children."

Clara Hellyer flushed with anger. "Don't mention those kids in the same breath with her. She deserted them, went whoring on the streets." She banged her small fist on the table. "She will never see those kids again, if I have anything to say about it."

"Where are they?" said Winnifred.

"None of your damn business," said Keith, pulling a can of beer from the fridge.

Mrs. Hellyer considered Winnifred dispassionately, and said nothing.

"I — it was just — I hope they're all right," said Winnifred. "They must be missing her."

Keith turned and studied her for a moment. "She's here to spy for that bitch." He popped the beer can open and took a drink.

Winnifred looked at him in horror. "No. No, of course I'm not. I'm here — I thought maybe you could see her, talk to her. But she doesn't even know I've come. Really — I hoped I could persuade you to let her see your children. That's all."

His eyes were dark brown, he had a large nose, and his eyebrows nearly joined. His ears were small, almost dainty, and lay flat against his head. Winnifred also noticed that he had a thick, strong neck, and acne scars had pitted the skin along his cheekbones. "She's a spy, Ma," he said, almost casually, but Winnifred felt very cold, looking into his eyes.

She stood up. "I'm not," she said, trying to keep her voice firm and strong. She picked up her handbag.

"Whether you are or whether you aren't," said Mrs. Hellyer, "you're making our Keith mad. It's just as well that you go now." She hustled Winnifred briskly down the hall and opened the front door wide.

Winnifred made her way down the steps and along the walk to the gate, trying not to hurry.

"You tell her to forget about those kids," Mrs. Hellyer called out.

Winnifred, climbing thankfully into Grey Greta, didn't reply.

Chapter
15

On Monday morning Gordon Murphy, naked, pulled a suitcase from the bedroom closet in a rented house two miles from Sechelt. He emptied it onto the bed and began looking through the contents.

He had come to Sechelt to acquire, with the utmost delicacy, essential information. Having accomplished this, he was now spending most of his time keeping out of sight. He had never in his life watched so much television. But he allowed himself to venture out for food and for exercise and — always safely in disguise — to take an occasional peek at Cassandra.

He had had to make one trip back to Shaughnessy to check on the workmen. This he did by bus, to downtown Vancouver, and then by cab — which was inconvenient, but his chocolate brown BMW was far too ostentatious; the little people of Sechelt would notice it, keep track of it, remember it. And if he had rented a car it might have been traced later. This was the simplest, safest way.

He had brought two suitcases with him. One was packed with his own clothes and toilet articles. The other held a selection of costume pieces: wigs, false mustaches and beards, eyeglasses with huge frames (and plain glass; Gordon Murphy's eyesight was perfect), oversize articles of clothing, ascots, a sturdy cane that folded up.

Crime begins, Gordon quoted to himself, with a carelessly worn beret. But he'd brought no beret. And besides, what he was doing was not a crime. He was, he admitted to himself, a criminal in the strictest sense of the world, in that he had committed acts that were unlawful. But the provocation, he recalled, shaking his head sorrowfully, had been intolerable.

He sat on the bed, still naked, his plans for the day temporarily on hold while he recalled the fourth time he thought he had found his soulmate.

Woman Number Four was a lawyer. He found her in the Yellow Pages; he had been having a civilized dispute with one of his neighbors. Her name was Julie Garcia. She did a good job for him, and one thing led to another...

It was after Julie Garcia that he was forced to see himself in a new light. He had prided himself on two things: that he was an excellent judge of character and that he enjoyed absolute control over every aspect of his life. Woman Number Four taught him that he had been overconfident in this regard; that there were things about himself that he hadn't known. Once he had recovered from the shock of this, and tidied up the mess that Julie Garcia had created, he decided that the fact that he still had unknown depths to plumb was something for which he should be grateful. He could still surprise himself, which was essential for personal growth. But it took him a while to learn these lessons and to figure out how the plan to find himself a mate had to be altered. Simplified.

The lawyer was a tall, strong woman with red hair cut in a bob. She carried herself well, dressed well, and didn't mind when the sex act developed a certain amount of boisterous intensity — although Gordon had toned down his act, too, demanding roughness only from professionals, cheerfully willing to pay plenty for it.

For almost a year, he was rapturously certain that he'd found the perfect woman. He had redecorated his house according to what he judged to be her taste, and laughed with

158

delight to see her gliding through his rooms, elegant and gracious, taking nothing for granted. Although she raised her eyebrows when he showed her his new private gym, she said nothing rude or critical, just smiled a little, humoring him. He didn't mind being humored. Occasionally.

One night, he proposed to her. Not before they had sex, which would have been in poor taste, but afterwards. They were sitting in bed, nude, drinking champagne and eating strawberries. Gordon didn't like strawberries, but it was, he thought, a casually sophisticated postcoital snack that suggested volumes about the life he wished to lead.

"Darlin'," he said to Julie Garcia.

"Hmmm?"

He climbed off the bed and knelt beside it, reaching for her hand. "Will you marry me?"

She looked baffled.

"Will you come with me and be my love?"

She blushed.

"Darlin'," said Gordon again, sentimentally, affectionately. "My own dear darlin'."

"Gordon," said Julie Garcia, withdrawing her hand. "This is terribly embarrassing."

He knew at that instant that dreadful news awaited him, but he forged on, pretending that he didn't. "Nothing is embarrassing," he rebuked her, "when two people love each other."

"But Gordon." She turned away, then back, to look him straight in the face. "I'm terribly sorry. But I don't love you."

Gordon Murphy was speechless. He was excruciatingly aware of his nakedness, of his vulnerable, dangling penis. He stood and turned his back to her, folding his arms across his chest. He continued to be unable to think of anything to say.

"I'm sorry, Gordon."

He turned swiftly around, to say who knows what, and caught a little smile on her face, rather a tender smile; but

159

fuck "tender," she'd been looking at his butt cheeks and finding them amusing.

He climbed into a pair of jeans, pulled a sweatshirt over his head, shoved his feet into loafers and combed his hair with his fingers. While he did this, she just sat there, talking to him. She told him how much she had enjoyed their dates, and that she had affection for him, blah blah blah, but she'd never thought he had anything serious or permanent in mind, blah blah blah, and certainly she was not ready at this stage of her life to settle down, even if he was the right person for her, which she was reasonably certain he was not, blah blah blah talk talk talk she even had another glass of champagne, the bitch, trying to get all she could out of him before taking off. The strawberries were all gone. She'd eaten all of them, all by herself, the pig.

"You misled me," Gordon said finally. His voice, he was gratified to notice, was as cold as ice.

"That certainly wasn't my intention," said Julia Garcia wearily. She pushed her hair away from her face and glanced at the clock on the table next to the bed. "I'd better get going."

"You aren't going anywhere." Gordon was rather surprised to hear himself say this — he was not conscious of having made a decision.

And this was the part of the plan that he later revised. It was an excellent idea, he knew that as soon as the words were out of his mouth. Keep her prisoner. Working hand in hand with the Stockholm syndrome, he'd soon have her under control. He even knew right away where he would keep her: in that room in the attic.

But he discovered that this was not the kind of idea you could act upon on the spur of the moment.

Julia Garcia tilted her head a little, frowning. "Excuse me?"

He strode to the bed and grabbed hold of her. It was lucky she was naked, he thought. She'd hardly run screaming from the house in her birthday suit.

Naked or not, though, this woman did not give up without a struggle. In fact she didn't give up at all; he finally had to choke her a bit, just enough to put her out, so he could pick her up and carry her into the attic.

Except that, once again, Gordon was a victim of not knowing his own strength. He ended up killing her. Inadvertent, accidental it might have been, but Woman Number Four was no less dead for that.

Gordon Murphy shuddered at these memories and refused to entertain more.

He focussed on the costume elements he'd dumped upon the bed and selected for today's disguise a pair of baggy black pants, a very large white shirt, a shaggy blond wig and a pendulous mustache that was light brown.

He dressed himself, combed his hair back and snugged the wig over it, applied glue to the mustache and affixed it to his lip. He stood back and gazed at himself in the swing mirror in the enormous dressing table that was the focal point of the bedroom. He turned left and right, studying himself critically. He looked older. He unfolded the cane, flourished it, set its rubber tip upon the floor and leaned on it, humping his back a little. Yes. He *did* look older. Good.

He stuffed his house key and some money in his pocket and walked toward the front door, practising a slight limp. He went outside and locked the door and started down the path that led to the road.

Gordon soon discarded the limp — he kept forgetting about it, and that would be noticeable, a man who limped and then didn't limp. He'd just take it slowly, pretending weariness, leaning on his cane.

He hummed to himself, walking along the roadside, heading for Sechlet. His mustache tickled. He could chew on it if he felt like it, the thing was that long. But he'd better not. Chewing on it might dislodge the damn thing.

A couple of people stopped and offered him a ride, but he refused, giving them a charming smile, saying that he needed his constitutional.

He got to town and perambulated slowly along the main street, turned a corner and tottered past the library, glancing casually in through the huge windows. He had done this before, in several disguises.

And there she was. Gordon Murphy stopped, went close to the glass and stared inside unabashedly, beaming behind his false mustache. And when she caught sight of him he actually waved, merrily, and was rewarded by the faintest of curious smiles.

Gordon walked on, more spritely than was wise for a cane-dependent man, but he soon checked himself. He rambled around the block, bought himself a copy of the local paper and read it while lunching in a fish-and-chip shop.

He stopped at the supermarket on his way back to the rented house. Carrying his bag of groceries along the dusty roadside, Gordon Murphy thought of the future, with Cassandra Mitchell installed there, thought about her future nights, peopled, as Jean Genet would say, by a voluptuous guard. He shivered, delighted and impatient.

Monday, July 26, 1993.

Mary Jefferson is a spirited woman of twenty-five who was painfully distraught when she gave me her statement: she had been robbed of something that meant a great deal to her. She had been robbed of a telescope.

Ms. Jefferson is not in a position to make use of the telescope, at this point, given her lodgings, which consist of a small apartment above the Piccadilly Fish & Chip Shoppe. It is however a beacon in her life, a gleaming symbol of hope and optimism, of her determination to thrive and prosper. The theft of this item has

dashed her hopes, driven her near despair. She feels violated, a reaction that I tried to explain was not uncommon, but of course this is not particularly comforting, as I ought to have known.

She is a woman of medium height and she moves with a rare grace, even when unhappy. Her hair is brown with a golden tint. Her blue eyes are clear and steady.

Ms. Jefferson kept the telescope in a box at the back of a shelf in her small laundry room. She showed me this location.

She had owned the instrument for nine months when it was stolen. She discovered the theft on Saturday, July 17. Unfortunately, the last time she had taken the box down to look inside was several months ago; she cannot remember exactly when, but it was sometime between Christmas and Easter. She provided me with the serial number of the telescope and I assured her that we will distribute it widely among those establishments where it is likely to be sold or pawned.

Close examination of the premises yielded no clues as to how — or when — this robbery might have been carried out.

Signed, Constable Garnet (Mike) Michaelson.

Chapter
16

Ronnie lay on his sofa after supper on Monday, his hands behind his head. He was planning another excursion, in spite of himself.

"Hey!" the old man had shouted, and Ronnie had known instantly what was coming. It had made him dizzy and breathless, frozen in his tracks, unable to breathe. Then he got a big rush of adrenalin, and only just barely managed to keep himself from bolting through the door and sprinting away down the road.

Here he was, though, undeterred, going through several excursion possibilities in his mind. He had managed to reduce them to two. Information arranged itself in his head differently now, because the purpose of the excursions was different. He now looked for people who were interesting in themselves, rather than for people who might have interesting things to steal.

The old guy at Shady Acres tended to get confused about things, so nobody had believed him. Ronnie didn't think he had anything to worry about. But — boy. He would *never* forget how it felt, to think for a few seconds that you were caught. Cornered. About to be moved in on, snatched up, thrown in the clink. His relief, when he realized that it wasn't going to happen, was immeasurable.

He knew he ought not to tinker his way into any more homes in Sechelt. He was pressing his luck — the old man's accusation pointed to the truth of that. Plus his instincts were telling him to desist, now that he'd made the decision to move on.

But he had this mental list. Of people he was curious about. Or felt challenged by. And he kept adding to it, too. He'd hear about somebody — the old woman who he'd been told lived with a whole houseful of cats, for instance. Or he'd see somebody — like the guy in the fish-and-chip shop today, wearing a wig and fake mustache. And Ronnie got real curious, and wanted to learn more about them, until he'd have enough information to plan an excursion.

It was going to be hard to move on. To leave his job, the town, the acquaintances he had here. Naomi.

When Ronnie got up from the sofa, it was night. He turned on some lights and pulled the curtains closed. If he had a dog, he thought, he'd take it for a walk now. Of course it wouldn't even be necessary to take the dog for an actual walk; he could just open the door and let him go off on his own. But he probably wouldn't. It was good for dogs to run free, true, but a lot of them got hit by cars and trucks. So Ronnie would probably go out with his dog. They'd wander down to the road or up to the woods — no, not there, he didn't want his dog eaten by bears. Down to the road, then, swinging along in the moonlight, his dog at his side. He had read the books over the weekend and was trying to decide between a black Labrador retriever and a German shepherd.

Ronnie went into the kitchen and opened the fridge, but saw nothing in there that interested him. He got a half-full bag of tortilla chips from the cupboard and went back into the living room to watch the eleven-o'clock news while chomping on the chips.

Almost three hours later, Ronnie approached Alistair McNeil's house from the lane that ran behind it. He padded along, wearing the grey jacket with all the zippers, his grey gloves, and a grey woollen hat pulled over his fair hair.

Alistair McNeil was a small man with a small beard who lived alone in a house with shuttered windows and tall hedges, with shrubbery huddled around it like somebody in bed pulls blankets up around his neck. He didn't have a dog.

A small *irritating* man, thought Ronnie, slipping through the gate into the backyard. But there was something very interesting about him, too.

He stood still for several minutes, until his eyes had adjusted to the even deeper darkness created by laurel hedges, lilac bushes and the tall fences that surrounded the yard. A breeze was clattering among the laurel, causing the lilacs to rustle and cooling Ronnie's sweaty face; it was far too warm for leather and wool.

He made his way across the lawn, staying close to the fence, and then crept toward the sliding doors that led from the patio to what Ronnie assumed was a living room or a family room, although he couldn't see through the curtains that covered them.

Ronnie dismantled the handle and slid the door open. He pushed the curtain aside and stepped in, sliding the door slowly closed behind him. He had to know immediately where he was. What if this was a bedroom? What if Alistair was sleeping quietly or, worse, lying quietly awake, just feet away? Ronnie's heart was whaling away in his chest so hard that Alistair might be phoning the cops at this very moment for all Ronnie knew; he couldn't hear a thing except the frantic laboring of his own body. He turned the flashlight on. Relief spilled through him: no bed, no Alistair. He turned off the light and straightened from the crouched position he'd assumed as he stepped through Alistair's back gate, and spoke to himself, silently but sternly, breathed deeply a few times. Then turned the flashlight back on.

Its slender beam fell upon an enormous mahogany desk with a glass top. There was a matching bookcase with glass doors and a library table, and over in the corner, a smaller desk. On the library table was a pile of books about sewing, tailoring, crocheting and needlework. To one side of the room was an old Singer treadle sewing machine. Bolts of fabric were stacked neatly on the table, and patterns were stuffed into its interior. The bookcase contained sewing supplies: thread on one shelf, in specially made boxes, each spool suspended from a little dowel; various kinds of scissors, cardboard boxes marked Hooks and Eyes, Velcro Fasteners, Ribbon, Seam Binding, and on and on. Upon the mahogany desk some kind of striped material had been laid out, with the tissue paper segments of a pattern pinned to it. It looked to Ronnie like a pair of pants. Striped pants?

Ronnie sat down at the desk and was about to start going through the drawers when he thought he heard something. He snapped off the flashlight, got up quickly and stood behind the door, back flat against the wall. He stayed like that for what felt like a very long time, but heard nothing more. Cautiously, he opened the door and slipped out into a hallway; he thought he'd better check out the rest of the house and make sure that Alistair was fast asleep somewhere. He hesitated, then turned left. He found the kitchen and then the dining room, and the living room straight ahead. All was quiet.

Ronnie moved silently back down the hall. He reached the doorway to the sewing room and opened the door immediately across from it, revealing a small bedroom, a guest room, he decided, because the bed was stripped of sheets and blankets.

There were two more doors, across the hall from one another, one closed, the other slightly ajar. Ronnie figured that the closed door was Alistair's bedroom and the other one, the bathroom. His whole body was so intently alert that he felt pain. He reached for the knob on the bedroom door. He stretched out his gloved hand — and from behind the door came the sudden explosive sound of a toilet flushing.

Ronnie pulled his hand away and backed down the hall and into the sewing room. He heard the bathroom door open. He rushed out the sliding door, through the backyard and into the lane, where he broke into a run.

He cursed himself all the way home. What the hell was the matter with him? He might as well retire, he thought, disgusted, driving along the road that led to his house. Look at me, he said to himself, here I am barrelling along, twenty K over the limit. He slowed down, took some deep breaths, tore off the woolen hat and unzipped his jacket.

Jesus, though. It had felt so good.

He pulled off the road into the driveway.

The adrenalin rush. Getting away by the skin of his teeth.

The grey Toyota crunched along the gravel. Once inside the garage Ronnie sat unmoving for a moment, relishing — before they died away completely — the variety of sensations that made up the rush.

He climbed out of the Toyota and closed the garage door. If he had a dog, the dog would be inside staring at the door now, with his tail wagging, waiting impatiently for Ronnie. He sometimes thought it would be good to have somebody waiting for him when he got home. Here, going up the back steps, he thought again of Naomi. But it couldn't be a woman, because what self-respecting woman would put up with thieving in her man?

Ronnie undressed in his bedroom and put the clothes he'd been wearing downstairs in Alf's room.

He poured himself a glass of cold milk and drank it, standing in the middle of his kitchen.

Then: Am I an addict? he thought suddenly.

He went to his room and got into bed. Some light came in through the curtain, from the yard light he kept turned on at night. Ronnie rolled to his side and closed his eyes. But they opened again, right away.

He hadn't made up his mind yet whether to get a grown dog or a puppy.

To what, exactly, *was* he addicted? And what did it mean, he thought, if he was addicted? What could he do about it? Did he *want* to do anything about it?

Corporal Michaelson felt a little thrill when he learned it was another robbery. "I'll be right there," he said to Isabella. He put the phone down, donned his brown serge jacket and hurried out into the reception area.

"This is Howard and Patricia Berkson," said Isabella. "Mr. and Mrs. Berkson, Corporal Michaelson."

He took them into the interview room, got them coffee and talked about the weather for a minute, to get them relaxed, but he soon realized that that wasn't working, so he said, "Tell me what happened."

"We're having a family reunion," said Mrs. Berkson, who was a woman in late middle age, with short grey hair, wearing bifocals, carrying a handbag that looked like it was made of zebra hide. Garnet/Mike Michaelson, noticing this, was momentarily distracted. If there wasn't a law against making purses out of zebra skin, there certainly ought to be. "It's happening three weeks from now," Mrs. Berkson was saying. "There's going to be about forty of us."

"It's her side of the family having the reunion," said her husband. "Not mine." He was a small, thin man with long streaks of black hair stretched over a bald pate. He cocked his head in Mike Michaelson's direction when he addressed him, but didn't look at him.

"I see," said the corporal. "Go on," he said to Mrs. Berkson.

"It's an occasion for the good china," she explained. "And the silver. Which I seldom use. But when I hauled out the silver chest — I was going to clean it, see, polish it, and then wrap it up in Handi-Wrap so it wouldn't tarnish again — well, it was empty. I could tell there was nothing in there but air as soon as I picked it up, actually. But I didn't believe it. Do you understand what I'm saying?"

"I think so," said Garnet/Mike Michaelson.

"So somebody's stolen my silver that I've had since my wedding."

"Her people gave it to us," said Howard Berkson, pointing his chin at Mike and squinting toward the ceiling.

"There's place settings for twelve," said Mrs. Berkson proudly. "Plus serving pieces."

"Black as soot, last time I saw it," said her husband.

"That's tarnish," she said severely. "That's why I was getting it out, to clean it."

"Okay," said Mike, writing in his notebook. "Wow, twelve place settings. How many items in a place setting?"

"Two forks, two spoons, two knives," she said promptly.

"So then we're talking six times twelve, plus — "

"There's a total of eighty pieces," she told him.

Mike whistled. "Wow. And what's the value on that?"

"I don't have the remotest idea."

"Okay," said Mike, writing. "That should be easy enough to find out. Now, what else did he take?"

"Nothing."

"Nothing?"

"It's a very strange thing," said Mrs. Berkson. "We have a TV and a VCR and a microwave — "

"Top of the line," said her husband, nodding at Mike, his eyes squeezed shut.

"— but he didn't take another thing."

"Not even my gold watch that's sitting there in my top drawer, plain as day." Howard Berkson shook his head. "Can't believe it."

Mrs. Berkson was staring at Mike. "Good lord," she said.

"What is it? Mrs. Berkson?" She had become very pale. He wondered if she was going to faint, and was pleased he'd taken all those first aid courses. "What is it?"

She got to her feet slowly. "I didn't think to check my jewellery." She turned swiftly and headed for the door.

Her husband stood up hastily. "We'll prob'ly be right back," he said over his shoulder as he scrambled after her.

Chapter
17

"*I* knew you'd see reason," Alistair yelled triumphantly from the sidewalk, using his hands as a megaphone.

"Shut up and mind your own business," Winnifred yelled back, but she knew it was wasted energy: from now until the day he died Alistair would take credit for the new siding that was going up on her house. She planted her hands on her hips and turned back to watch the workmen, suddenly worried that the yellow she'd chosen might be too bright. But too bright for whom? she thought. Too bright for what? If I like it, that's all that counts. And I like it, she decided, after studying the siding for another minute or two.

"I'll bring you guys some coffee in a bit," she said to the workmen, who seemed to like that idea, and she went inside to make it.

While the coffee burbled and dripped she called Miriam, who confirmed that it was a slow day, with nothing booked except Helen Mitchell at Shady Acres, who was getting her hair done again, at two o'clock. Winnifred hung up and checked on the coffee. She felt herself to be hovering, anxious in her kitchen, which was inexplicable. She noticed that her eyes kept moving to the hallway, so she went down there and was led to the closed door of the guest room.

Winnifred put out her hand, turned the knob and pushed the door open. She went into the room and began methodically going through Naomi's dresser drawers and the clothes hanging in her closet, and the drawer of the bedside table. She wondered as she searched what the house or apartment was like in which Naomi lived, or had lived, with Keith and the kids. Had they left behind clothes, furniture, personal things like photo albums and scrapbooks? Children's toys? Bicycles? Maybe one of them had packed up everything and taken it away to be stored somewhere. Though she couldn't imagine Naomi being that organized. As for Keith — Winnifred shuddered, thinking about his rudeness, his downright hostility.

Naomi had acquired things since coming to stay in Winnifred's house. She would no longer be able to stuff all her possessions into the small suitcase with which she'd arrived in Sechelt. Winnifred would help her pack the excess into a cardboard carton when she moved out.

If she moved out.

Winnifred found nothing unusual among Naomi's things. Clothing, makeup, shoe polish, a couple of paperback romance novels — that was about it. She wondered if it was unusual for someone who had been a prostitute to read romance novels.

She was careful to put things back as close as possible to the way she'd found them, before leaving the room and closing the door.

Winnifred checked her watch and began moving a little faster, so as not to be late picking up Helen Mitchell. She poured three mugs of coffee and put them on a tray with a sugar bowl and a small pitcher of milk. She carried the tray and a plate of peanut butter cookies outside, where she set them down on a tree stump that had been evened off to serve as a table. "Come and get it," she told the workmen, and hurried inside to snatch up her handbag.

A few minutes later she parked in front of the comfortable sprawl that was Shady Acres. She went through the automatic doors into the foyer and looked around for Helen, even though unlike most of her clients Helen was never ready and waiting — Winnifred always had to go looking for her. And today was no exception. From the lounge adjacent to the foyer she heard music, so she headed in that direction.

Standing in the entrance, she scanned the assembled senior citizens, who were seated in several long rows facing a piano next to which stood a choir composed of people not much younger than they. Halfhearted applause for "Moonlight Bay" was dying out when Winnifred spotted Helen Mitchell.

"Thank you, folks," said a man with hands so large they looked like they'd been attached to the wrong boy. "We're gonna do one more set, as they call them, and then it'll be sing-along time, and it'll all be up to you."

"Helen!" Winnifred hissed, but nobody heard her. She couldn't barge through to poke her in the shoulder because there were a lot of wheelchairs between her and Helen Mitchell, and a lot of people who Winnifred knew from experience could get very cranky if they thought they were being interfered with in any way. She sighed and sat down in an easy chair; she'd get one of the aides to fetch Helen when the next song was over.

The women in the choir outnumbered the men two to one, she noticed — just as they did in the room at large. Although it was a man who spoke for them, their conductor was a woman. Her demeanor was authoritative enough and her voice, which could be heard above everyone else's, was clear and pleasant, but Winnifred found her conducting technique baffling: the woman did nothing but point spiritedly at the choir with the index fingers of both hands, in time with the music. It was all kind of beside the point anyway, Winnifred decided, since hardly any of the singers ever looked at her.

Even though they were all holding music books, they didn't look at them, either — they were singing "Schooldays" and they knew the words off by heart. No, they weren't looking at the conductor, and they weren't looking at their music. They were looking at the inmates of Shady Acres, their eyes darting among them, furtive glances sliding off them, and Winnifred knew exactly what they were thinking because she couldn't help it, she had that thought, too, every single time she had occasion to come here, and that thought was god help me I'm never going to end up in a place like this. But she didn't mean exactly that. What she meant was please god don't let me need to end up in a place like this.

Not that there was anything wrong with Shady Acres, for those who *did* need such a place. It was bright, comfortably furnished, well maintained, prettily landscaped; the staff were capable, usually cheerful, tolerant...

"Taught to the tune of a hick'ry stick," warbled the choir as Winnifred watched a man at the fringe of the audience working hard to remove one of his socks. He was loosely belted into a wheelchair. He'd gotten his right slipper off and was now working on the sock. He was completely absorbed in this activity, despite having little success. Either his fingers weren't strong enough to push the sock down over his ankle or his mind had forgotten what movements were necessary to achieve this.

"You were my bashful, barefoot beau," carolled the choir.

"What the hell's going on here?"

Winnifred turned, startled.

An old man, red-faced and furious, standing in the entrance to the lounge, lifted his cane and waved it at the choir. Winnifred recognized him — Reginald Dutton.

"What the hell are you people doing here?" he shouted.

Their voices trailed away and they gawked at him. He had the attention of everyone in the room — except the man trying to take off his sock.

Helen Mitchell, having turned around like everybody else, spotted Winnifred and waved. She murmured something to the woman sitting next to her, patted her shoulder and stood up; Winnifred noticed that she had her handbag with her.

"Get the hell out of my living room," hollered Reginald Dutton, shaking his cane and moving directly in front of Winnifred's chair.

Several aides materialized. "Come on, now, Reginald," said one of them, a young man no taller than Reginald but considerably bigger around, "that's not very hospitable."

Winnifred peered around Reginald and saw that Helen had almost extricated herself from the assemblage, so she got to her feet. "Excuse me, Mr. Dutton," she said, "I've got to get by here."

He whirled around and stared up at her. "How do you know my name?"

"You used to ride in my taxicab sometimes."

"What do you mean, I used to? You mean I don't any more?"

"You haven't for a while," said Winnifred, glancing at the aide.

"Since when?" Reginald Dutton demanded. "Why?"

"Well, uh — I don't know. I can't remember.'

"*I* know," he said. "*I* know." Exhaustion settled upon his face. "*I* know," he said dully. He was looking into Winnifred's eyes. Then he turned away. "I want a cup of tea," he said, shaking off the aide's hands. "Get these people out of here," he ordered, gesturing at the choir. He limped slowly out of the lounge, leaning heavily on his cane, and disappeared down the hallway. Winnifred and Helen watched him go.

"This place is a madhouse," said Helen. "Come on." She headed for the automatic doors, and Winnifred followed.

"It's the ones whose minds are going. Or gone," said Helen in the cab on the way to the hairdresser. "They're the ones you don't like to consider."

She was a short woman and she used to be overweight, but moving into Shady Acres had caused the pounds to melt away. Winnifred wondered if the food was bad or if the place just took away a person's appetite. "How're you doing in there, anyway?" said Winnifred.

"I've got my own room," said Helen, gazing out the side window, holding her handbag. "And some of us get together to play bridge, or canasta." She turned to Winnifred. "It's important to get out. Very important to get out."

"I can see that it would be," said Winnifred, pulling up in front of Arnold's Styling Salon.

"I get out several times a week. Once to get my hair done. A couple of times to shop. Every Sunday Cassandra and I have dinner somewhere."

"That's good," said Winnifred. "It's good to keep busy. What time should I pick you up?"

"About three-fifteen, I think."

"Okay. Can you manage the door? Okay. Three-fifteen it is. See you then." She waited until Helen was safely out of the cab and in the salon. Helen waved through the window, and so did Arnold, standing behind her. Winnifred grinned and waved back.

At home she was surprised and pleased to see that one whole wall of her house was now sunny yellow. Last week the window people had come and replaced all of the windows that weren't double glazed; what with that and the new siding she could count on much lower heating bills this winter.

She went inside, thinking she just had time to get a tub of laundry going and maybe write up her shopping list before taking Helen home.

She had the washer loaded and was dumping a scoop of detergent on top of it when she heard the front door open.

"Winnifred? It's me," Naomi called.

Winnifred, irritated, looked at her watch. "In here," she called back. "The laundry room." She closed the lid of the washer and turned on the water.

"Hi," said Naomi from the doorway. Her face was less pale than usual, and her eyes were extremely bright. "You were right about the playschool," she said.

Frances Cox had told Winnifred about two new kids who'd started coming to her three-year-old's summer playschool. They were the right ages to be Naomi's kids. "Maybe you should stroll by one day and have a look," Winnifred had suggested to Naomi. "Satisfy yourself that they're okay. If they turn out to be yours."

"Was I?" said Winnifred now, beginning to smile. "Good. Did you get a peek at them then?"

Naomi stood aside, half turned around, and made a little beckoning motion.

Two children emerged from the dimness of the hall. The girl looked to be about five years old; the boy, a year or so younger.

"This is Tiffany and Walter," said Naomi. "Kids, this is Winnifred."

Winnifred stepped back and leaned against the washing machine. She fixed her attention on the sound of the running water. "This," she said to Naomi, and to the world at large, "is not what I had in mind."

"Say hello to Winnifred," said Naomi, smoothing long strands of hair away from Tiffany's forehead.

"Hello," said the children obediently. They were wearing jeans and sneakers and T-shirts.

Naomi looked at Winnifred, smiling. "I only need to keep them here for a couple of days," she said. "Until I find a place of my own."

Wednesday, July 28, 1993.

The report I am about to make, when considered along with four earlier reports submitted over the last seven and a half weeks, suggests to me that we in Sechelt are experiencing a virtual epidemic of break-and-enter offences.

178

For the fifth time, I have interviewed a victim — in this case two victims — of robbery.

What we have here, in my opinion, is no garden variety burglar.

First, the most recent of the crimes.

On Tuesday, July 27 (yesterday), Mrs. Patricia Berkson discovered missing from her home a sterling silver service for twelve, consisting of eighty pieces, in total, including serving pieces. She opened the large chest in which they were kept — and found it empty. She was, as she expressed herself to me, dumbfounded. Despite the evidence of her eyes she actually looked for the silverware, looked all over the house, as if she or someone else might have absently emptied the chest of the silverware and put it someplace else and forgotten all about it.

She did not, of course, find it.

She informed me that she had been going to clean it, in preparation for a family reunion. The silver was seldom used, she said. The last time she had used it was at Christmastime. She would have used it at Eastertime, ordinarily, but this year she and Mr. Howard Berkson spent Easter with relatives in Vancouver. The silver could have been stolen, then, anytime between Christmas and the date she noticed that it was gone.

In the middle of our first interview, Mrs. Berkson suddenly blanched. She had some jewellery, too, she said, which she kept in a box in her closet. She hurried away, followed by her husband. They returned less than half an hour later. The jewellery, too, was gone. This jewellery consists of one three-strand pearl necklace with matching earrings and an amethyst ring surrounded by diamonds.

Close examination of the premises yielded no clues as to how this robbery might have been carried out.

I add here the report made yesterday morning by Mr. Alistair McNeil, who upon investigating noises in his house on Monday night discovered that the locking device on a pair of sliding glass doors had been dismantled. It is his opinion — with which I concur — that he unwittingly interrupted, when making a trip to the toilet, a theft in progress.

Close examination of his premises yielded no evidence as to the identity of the perpetrator.

I respectfully suggest that the robberies of Reginald Dutton, Earl Chan, the Sechelt Public Library, Mary Jefferson, and Mr. and Mrs. Berkson, and the attempted robbery of Alistair McNeil, might well have been executed by the same perpetrator, and ask permission to devote all my energies and attention to this case, to the exclusion of other duties.

Signed, Constable Garnet (Mike) Michaelson.

Chapter

18

"Can you rent *Dragnet*, do you know?" Alberg asked Sokolowski on Wednesday. He took off his reading glasses and rubbed the bridge of his nose. "The series, not the movie."

"I don't know," said the sergeant. "Why?"

"We're going to have to take drastic action here." Alberg tossed Mike Michaelson's most recent reports across his desk toward Sokolowski. "I thought if we locked him in a room with Joe Friday for a few days, maybe he'd get the message."

"I'll talk to him again," said Sokolowski, reading. "Jesus."

Alberg stretched, wincing, and massaged the small of his back. "Tell him no he cannot devote all his energies and attention to the robberies." He put his glasses back on and peered at the paperwork. When I'm not here, he thought, this stuff copulates. And achieves instant procreation. "He can spend all his leftover energy and attention there, though," he said. "I think he's right. It does sound like it's one guy."

Isabella knocked. "How many hours left until you leave?"

"Two days," said Alberg promptly. "I'm not counting the hours, Isabella. Not yet. Is Dutton out there with his damn sign?"

Isabella shook her head. "Nope. I'm here to find out when the sergeant plans to take his holidays."

"I'm not taking any," said Sokolowski.

"That's not allowed," said Alberg.

"Yeah, well, I don't care if it's allowed or not. I got no place to go. Nothing I want to do. I'm not taking any leave. Give mine to somebody else."

Isabella looked from one to the other. "Let me know what happens," she said and disappeared.

Alberg looked at Sokolowski intently for a minute. "You need to get out of here." He stood up. "Come on."

"I don't need to," said the sergeant plaintively.

Alberg went around his desk. "Come anyway." He left his office and headed for the parking lot, and Sokolowski reluctantly followed.

Alberg took them to Earl's, where they sat at a table by the window. Alberg ordered two coffees from the new waitress.

It was late afternoon, and there weren't many other people in the place. Alberg saw no sign of Earl. He recognized a teller from the Bank of Montreal occupying one of the stools at the counter, reading one of the morning papers. A bearded man wearing coveralls sat at a table near the door with an elderly woman, maybe his mother. At a table where smoking was allowed, four mill workers from Port Mellon were playing cards.

"Okay, Sid," said Alberg. "What's up?"

Sid looked at him bleakly.

Alberg leaned over the table and said it again. "Sid. What's up? Come on."

"I don't think I can talk about it."

"It's serious," said Alberg. "That much I can see. I don't want to pry into your private life, Sid, for Christ's sake — you know that."

"I know."

"But — " He broke off when the waitress approached with their coffee. "Thanks," he said to her.

"No problem."

When she had retreated, Alberg went on, quietly. "But, Sid, you can't go on like this."

The sergeant's unhappiness had been growing for weeks. Isabella had noticed it first. "Are you sick?" Alberg had heard her say to Sokolowski, who hadn't immediately replied. "You sure *look* sick."

"I'm not sick," Sid had snapped.

Alberg had turned from the coffee machine; while he protested his wellness, there was pain in the sergeant's voice. Alberg had looked carefully at Sid Sokolowski, and seen that he had grown less enormous, and that his face was drawn; noticed the air of distractedness about him.

Sid had removed his service cap and placed it on the empty chair next to him. Now he rubbed his close-shaven head with both of his huge hands. "I know I gotta do something. I'm starting to forget stuff."

"I noticed."

"I'm really sorry about that, Staff." He sounded miserable. "I've never forgotten to go to court in my life before. Never."

"I know, Sid."

"It's very humiliating."

"I know. Is somebody sick? Elsie? One of the kids?"

But the sergeant was shaking his head.

"Is it money, then?"

"No, Karl." He sounded indignant. "It's nothing like that." He picked up his coffee cup, but put it back in the saucer without drinking. "It's a personal thing. An emotional thing."

"Okay," said Alberg, nodding. "Okay. So how about — do you think you need to see the shrink?"

Sokolowski considered it. As Alberg studied his face, he thought he saw a flash of hope rise and fade. "Not me."

"Why not you? It's okay for the rest of the world to need a shrink from time to time, but not for you? Is that it? How come you think you've got to be stronger than everybody else, just because you're bigger than everybody else?"

Sid was shaking his head. "That's not what I meant."

The door of the café flew open and a small, red-faced, middle-aged woman burst in. She was wearing a short-sleeved cotton dress with polka dots and open-toed sandals.

"I mean," Sokolowski was saying, "it's not me who needs the shrink, it's Elsie."

"What's the matter with Elsie?"

The woman was gripping the edge of the counter, getting her breath, when the waitress emerged from the kitchen. "Where're the kids?" she yelled at the waitress in a faded but still recognizable north country accent. "What've you done with our Keith's kids!"

Sokolowski glanced at her, then back at Alberg. "She — I haven't said this out loud to anybody, Karl."

"Uh-huh," said Alberg. Earl opened the door from the kitchen and peeked out.

The waitress folded her arms and stared stonily at the older woman. "Your Keith's an asshole. You know he doesn't deserve to have those kids."

Alberg turned in his chair and watched the two of them. The whole café was watching them.

Earl came through the door. "What's the trouble?"

"Elsie," said Sokolowski, his eyes on the tabletop, "she says she wants to — to be on her own for a while."

The older woman pounded the counter with her fist. Alberg noticed she wasn't carrying a handbag.

"You give me back those kids!" she shrieked, pounding. "Tart! Whore!"

Earl came around the counter to stare up at her, horrified.

The bearded man in coveralls stood up, uncertain, and looked around for help.

Alberg reached across the table and laid a hand on Sokolowski's arm. "Sid. Shit. I'm damn sorry, but I think we're needed here."

"Her son's an asshole," said Naomi, breathless and dishevelled. "And she's no better."

"That kind of talk isn't going to get us anywhere," said Alberg. He and Sokolowski were sitting at one of Earl's tables with Naomi and her mother-in-law. "Let's see if I've got this straight. You and your husband lived in Vancouver. Two months ago he left you, and took the kids, and came here to live with his parents."

"Yeah."

"Is this a legal separation?" Sokolowski asked.

"No, for god's sake. He just took off. Took off for here, this hole-in-the-wall town, just *took off*," she said, her voice rising, "the damn *druggie*, with *my damn kids*."

"And why? Tell them why he took off, Missy," said Clara Hellyer, patting her greying hair into place. "Tell them about your whoring down on Granville Street." She pointed a finger at Naomi, nodding her head, looking at Alberg.

"And what about your damn son?" said Naomi. "Keith the druggie? What kind of a guy is that to bring up kids?"

"Keith doesn't do that any more," said Clara Hellyer furiously, with a glance at the uniformed sergeant. "And he gets help bringing up his kids from me and his dad."

The rest of Earl's patrons were listening with keen interest.

"Okay," said Alberg. "I think we need some help with this situation."

"We gotta get the Social Services people in on it," said the sergeant.

"We don't need no government intervention," Clara snapped. "Keep the government out of it."

"I'm afraid we can't," said Alberg. "They'll have to help decide what's best here. For your grandchildren."

"And meanwhile? Meanwhile? Meanwhile, *I* want them." Clara pounded the table. "Now." She whirled on Naomi. "You go get them. If I go home without those kids — "

Alberg looked at her thoughtfully. "Yes? If you go home without them? What then?"

She snapped her mouth shut. "Our Keith'll be broken-hearted," she said. "That's what then."

"Where are these kids?" asked Sokolowski.

Naomi darted a glance at her mother-in-law. "Winnifred's."

"Winnifred Gartner?" said Alberg.

"I knew she was in on this!" said Clara.

"Yeah," said Naomi defiantly. "What of it?"

"Are you planning to go back to Vancouver, Naomi," said Alberg, "when this business has been settled, one way or the other?"

She looked surprised. "I haven't thought about it. Maybe not right away. I got me a job here, now. Unless the asshole's mother here lost it for me, coming in and making trouble like she did." She looked uneasily at Earl, who had taken over behind the counter.

"If you get to keep them, who's going to look after the kids while you're at work?" said Alberg.

"I haven't figured that out," she said. "Winnifred got me a sitter for this afternoon. Beryl, her name is. Maybe she could do it regular."

Alberg pulled out his wallet and left some money on the table. "Okay. I'm going to call Social Services."

"They'll be closed by now," said Naomi. "Won't they?"

"There's an emergency number," said Sokolowski.

"I don't like this," said Clara. She pushed her chair away from the table and stood up. "And our Keith's gonna like it even less. You mark my words," she said, nodding vigorously at Naomi. "You're gonna be sorry, Missy. Very, very sorry."

It was wind, thought Winnifred the next morning, that made a day seem real. Wind gave a day a personality. It felt like something alive and separate, a day did, when there was wind in it; wind to give it life, and power.

Today it was coloring the sea a dark, dark blue and ruffling it with white. Winnifred felt the wind cuffing her cheek and tossing her hair around and unsettling the sand, sparse among the rocks on the beach. She was sitting on a log and looking out over the bay to the Trail Islands, mulling over the years she had lived in Sechelt and the people she knew there. Winnifred was heavy with a grey weight of something sad and ominous and hadn't yet been able to slip out from under it.

She looked at her hands, spread upon her knees, as if they were a stranger's hands. They were large and rough. She obviously hadn't looked after them for a while. Her cuticles needed pushing back and the nails needed tending with an emery board. At least they were clean, she thought, at least there was no dirt lodged under them.

The skin of her hands was the only skin she could see. She had put on a red blouse in an attempt to lift her spirits — which meant she must have started the day feeling out of whack. She picked up a handful of stones and tossed them one by one toward the sea. But she was sitting too far back, and they landed short of the water.

Winnifred reached into her big black bag for her notebook, and in doing so noticed that the bag was dirty on one side, as if it had been splashed with muddy water. She dug out a couple of tissues and got up to moisten them in the sea. She felt very heavy to herself when she stood up, had to press her hands hard on her knees to lift herself up, and trudged the several steps to the water feeling as if she'd put on about a ton of weight since the last time she felt happy. She wet the tissues in the seawater, returned to the log, dropped down upon it and rubbed at her bag with the wet tissues until the marks were almost gone. It'll do till I get home, anyway, she thought. She glanced up and down the empty beach, then stuck the tissues under a rock.

She stared out at the water for a while. It was such a very dark blue, almost as dark as the blackberries that were starting to ripen everywhere you turned. Little glints of sun shone off the water like sparks of fire. The sky was blue too, but you'd hardly know there was just the one word for both of those colors, Winnifred thought; they were so different from each other today. In the winter sometimes the sea and the sky were both grey, and the one would bleed into the other, so you couldn't hardly tell where the horizon was, and you surely couldn't see the islands on it because they were grey and foggy too. Not today, though, she thought, gazing upon the world. Today those islands were marching across the horizon clear as anything, layers upon layers of them, in different shades of purple and blue. She hauled out her notebook and began another letter to the twins with these observations.

She had thought to use this letter, as she'd used so many others, to help her work things out. Winnifred often visualized her letters to the twins as a blackboard and saw herself up there with a piece of chalk, like when she was in school working out a mathematics problem and being praised by the teacher for the precision of her thinking. But her thinking had lately become muddled, which had eroded her confidence, and this was attacking her self-esteem, thereby making her depressed. Winnifred read a lot of magazines and when she could, watched a lot of daytime television. She thought that what was called pop psychology could be very useful, and pop psychology was always urging people to communicate. It apparently wasn't working for her today, though. She couldn't bring herself to talk again to the twins about her problem. She concluded the letter rather abruptly, signed it and tucked the notebook back in her handbag.

Winnifred reached down to where she'd leaned her lunch against the log. She hadn't bothered with breakfast this morning. Just wanted to get out of the house quick. And now she was too hungry to wait for noon. She unwrapped a tuna salad sandwich and removed the cap from a bottle of Summer Peach fruit juice and mineral water. As she ate, she watched the traffic on the water: tugboats, a couple of fishboats heading north.

She knew that if necessary she'd take matters into her own hands. But she hoped it wouldn't come to that.

The Social Services woman who'd come over last night couldn't make head or tail of the situation. So she'd left the kids temporarily with Naomi, because they were very happy with Naomi, anybody could see that.

But more investigating would have to go on before a decision was made. And while that was happening, it looked like Winnifred was stuck with all three of them.

Winnifred shook her head wearily and stuffed the sandwich back into its plastic bag. She'd had only three bites and wasn't a bit hungry any more, not even for the peanut butter cookies she'd also brought.

She picked up the remains of her lunch, the bottle of juice and her handbag and plodded back to Grey Greta, parked off the highway across the street from the take-out place. Once inside the cab she called Miriam.

"I'm taking a couple of hours off," she told her. And she hung up quickly, before Miriam could tell her how many fares she had waiting.

The ferry must have just docked at Langdale, because there was a stream of traffic northward. Winnifred waited for it to trickle away, then wheeled the cab around and drove up the hill into Sechelt.

Winnifred had deep reservations about Naomi's mothering skills. She had been hoping against hope that either Naomi would get back together with her husband or else she'd give up on the kids and return to Vancouver. But now — the little shivers in Winnifred's spine that had warned her against Naomi were nothing compared to what she'd felt when she'd met Keith.

Winnifred pulled up in front of her house, which she knew was empty because Naomi was at work and Beryl had taken the kids to her house for the day. Naomi had decided they'd better not go to playschool, in case Clara tried to steal them back.

Winnifred got out of the cab and took her leftover lunch and her big black bag into the house, where she sat in the middle of the cushioned pine sofa for a long time, thinking some more.

She emerged from this reverie feeling no better.

Winnifred reached into her bag for the notebook and tore off the pages on which she'd written to the twins. She pushed herself up from the sofa and went to the desk in the corner and took an envelope from the drawer. "Roland and Polly Gartner," she printed on the front. She folded the letter and put it inside, licked the flap and sealed it.

Then she went into her bedroom. On the top shelf of her closet, way at the back, was a hatbox. Winnifred took this down and opened it. The box had been made to accommodate a cowboy hat, a tan felt one she'd had once, when she was a lot younger. Now it held only a straw hat with flowers stuck in the hatband.

Winnifred took the hat out, lifted up the cardboard false floor of the box and placed the letter to the twins in the compartment. She pushed gently at the pile of letters there, moving them around, making room for one more. Then she put the hatbox back on the closet shelf.

She locked up the house, returned to Grey Greta and called Miriam to tell her she was back at work.

Chapter
19

"Her grandmother on her mother's side was English," the sergeant called out to Alberg. "Did I ever tell you that?" It was Thursday evening.

"I don't think so, Sid," Alberg called back from the deck of *The Sea Nymph*. "Is it important?" He dunked the mop in the pail of soapy water and continued scrubbing.

"Well, it's back to the hereditary thing." Sokolowski was wearing casual khaki pants and a yellow polo shirt. Alberg wouldn't let him on board because he had on black-soled running shoes.

"The hereditary thing? What hereditary thing?" Alberg stepped up onto the cabin top, mop in hand.

"I mean, those English, they tend to be uppity. Selfish."

"There's nothing uppity or selfish about Elsie, Sid," said Alberg, scrubbing energetically.

"Well, I figure that with her, it's just coming out in her now. As we get into her declining years."

Alberg straightened up and looked at him. Sokolowski's hands were in his pants pockets and his shoulders were sagging. Alberg considered him for a moment, then squinted up into the evening sunshine, which felt warm and loving on his face. He cast an exasperated eye upon his sailboat and picked up the pail and mop. "Here."

Sokolowski took them from him. "Finished?" he said hopefully.

"Yeah. Finished. I just have to hose her down."

While he did this, Sokolowski emptied the pail into the ocean and turned it upside down on the dock to dry out.

"Okay," said Alberg when he'd turned off the water and coiled up the hose. "Let's head up to the pub."

The place was crowded, so they had to sit at the bar, but Alberg kept his eye on the window tables and as soon as one was vacated he swooped in on it; Alberg hated sitting at a bar.

"Order some food," he instructed Sokolowski, who shook his head. "Then I'll do it for you," said Alberg. "He'll have the clam chowder," he told the waitress. "And I'll have fish and chips. Is it cod or halibut?"

"Halibut."

"Halibut," he said with satisfaction. "Good. Two pieces, please. And two more beers," he added. "Now," he said to Sokolowski when the waitress had left, "what is this shit about Elsie's declining years?"

Sokolowski shoved his chair back from the table a little and rubbed his bulky thighs, as if they were aching. "It's the only thing I can think of, Karl. Sometimes, when they get to a certain age, women — well, they can have a variety of troubles. And Elsie, she's — I guess taken leave of her senses would be a good way to describe it."

Alberg was sitting back with his elbows on the arms of the chair, fingers steepled, gazing at Sokolowski and trying not to be distracted by the sounds and smells of the harbor coming in the open windows. If he was to turn his head slightly more to the left, he'd just about be able to see his boat.

"I told her maybe she should see a shrink." Sokolowski winced a little, remembering. "But she said no." There was a lot of loud talk and laughter coming from a table near the front of the pub, where a crowd of young men and women were drinking beer, eating hamburgers and watching the TV above the bar.

"How did she actually put it to you, Sid? When she told you she wants to move out?"

"She said she wants to be on her own for a while."

Alberg drank from his glass of beer. Sokolowski had dumped some salt onto the tabletop. Alberg watched as he licked his index finger, stuck it in the salt and licked it again. Their table was in a corner, far enough away from its neighbors that they couldn't be overheard. Not that anybody was listening anyway.

"She must have given you some reason," Alberg said gently.

Sokolowski looked up at him. "She wants to live her life on purpose and not automatically." He shrugged. "She said a bunch of stuff. That's all of it I really remember."

The waitress arrived with their orders and another two bottles of beer. "You guys're off duty, I guess."

"You're right," said Alberg.

"Or you wouldn't be drinking beer."

"Right again."

"Not out in public, anyway."

"Not anywhere," said Sokolowski, with a trace of his former righteousness.

"You mean you don't have a fridge full of beer over there at the cop shop?" said the waitress, feigning astonishment.

Alberg grinned at her. Sokolowski didn't.

"Well, what a disappointment." The waitress moved swiftly to the next table, to clear it and wipe it clean before the group waiting at the door could get over there.

"Are you sure you don't want to take some time off, Sid?" said Alberg, squeezing a wedge of lemon over his halibut.

Sokolowski looked at him miserably. "I wouldn't know what to do with time off, Karl. I'd just follow her around from home to work and back again asking her questions she won't answer."

Alberg sprinkled malt vinegar on his chips. "It's good that your kids are grown, at least." The Sokolowskis had five daughters. "You don't have to worry about how this will affect them. I think my kids still haven't forgiven Maura and me." Even as he said this, Alberg realized that it was only him they hadn't forgiven. Because even though it had been Maura who'd ended the marriage, his daughters had thought she'd had good reason.

He reminded himself to call Janey. He wanted to put things right between them before he left on Saturday morning.

The sergeant picked up a soup spoon and tried some of the clam chowder. "The kids are mostly bewildered, I think. They don't want to say much until they've got more information." He gave a bitter laugh.

"It sounds like Elsie needs some time to herself, Sid," said Alberg, chewing on a french fry.

"She could quit her damn job at the damn dry cleaner's," said Sokolowski, "and stay home all day, she could have all damn *day* to herself if she wanted." He pushed his soup bowl away from him and slumped back in his chair. "Jesus, Karl. It hurts, you know? And I'm so damn *mad*, at the same time."

"I know, Sid," Alberg said quietly. "Believe me. I do. But there's not a thing you can do about it."

"I'm telling you," said Sokolowski grimly, "I feel pretty belligerent about this. My marriage is the most important thing in my life. I'm not gonna hang around and do nothing while it falls apart."

"Can I make a suggestion?"

"Yeah. Of course. That's why I'm here. You're a man with some experience in this area."

"Your case is different from mine, though," said Alberg. "Maura left me because my marriage was *not* the most important thing in my life. The job was." He leaned toward Sokolowski. "This is my suggestion. Support her in this. Let her go." The sergeant was shaking his head. "Sid, think about it — "

"I can't." He pushed himself up from the table. "Can't do that. Can't do it, Karl."

Alberg watched him lumber slowly through the pub and out the door.

Cassandra couldn't look at her. It was Friday afternoon, and she was visiting her mother. She kept her eyes fixed on *General Hospital*. She would pretend not to have heard. But she knew this wouldn't work for long: her mother would just say it again, and again, until Cassandra acknowledged her. So finally she turned. "What do you mean?" she said weakly.

Helen Mitchell shook her head impatiently. "You know very well what I mean. I spoke English, didn't I?"

"I don't think it would be a very good idea," said Cassandra.

"I think it's an excellent idea. It would be a nice change for me, and for you, too." She uttered an indelicate snort. "Separate holidays. What an astonishing idea. I imagine you're very hurt, Cassandra. You certainly ought to be."

"I'm not hurt at all, not in the slightest — it was my idea, for god's sake. I don't like boats. I get seasick on boats." She didn't get seasick at all, she got frightened, but she wasn't going to tell her mother that.

"It's extremely selfish of him to go off on a holiday without you, I don't care what you say."

"Mother," said Cassandra wearily, "I've told you, he's only going to be gone for a week. We've both got another two weeks after that, and that's when we're going to do something together."

"Still," said Helen. She looked down at her hands, folded in her lap. "I could be very useful to you."

"I know, Mom. Sure you could." Her mother had fashioned a sitting area by arranging the two armchairs and the coffee table between the bay window and the bed. But the bed continued to dominate the room, as if it were somehow certain that eventually her mother wouldn't need anything else.

"Well, then?" said Helen.

"Look. It's not my house. It's Karl's house. I don't think I should invite anybody else to stay there."

"What if you were married?"

"What do you mean?"

"I mean, would it be all right to invite your mother to stay if you were married?"

"I don't know. I guess so."

"I don't see the difference."

She could be honest and upfront about it, thought Cassandra. She could say, Mom, you've stayed with me before and I didn't like it. I don't want you to stay with me because we'd fight and I'd be unhappy. I don't want you to stay with me because I don't like being with you all that much. I don't want you to stay with me because you love my brother more than you love me.

"Maybe there isn't any difference," said Cassandra quietly. "But that's the way I feel."

They turned back to the television set.

"I hope you at least plan to stay for tea," said Helen querulously.

"Of course," said Cassandra. "Tea on Fridays. Dinner out on Sundays." She smiled at her mother, who did not smile back.

"There's a fella out here wants to talk to you," said Isabella that afternoon.

"I'm counting the hours now," said Alberg, looking up from his paperwork. "There's less than two of them to go. Please. Don't tell me it's Reginald. Please."

"Nope. This guy's name is Morton."

Alberg took off his glasses and tucked them into their case. "Please tell Sokolowski to join Mr. Morton and me in the interview room," he said, picking up his notebook and a pen.

"See," said Frank Morton a few minutes later, "Nathan was pokin' around, tryin' to find out who was muscling in on us."

"On your delivery business," said Alberg. "Pizza, wasn't it?"

"Come on, man," Frank Morton said wearily, plucking at the tufts of hair that sprang sparse and aimless from his freckled scalp. "You wanna hear this or not?"

"Go ahead," said Alberg, settling into one of the metal folding chairs. Morton sat in another. Sokolowski, standing, loomed in a corner, near the door. Alberg tossed his notebook and pen onto the table.

"So Nathan, he's talkin' to everybody up and down the Coast, see? Clients, like. Askin' where they're gettin' their shit, 'cause they sure ain't gettin' it from us."

"And did he find out?"

Reflexively, Morton wrapped his arms around himself, hunching his shoulders.

"Frank?" said Alberg. "What did he tell you?"

Morton, his eyes fixed on the battered tin ashtray next to the tape-recorder, said, "Okay if I have a smoke?"

"Sure," said Alberg and watched while Morton lit up. "So? What did Kijinski tell you, Frank?"

Morton's owlish eyes, round and dark, with lashes and brows so light as to be almost invisible, looked at him sorrowfully. "Call him Nathan, willya?"

"Okay. Nathan. What did he tell you?"

"I gotta start at the beginning." Morton took another drag, and tapped the ash into the ashtray with a surprisingly graceful, somehow sophisticated gesture that made Alberg think of Cary Grant movies. "We been in business together awhile now," said Frank. "Nathan looked after the Coast. Me, I did Horseshoe Bay up to Whistler." He talked, smoked, talked, smoked. "So everything goes along tickety-poo until all of a sudden, about, I dunno, a coupla months ago. Whatever. Business starts droppin' off." The cigarette didn't seem to be soothing his obviously ragged nerves: his heel drummed the floor with an increasingly anxious beat. "Well, we knew the clients was still out there, still, ya know, still needin' the product, like. So they was getting it someplace else."

"Was business dropping off in your neck of the woods as well?" said Sokolowski, who had moved from one corner to another.

"Yeah," said Morton, glancing up at him. "You're damn right it was." He stubbed out his cigarette and clasped his hands in his lap.

"And you didn't see this as casual, or temporary? You figured it was serious competition moving in on you?" said Alberg.

Morton nodded vigorously. "And we was right, too, wasn't we? Nathan turning up dead's proof of that."

"Go on," said Alberg. "What did Nathan find out?"

Morton lit another cigarette. His heel was tapping frantically. "See, it scared the shit right outa me when he got killed. I'm next, that's what I thought. That's why I took off. But shit." He squinted pathetically at Alberg. "What am I gonna do in Calgary the rest of my life? I don't know a fuckin' soul in Calgary. So then I go, okay, what if I change my mind, tell the cops what I know, they get this guy, they send him away, and I'm okay."

"Back in business," said Alberg.

"Right. Well, no, get me a job, that's what I figure to do. Get me a regular job." He pushed his shoulders back and crossed his legs, his heel for the moment quiescent.

"Okay," said Alberg. "So here you are, and here we are. Tell us what you know."

"Okay. Right." Morton pulled deeply on the cigarette. He put his feet flat on the floor again and leaned forward slightly, lowering his voice. "So Nathan calls me up on whatever day I don't remember and he says he talked to two guys who told him they been makin' buys from this guy named Keith. He's undercuttin' us, see?" Morton sounded indignant. "That's how he's gettin' our customers. He's chargin' them less. So

Nathan, he called up the guy, this Keith guy, says they need to talk, come to some arrangement or somethin'. So the guy says sure, fine, and Nathan tells me on the phone they're gonna meet that night and then he'll call me, say how things went." He looked sadly at Alberg, smoke drifting toward his face from the cigarette held in his right hand, resting on his knee. "But he never called."

"Keith," said Alberg, looking at Sokolowski.

"This Keith," said the sergeant. "He got a last name?"

"I don't know what it is," said Morton. "Nathan never said."

"Did he say anything else about the guy?" said Alberg. "Anything at all?"

Morton shook his head, took a final puff on his cigarette and crushed it in the ashtray. "That's it. His name's Keith. That's all I know."

"Where does he live?" said Sokolowski. "Sechelt? Someplace else on the Coast?"

Morton shrugged. "I think someplace on the Coast. But I don't know for sure."

"Had Nathan ever actually seen him?" said Alberg.

"Sort of," said Morton. "This client, he pointed him out to him, but Nathan only saw the side of his head, like. Through the truck window."

Alberg and Sokolowski looked at each other.

"Was Keith driving this truck?" said Alberg.

"Yeah. An '88 Ford pickup. Black."

Chapter
20

Cassandra drove Alberg down to the harbor in his Oldsmobile Saturday morning and helped him unload the car and put the stuff — his provisions and personal effects - in the boat.

Alberg was still somewhat preoccupied with work, but he knew that would vanish once he was on his way. Sokolowski had called late last night: Motor Vehicles had confirmed that Keith Hellyer drove an '88 Ford pickup and that he was the only Keith on the Sunshine Coast who did. Sokolowski and Jack Duggin would pick Hellyer up for questioning this morning.

"It's a great day for it," said Cassandra, smiling up at Alberg from the dock, shading her eyes from the early morning sun. She wore yellow shorts and a blue and yellow top, and a big leather bag was slung over her shoulder.

"How come you never use the handbag I gave you?" said Alberg, starting the motor. He had been eager to go. Now he was suddenly unwilling, looking for reasons not to leave her.

"You mean the one that looks like it belongs to Queen Elizabeth?" said Cassandra, and she laughed. "Come on. It's not my style, Karl, I told you that." She looked at the ropes tying *The Sea Nymph* to the dock. "Now what do you want me to do here?"

Alberg was full of uncertainty, looking at her. "Just undo those ropes and, when I tell you, throw them on deck. Hey. I didn't kiss you goodbye."

Cassandra kissed her fingertips and blew. "I'll call you tonight." She undid the ropes. Alberg put the motor in reverse and backed slowly out of his slot. She watched, waving, and moved along the dock so that she could continue to watch as he motored slowly out of the harbor.

Then she parked the Oldsmobile in a lot near the marina and walked home, up the hill.

Gordon Murphy caught the first ferry to Horseshoe Bay that morning and made a quick trip back to Vancouver, to check out the work on the house. He was pleased to find that the job had been completed and was every bit to his satisfaction.

He put fresh flowers in the room that would be Cassandra's and left in his BMW, which he had greatly missed. He stopped to get his hair trimmed and styled, and in the afternoon returned to the Sunshine Coast, to the rented house that he'd been occupying for the last eight days. He packed his bags, checked the place over carefully to make sure he had left nothing behind, tossed the bags into the back seat of the BMW, slid behind the wheel and drove away.

"Good morning, ma'am," said Sid Sokolowski, removing his service cap. "Is this the residence of Keith Harvey Hellyer?"

She looked behind him, peering around his shoulder into the patrol car parked on the street. "Did you come with those kids? Did you come to return those kids to their dad?"

"I'm sorry, ma'am, no, we didn't, I don't believe that matter's been sorted out yet."

"Well, what do you want with our Keith, then?" said Clara Hellyer.

"It's a routine matter, ma'am. Is he at home?"

"No, he's not at home."

"Can you tell us where to find him?"

"I don't know where he is. Could be any place, post office, supermarket, bakery, getting his shoe fixed. Any place." She hesitated. "He's not in any — trouble, is he?"

"We just want to have a word with him, ma'am," said Jack Duggin. "When do you expect him?"

"I expect him for supper, don't I. Like always. What's this about, anyway? I demand to know."

"It's just routine," said Constable Duggin soothingly. "Thank you for your time, ma'am."

Cassandra was slightly depressed when she got home, and started to become more so as she wandered through the house, very much aware of Karl's absence. So she got brisk and stern with herself; after all, the man was only going to be gone for a week and she'd managed on her own just fine for a whole lot of years before he came along, thank you very much. She decided to do something physical. She would houseclean the bedroom.

She dusted, and cleaned the window, and polished the wardrobe, and vacuumed, and then began reorganizing the closet, a job she'd been putting off for weeks. She got the stool from the kitchen and started with the high, dusty shelf on which were arrayed some of her handbags. She looked at the one that had been a gift from Karl. It was brown, and boxy. She took it down, emptied the contents of the shoulderbag onto the bed, transferred them to the brown one and put the shoulder bag up on the shelf.

She noticed a cardboard box up there as well: she hesitated, then took it down and removed the lid. Inside were a half-full bottle of cough medicine, a tube of antacid tablets, a ball point pen and an old pair of jockey shorts. Cassandra looked at this collection of objects for several minutes, her mind working busily. Finally she replaced the lid and put the box back on the shelf.

She took the stool back into the kitchen and poured herself some lemonade. What the hell *was* that stuff?

She took her drink into the backyard, having lost her enthusiasm for housecleaning. It was a pointless task anyway; Bernie had been there just yesterday. Cassandra decided to enjoy what was left of the day, reading, drinking lemonade in the shade and thinking about Karl "gunkholing around" among the Gulf Islands.

She went indoors about five o'clock, had a bath and put on a cotton skirt and a short-sleeved blouse. She would ask Phyllis if she'd like to go to a movie. Or rent one and order in Chinese food.

The doorbell rang just after six. Cassandra was in the kitchen, about to pour some milk for the cats. She noticed the time because she'd been looking at the clock on the kitchen wall when the bell sounded, wondering if Phyllis would be home from shopping yet.

Cassandra went to the door, glancing casually out the window, looking for a car, but she didn't see one.

"Hello, Cassandra," said Gordon Murphy, smiling, when she opened the door. "Oh! The look on your face!" He tossed his head back and gave a hearty laugh.

Cassandra tried to close the door, but his hand shot out and grabbed the edge. "Is your boyfriend at home?" he asked.

"Yes," she said quickly.

"Good."

She stared at him.

"Well?" he said.

"Well, what?"

"Where is he? I want to talk to him."

"He's not here just yet," she said. "I mean, he's on his way here. From work. He's a policeman — did you know that? Did I tell you that?"

Gordon laughed again.

"I'm not kidding," said Cassandra. "He is. He's a Mountie."

"I know that." Gordon pushed the door open, wrenching it out of her grasp, and stepped into the house. "Oh boy," he said softly, looking around. He gave a low whistle. "This place certainly is not you."

"Gordon. I'd like you to leave."

"Can't."

"Please."

He wagged a finger at her and sat down on the sofa, resplendent in white shorts and T-shirt, white socks and sneakers, white jacket; he knew he looked wonderfully brown and sexy against the bright white of his summer clothing.

He smiled his dazzling smile and said to her, "I know he's a policeman. I also know where he is. Out on a sailboat."

"You're wrong," said Cassandra. "He *was* out sailing, but he's on his way home now. He'll be home tonight. This evening. Very soon."

"Any minute now," said Gordon absently. He looked at her for a long time. He had hoped that logic would convert her here and now, and that if logic failed, sex would triumph. But he had accepted the possibility that she might prove difficult to convince at first. "Oh well," he said softly to himself. He was prepared for that, too, of course.

Chapter
21

$\mathcal{W}$innifred, outside in her front yard on Saturday afternoon, watched gloomily, her hands in the pockets of her baggy black sweatpants, as Walter and Tiffany painstakingly planted plastic daffodils in the grass around the front porch.

She heard a noise behind her and turned to see Alistair McNeil standing at her gate. They looked at each other in silence.

"How's your head?" she said finally.

"It's fine." He glanced toward the home of her neighbor the dope addict. "Thank you for asking."

There was another awkward silence.

The stems of the plastic flowers were green spears that sank easily into the soil and would have sunk as easily into flesh, so Winnifred was keeping a close eye on Naomi's kids.

"I let them rummage around in my storeroom," she said. "And they found this box. I don't know where the hell it came from. I don't remember buying this stuff." She gave a little kick to a carton lying nearby. "There's a whole bunch of them in here. Tulips, too."

"Are they your grandchildren?" said Alistair.

Walter, on his haunches, holding a tulip, struggled to turn around, and fell onto his bottom.

Winnifred gave Alistair a long look. "No."

They watched for another few minutes. Tiffany jumped up from her squatting position near the house and ran to the box, to collect another handful of flowers.

Eventually Alistair McNeil said, "Good day to you then, Mrs. Gartner," gave Winnifred a little bow and walked off toward his house.

I should have offered him coffee, she thought. Or a cup of tea.

In Karl Alberg's office, Sid Sokolowski looked across the desk at his wife. "For how long?"

"I don't know, Sid. I told you. I'll be in touch when I find a place."

"Sit down, Elsie, will you? I want to talk."

"There's nothing to talk about." She stood and reached out to place a set of keys on his desk.

"Keep them."

She shook her head and took a step backward, toward the door.

"Elsie, I don't want you to go. Goddamn it, Elsie — " Sokolowski started to get to his feet just as somebody tapped on the office door.

"Sarge," Mike Michaelson began.

"Get out," Sokolowski shouted.

"Sid," said Elsie. "Please."

"Out!"

"Sorry," said the corporal, retreating. He closed the door.

Sid rubbed his face and scalp with both hands. "Christ."

Elsie stayed where she was, suddenly indecisive. "Do you want me to wait until Karl's back?"

He dropped his hands. "No." He took hold of the edge of the desk, struggling to control himself. "You want to go? Go." He breathed in and out, and spoke quietly. "Go now."

And so she did.

Alberg sailed across the Strait of Georgia that day.

The wind was strong and the sea was choppy, and the boat required his full attention. It took him several hours to make it across from Gibsons — it was late afternoon when, tired but exhilarated, he approached Gabriola Island. He had intended to go through Gabriola Passage and look for moorage in Pirates' Cove, but the tide looked better in the morning, so he decided to put up at Silva Bay.

He started the motor, turned up into the wind and dropped the foresail. He stowed it, pushed the bag through the hatch into the forward berth and dropped the main, which he secured to the boom. Then he tied on the fenders and returned to the tiller, put the motor in gear and puttered toward the entrance to the bay.

He was wearing a khaki denim hat with a brim and he'd slathered his face with sunscreen several times during the day. But not often enough, apparently; his skin felt stretched and sore, and it radiated heat.

Alberg turned *The Sea Nymph* into Silva Bay and saw a bright scattering of boats, some drifting lazily at anchor in the middle of the bay, others moored to wharves. He idled across the water and squeezed in between a Cal 27 and a San Juan 24.

He tied up and turned off the motor, and began straightening up below. He was pleasurably aware of the sounds of seagulls, the breeze in the rigging, far-off laughter and the water plucking curiously at hulls and piers and beaches.

Tomorrow he'd catch the high tide at the passage early in the morning, meander the day away, maybe poke around in Pirates' Cove, and figure on spending the night at Ganges, on Saltspring Island.

Alberg turned on his radio telephone and set the channel, then lit the charcoal in the hibachi secured to the rail. He took a beer from the ice-box and, ignoring his sunburned face, settled himself on cushions in the cockpit and gazed out over the bay. The sun had drifted almost to the horizon; he could see it glinting behind the trees on the western side of the bay. The water was very still. A red dinghy was being lowered from an enormous powerboat anchored twenty-odd feet away; a middle-aged couple climbed down the ladder, got in and rowed toward shore. Alberg sighed, drank some beer. He closed his eyes.

When the charcoal was ready he opened the icebox and pulled out a hamburger patty, a tomato and a cucumber. He put the burger on to grill and got a bun from a bag in his food cupboard.

He drank a second beer with his food, and checked the time. He'd told Cassandra and Sid Sokolowski that he would monitor the radio between seven and eight every evening. It was after eight now. He wasn't surprised not to have heard from Sid. But he had expected that Cassandra would call. He waited a few more minutes, then picked up the mike. When the marine operator came on the line Alberg gave her his call sign, his B.C. Tel identification number and his home phone number in Gibsons.

"I'm sorry, no answer," said the operator after a minute.

She was probably out for dinner with somebody. Phyllis, maybe, or Paula from the library.

He wouldn't turn off his radio yet, though.

Alberg washed and dried his dishes, wiped the sink and the tiny counter and stowed everything away.

He returned to the cockpit. The light was fading rapidly. Lights burned in most of the boats now, and the air was much cooler. He stowed the cushions in a locker so they wouldn't be dew-soaked in the morning and went below to make up his berth.

He was uneasy, though he knew this was irrational. She had said she would call, though. And this wasn't something she'd forget to do — not Cassandra.

But maybe he'd misunderstood her. Maybe she'd said she would call, not meaning tonight but tomorrow or the next night.

Alberg put in the hatch door but left the cover open. Then he stripped to his shorts, found his glasses and his paperback, got another beer and climbed into bed.

No. He was sure she'd said she would call him tonight.

He reached up for the radio and tried again. Still no answer. Shit. This was ridiculous. If anything had happened to her, somebody would have let him know.

He'd try again first thing in the morning, and if she still didn't answer he'd call Sid, have him take a look around.

He turned off the radio, settled in against the pillow and tried to get absorbed in the book, and eventually he did.

Gordon Murphy, in his basement exercise room on Sunday morning, wearing sweatpants and a sweatshirt, skipped energetically with a leather rope. He had become adroit with his skip rope. He had learned to cross it in front of him and behind him, too, without missing a beat.

He started his workout slowly, gradually built up speed and then continued at a steady pace, enjoying the sound of the rope knifing through the air. Soon he had to stop for a minute to strip off his sweats, under which he wore gym shorts and a muscle shirt. Then he resumed skipping. Every so often he turned the rope as fast as he could; the noise became dense and furious, like a crowd of angry birds beating the air to death. Then he slackened off again, steadying his pace. He skipped for a minimum of twenty minutes, and on this day he did thirty.

He was dripping with sweat when he finished. He dropped the rope and wiped himself down, admiring himself in one of the full-length mirrors installed around the room. Next he did two circuits of the twelve weight machines, which along with an exercise bicycle, a treadmill, a rowing machine and a warmup mat made up his own private gym. He found it extremely satisfying to have achieved a pinnacle of fitness and then to keep himself there.

211

After his workout Gordon Murphy sprinted up the two flights of stairs to what he called his suite, which consisted of bedroom, bathroom and dressing room. He showered, shaved and dressed, thinking about the day. He didn't have much of a plan. Wanted to do the garden thing, but that was about all. He knew he had to take it slowly. It was important not to rush. Have patience and tolerance, he reminded himself, show her your firmness but also your affection; let her see the future in glimpses, only in glimpses, and eventually she will be tantalized — fascinated — enthusiastic — enraptured. It might be a long, slow road; but they'd get there in the end.

It was a sunny day, he observed with satisfaction; his garden always looked better in sunshine.

He chose his clothes carefully, intent upon looking casual but rich.

Gordon Murphy had two walk-in closets. His dressing room also had shelves for sweaters; shelves for shoes; shelves for hats; and drawers for underwear, scarves, gloves, handkerchiefs, socks and dress shirts, laundered and packaged. There was a special section for workout clothes. He wondered if she would shiver to see him in shorts that revealed his genitals, in a muscle shirt cut low front and back and under the arms. Maybe he'd take her down into his gym one day, he thought, shuffling through his closet. He put on a pair of jeans and a blue cotton shirt, and sneakers with no socks — and as he tied his shoes he imagined her kissing his ankle, her lips pressed into the hollow below the bone, her lips stroking the skin there.... He warned himself again not to rush things. The plan as outlined, in detail, was a good plan and he must not rush it. He slapped aftershave on his cheeks and washed his hands, whistling to himself, studying his image in the mirror. Then he winked, dried his hands and skipped downstairs to the kitchen.

Gordon Murphy had a kitchen that was almost completely white. It had a butcher-block island and so many small appliances that there were some he had never used. They were arrayed on the countertops, suspended under cabinets, stashed away in cupboards, affixed to the walls.

He got the coffee started, then made himself a banana breakfast drink in the blender and gulped this down with a selection of vitamin pills. Next, he pulled out a frying pan, and got bacon and eggs from the fridge, and two pieces of brown bread from a sliced loaf in the freezer. He turned on the fan over the stove, because he couldn't bear the smell of bacon; he breathed through his mouth as he cooked it for her. He kept the bacon warm in the toaster-oven while he cleaned out the pan, added butter and cracked two eggs into it. One of them broke, so he decided to scramble them. He chopped fine a couple of green onions and dropped them into the egg mixture, moving it around with a fork until it set. Then he buttered the toast, arranged everything on a platter and added a glass of orange juice and a mug of coffee.

He couldn't remember if she took anything in her coffee — cream or sugar or both — and for a moment he experienced a flicker of uncertainty. He looked down at the platter, and out the window at the blue and gold August day; thought about his gym and how he looked in the mirrors there; tasted nausea at the back of his throat... But it's just the damn bacon, he told himself, just the fucking bacon.

He took the vial of ground-up Halcion from the vitamin cupboard, shook some of it into the orange juice, stirred it vigorously and proceeded upstairs, bearing the tray.

Chapter
22

"There was police here," Clara said indignantly on Sunday morning, fixing her gaze on Keith, who had just arrived home. It wasn't the first time he'd been out all night.

He whirled around.

She saw the fear in his eyes and put a hand over her mouth. "Keith. Oh no. Your dad'll be beside himself. You said you weren't doing that no more."

He hurried into the living room and looked outside. "Come here," he said to his mother, and when she got there he said, "Watch out this window. If those fuckin' cops show up again, yell." He moved toward the stairs.

"Oh, Keith, what're you doing?"

"I'm gettin' out of here," he said, taking the steps two at a time.

Then he yelled down at her, "Find that woman's address in the phone book. Where Naomi's at."

Clara hurried off to do it. Then she stood by the window, pulling at her fingers until they cracked, making whimpering noises.

There were tears in her eyes when he came banging downstairs carrying two suitcases and a gym bag.

"What's the address?" he said, and she gave it to him. "That bitch, she's not getting to keep those kids."

215

Clara was out and out crying as he tossed the bags into the back of his truck.

He gave her a swift hug. "I'll be in touch," he said, and he drove off.

The pain in her heart, Clara noticed, was tempered a little by relief.

In Cassandra's dream there was a very big long-handled axe whose name — Thunder — was carved into the head. She was shown how to light it, by banging the head against concrete, which created sparks. Cassandra, in her dream, was told that she might use this axe, twice. And the unseen someone or something that was the benevolent custodian of the axe watched, encouraging her, as she picked it up. She wielded it confidently, banged it joyously against concrete — there was a whooshing sound and sparks flew, ordered fragments of fire. As she swung it high aloft, the axe threatened several things or people — evil and dangerous things or people — and they slunk away.

But when she took her second turn Cassandra got only fizzles of sparks, no matter how hard she banged and banged the axe against concrete. She became disgusted then, and threw it aside.

Next she was in a wooden room at the top of a flight of rickety wooden steps, and her brother was there, too. The door was closed — they were hiding. And then they heard terribly loud footfalls on the stairs and Cassandra knew who was coming and she was terrified, and so was her brother. The door flew open, admitting a burst of golden sunlight with motes in it that made Cassandra think of sawdust — and the axe was standing there, huge and towering, brandishing itself: it had metamorphosed into a human-like creature that could wield itself. It stood still in the doorway, holding itself aloft, and looked first at Cassandra and then at her brother, and she knew that it would attack her brother first, and as it moved toward him she was flooded with relief, and ducked around it, and ran out the door and down the steps and into the darkness outside. And she heard the thwacks and heard her brother screaming and *I did not help him did not help him* —

Cassandra woke with her heart pounding, sweaty, filled with terror and shame. She sat up quickly, panting, staring at the wall, fighting the dream. There were tears in her eyes. She would have liked to go back into the dream to relive the end of it and save her brother, but she was too frightened, too relieved to be awake, to be safe.

But gradually the dream retreated and the real world made a stronger and stronger claim upon her consciousness, and Cassandra remembered that she was not safe after all.

She was in a small, bright room in the top of a house. Three walls had no windows. The fourth wall was the downsloping roof in which three long windows had been installed. Through these windows Cassandra could see the tops of some Lombardy poplars and the sky, and a seagull treading scratchily across the roof. She imagined the bird looking in and wondering about her.

Cassandra sat on the daybed blinking at the sunlight. She was profoundly reluctant to get up and cross the room to the door. Of course it wasn't locked, she told herself. Of course I'm free to leave.

Her mouth, she realized, was very dry. She reached for the glass on the bedside table. She put the glass to her lips, tipped it up and extended her tongue, keeping her lips wrapped tight around it, letting a drop of the liquid in the glass touch the very tip of her tongue. She identified the liquid as water, and let herself drink.

Cassandra put the glass back and swung her feet over the side of the bed. This took a great deal of energy. She was astonished and confused to find herself so weak. She stood, slowly, and almost immediately sank back down on the bed. Her legs weren't strong enough to carry her anywhere, and she wondered how the hell she was going to get down two flights of stairs — how had she known there were two flights of stairs?

Through a half-open door she glimpsed a bathroom. She got to her feet again, leaning heavily upon the night table, took a step, reaching out for the arm of a stuffed chair, and made her way slowly, uncertainly, toward the bathroom. Her legs felt like spaghetti — that's exactly how they felt; she wouldn't have believed it but it was true. She thought about Scarlett O'Hara: if she could put off considering her situation for even a few minutes, she could perhaps stave off panic. Don't try to think, she told herself; don't poke around in your head for information; one thing at a time — get into that bathroom. And she did so, with the help of various pieces of furniture — it's really rather cluttered, she thought, this little room. She got into the bathroom, closed the door behind her and almost toppled to the floor in there — but didn't.

She used the toilet and sat there for a long time afterwards. Maybe I'm falling asleep again, she thought; no, I'm just gathering my strength. She stared between her knees at the floor, which was made of black and white tiles. After a while they began to grow, and then to shrink, and their edges started to move around, and they seemed to clatter against each other down there, like a handful of dominoes thrown to the floor. She blinked several times, stood up unsteadily, pulled up her underpants and flushed the toilet.

Cassandra turned to the sink. She washed her hands and face thoroughly and dried them on a black hand towel. There was no mirror in the bathroom. Where the mirror ought to have been, right over the sink, there was a watercolor of a vase full of flowers, huge sunflowers in shades of yellow, orange and gold, with a few lilacs mixed in among them. This bothered Cassandra enormously. It hurt her brain to see sunflowers and lilacs together. It wasn't right. But she couldn't remember why.

She was clutching the sink with both hands, resting most of her weight on it. She let go with her left hand for a second, to open the bathroom door, and looked through into the bedroom, and saw some clothing she recognized, folded neatly in a pile on what seemed to be a small desk. She looked down at herself and saw that she was wearing a thigh-length nightgown with short sleeves, green-and-white striped. This garment she did not recognize.

Cassandra turned on the tap and scooped handfuls of cold water into her mouth, and over her face and on her neck. She pulled the nightgown off and splashed more water onto her breasts and all over her body, until she was shivering. Then she turned off the tap and patted herself dry with the small black towel. She was more awake now, and a turmoil of information clamored for permission to dump itself out of her unconscious brain, to spread-eagle itself for her edification. She cautioned it, though: hold off, hold back, let me get my own clothes on first — this was necessary because of vulnerability, and a need for courage.

She made her way — more surely, this time — across the room to the desk and in bright gilded knife-edged sunlight put on a bra, a cotton skirt, a short-sleeved yellow blouse and sandals — clothing that was oh so familiar. Her breath stumbled in her throat and her eyes filled with tears as she touched these things. She handled them with tenderness, as if they were live things to which she owed love and protection. Cassandra dressed herself, lovingly, girding herself. With her face in the sunlight, her eyes closed against its brilliance, she ran her fingers through her hair.

She turned at the sound of a tap on the door, opened her eyes, saw the door open and a smiling face peek around it. Gordon Murphy stepped in, holding a breakfast tray. "Good morning," he said, smiling.

The scent of his cologne was stronger than the smell of bacon, eggs, toast and coffee. A convulsive shudder occurred

219

in Cassandra's stomach and moved up into her throat. She saw that there was a bud vase on the tray, and that it held a red rose. She was certain that if he was to take a single step closer to her, holding that damn bacon and eggs, carrying that damn rose, wearing that nauseating cologne, she would throw up. I'll do it onto the tray, she thought, or better yet, onto the front of his blindingly white T-shirt.

"I want to go home," she said. "Immediately."

He didn't speak for a moment, or move, just stood still and looked at her. She couldn't read his face.

"You *are* home," he said finally.

"It's a beautiful day, isn't it?" said Gordon later, beaming appreciatively upon the afternoon. "I do a certain amount of the work myself, yes," he said as if she had asked him a question, "but not most of it. Somebody else does most of it. Now here, you see," he said, gesturing across the sweep of lawn toward the stone fence that divided the property from the neighbor's to the west, "when I moved into this house, this was a mass of blackberry bushes. The whole place had been allowed to go wild. To rack and ruin." He turned full circle, scanning, momentarily puzzled. He had said that so easily: "A mass of blackberry bushes... rack and ruin." He clamped his teeth together. He didn't remember any blackberry bushes. He didn't remember any rack and ruin.

They moved off the patio onto a wide concrete path. "This goes around the whole house," he told her. "I'm taking you on a tour. Now obviously," he said, manoeuvring past a grouping of low-growing azaleas, "we can't go to the far reaches out here. Not today. Someday we will." He squeezed her shoulder. "I'm trying very hard to keep my happiness in check." He threw back his head and laughed, letting the sound chuckle out of him deep and warm. He knew it was an extremely pleasant sound, because of the breadth of his chest and the voluptuous timbre of his voice; he knew his voice was one of his more engaging attributes. "And I will, too," he continued. "I won't rush you. We'll take our time." But he couldn't resist laying a kiss upon her hair, just above her temple, and he let himself growl softly into her ear, too, a seductive allusion to what was to come. "Oh, baby," he said softly, straightening. He liked the sound of that. It had a cheerful, reckless quality that he thought appropriate. "Baby, we are going to have such a life." He moved briskly along the walk and around the corner of the house. Here he stopped and gestured again, toward a bank of rhododendrons ten feet high and extending the width of the property, effectively screening the house from the street. "These are gorgeous," he said, "in the spring. You'll love them. And in the middle there," he said, pointing to a circular garden about eight feet in diameter, "where the driveway curves around, there are tulips in the spring, bright red ones, with a border of grape hyacinths. And when those are done, the annuals go in." He proceeded across the front of the house and along the other side, past plantings of chrysanthemums, and came to a halt again at the northwest corner. "There's the rose garden," he said sentimentally. "Twenty-four plants. Mostly hybrid teas. The flower I brought you this morning, it's a 'Mr. Lincoln.' I'm very partial to roses." He bent to press his cheek against hers. "I knew you would be, too." He stood straight again and moved around the corner and back onto the patio. "It's such a beautiful afternoon," he said happily, "I think we should sit out here for a while. Maybe have some iced tea. Would you like that? Or some lemonade? Would you prefer lemonade?" He squatted in front of the wheelchair, smiling at her. "Your wish is my command. Just nod your head. Tea? No? Lemonade? No?" His smile was fading. He was beginning to feel impatient with her.

He stood up and with his hands in his pockets looked around at the tubs overflowing with marguerites and petunias and heliotrope, at the baskets dripping with fuchsias and lobelias and ivy geraniums. Tables and chairs were scattered across the length and width of the patio, as if he'd been expecting a deluge of visitors. And in fact one of his fancies was to host a neighborhood barbecue with this woman — Cassandra — at his side, smiling, flushed with happiness. He looked down at her, sullenness making his bones heavy and his flesh sag. He felt like leaving her out here. All day and all night, until she peed her pants and starved to death. Nobody could see her unless they climbed over the stone wall, and there wasn't much chance of that. Shaughnessy was a place where if you didn't already know your neighbors when you moved in, there was little chance you ever would. People ignored their neighbors in Shaughnessy, unless one of those neighbors ripped down the house he'd bought and put up a great pink fucking monster and there wasn't any chance that Gordon Murphy would do that; all Gordon Murphy wanted was to be ignored by his neighbors and to have the love of a good sexy decent woman — "Is that too much to ask, for fuck's sake?" he shouted at her.

And then he made a big, helpless gesture with his arms. Because he was a loving, expansive, caring person. "And I'm fucking *rich*, too," he said, grabbing the wheelchair handles, propelling her roughly toward the house. He noticed that her hands were gripping the arms tightly, as if she was afraid the thing might topple over, as if the scarves binding her wrists snugly to the chair arms, and the belt that embraced her firmly from left shoulder to right hip, weren't enough to keep her in place.

He hauled open the patio door and pushed the chair up the shallow ramp and into the living room. He sat down on a hassock and stared at her eyes, which were a little glassy, but intelligent and aware. He reached toward her; she flinched and closed her eyes tightly. This depressed and disgusted him, but he ignored it.

He pulled off the scarf that he'd tied around her mouth. "So?" he said coldly. "What's it going to be? Are you going to be my love? Or what?"

Chapter
23

$\mathcal{W}$innifred went to church that Sunday, for some unknown reason. People were surprised to see her there, the minister included. But they weren't any more surprised than Winnifred herself.

When she got home, Naomi's kids greeted her as if she'd known them a lot longer than she had. Kids were like that, of course, they either liked you right away or maybe they never would, but she wished they were less exuberant with their affection. Poor little tykes, she thought, paying Beryl, who was babysitting while Naomi looked at a couple of apartments to rent, pulled this way and that, don't know where they'll be from one day to the next.

She got them settled in front of the TV and found a program for them, one about animals, how to take care of housepets. Then she went into her bedroom to change. She put on a cool short-sleeved robe that was made of cotton and hung long and loose to her feet. It was blue, with large orange parrots all over it. Winnifred had bought it at a garage sale down in Gibsons last summer.

On her way past the guest room she glanced in. The bed wasn't made, and the sleeping bags the kids were using hadn't been rolled up and stowed away in the closet like Winnifred had asked Naomi to do. Winnifred stood very still. She let a hot surge of rage make its way, untrammelled, through her chest — thinking, perhaps, that it would spend itself. But it didn't. Her toleration of it only made her anger grow.

She quickly made the bed, quickly rolled up the sleeping bags. She scooped toys from the floor and dropped them into the carton she'd placed against the wall, next to the dresser, and picked up Naomi's brush, and opened the top dresser drawer, and let it fall in there on top of a box of condoms.

Winnifred had the drawer almost closed when that registered. She yanked it open again and stared inside. Yes. Condoms.

"Winnifred!" called Tiffany. "Winnifred!"

Winnifred ran up the hall and into the living room.

Tiffany, on her knees on the sofa, was pointing out the window. "Daddy's here." She looked at Winnifred, her face solemn. Winnifred thought Tiffany's face looked like a flower. A pansy, she thought, blooming sweetly from the soft tangle of her hair.

Keith got out of his truck and ran up the walk to Winnifred's front step, and started banging on the door.

The woman on the television was explaining how to brush your dog's teeth. Winnifred couldn't imagine doing such a thing.

"I've come for my kids!" Keith hollered. "Open up!"

Winnifred walked to the fireplace and took down one of the crossed swords from the wall above the mantel. They'd been her father's, from when he was in the army; dress swords, worn in a scabbard on his belt. She didn't know how he'd come to have two of them. She'd only ever seen him wearing one at a time.

"Open up!" He banged again on the door. "I'm in a fuckin' hurry here!"

Winnifred raised the sword to waist height and opened the door. "No."

"What the fuck is this?" Keith attempted to shove past Winnifred.

But she thrust the sword into him. He let out a cry of pain and disbelief and fell onto her porch.

"You don't deserve to have children," said Winnifred.

She pushed his foot off the threshold, closed the door and locked it.

"If I have a hero," said Gordon Murphy, "it's Jean Genet. Do you know who he is?" He waited politely. "Of course you do. He talks about the importance of dreaming in the life of a hoodlum. I guess he means in the life of a man in prison. I think of myself as a hoodlum. Even though I'm not in prison." He assumed a position of openness and invitation, his arms spread along the back of the sofa, his knees casually apart, his smile gentle and warm. "Genet's hoodlum has dignity, and fierceness, and a terrifying, thrilling beauty." He leaned forward now, resting his forearms on his knees. "'Your dead man is inside you;'" he quoted, "'mingled with your blood, he flows in your veins, oozes out through your pores, and your heart lives on him, as cemetery flowers sprout from corpses.... He emerges from you through your eyes, your ears, your mouth.' Isn't that great stuff? Isn't that fucking *great*?"

Now he sprawled on the sofa, suddenly impatient, restless. "I'm wanting sex pretty badly," he said, his eyes roving around the room. "This whole house, it's been redone just for you. Did you know that? Have I already told you that? The little room upstairs, that's just temporary, you're only going to be there for a few days. Until we can dispose of all this shit," he said, waving at the wheelchair, the bindings, the gag. "You have no idea how incredibly frustrating it is not to have sex, or conversation, or companionship with you. The sooner this part of the thing is over with, the better."

He knelt in front of her and put his hands on her waist, on her breasts. "I could make you come." He opened her blouse and slid it from her shoulders, and did the same with the straps of her brassiere. He pulled down the bra. "Sitting right here." He placed his mouth on her nipple and swiped his tongue across it, and again. He lifted his head and looked into her eyes. "I don't rape people," he said sternly, "whatever you might think. I don't intend to have sex with you until you're ready." He licked her other nipple. "But I could make you come, now," he said, "with my tongue, and my fingers." He moved his mouth back and forth from one nipple to the other, licking, sucking, kneading her breasts with his hands, and he began to moan, and his moans became louder, and came faster, and finally he shuddered and collapsed in her lap. "Shit. Fuck. I came in my goddamn shorts."

He got to his feet and strode out of the room. He took the stairs two at a time and ran into his dressing room, where he pulled off his shorts and tossed them into the laundry hamper, then went into his bathroom to clean himself up. He put a little talcum powder down there and took a minute to look at his penis, wondering if it was bigger than Jean Genet's. Then he put on clean shorts and went back downstairs, where he adjusted Cassandra's clothing, flicked off the wheelchair's brakes and pushed her into the kitchen.

"Lunchtime," he said thoughtfully, bending over to look into the fridge. "What shall we have for lunch? A rhetorical question," he said, grinning at her over his shoulder. But then he looked at her more intently and stood up straight, letting the fridge door close. "What's the worst thing that could happen, I ask myself, if I were to take off that gag now, right this minute. She could yell and scream at the top of her lungs, I answer myself. If she did that I'd put the sucker right back in her mouth and tie it good and tight, good and tight, *much* tighter than it's in there now. Nobody could hear you anyway, Cassie. But I would find all that noise extremely irritating." He leaned closer to her. "Your eyes are getting *so* big, and your head is bobbing up and down like a woodpecker's." He threw out his arms. "What the hell," he said expansively.

"You're all drugged up anyhow. Probably we only need that in there when we go out into the garden." He untied the scarf.

Cassandra gasped. "Thank you," she croaked.

"You're welcome," said Gordon Murphy, grinning.

"Can I please have a glass of water?"

"'*May* I have a glass of water,'" he said, wagging his finger at her. "'*May* I.'"

"May I please have some water?"

"Of course, my dear. I aim to please." He filled a glass with bottled water from the fridge, got a straw and held the glass while she drank. "'Eyes blackened by fists are the pimp's shame,'" he quoted, "'but Darling says: "My two bouquets of violets."'" When she was finished he leaned down to kiss her temple tenderly. "Don't pull away, my darling," he said softly. "Pulling away is a very bad thing."

He went back to the fridge, humming to himself, and inspected its contents for several minutes. "A salad, I think." He got out a head of butter lettuce, three plum tomatoes, a small zucchini, two hard-boiled eggs and a bottle of commercial salad dressing. From a cupboard he took a can of salmon. In the freezer compartment of the fridge he found two sourdough rolls, which he removed from their plastic freezer bags and placed on a piece of paper towelling to thaw. He poured himself a glass of white wine and set to work putting the salad together.

"What did you mean about redoing the house?" Cassandra said hoarsely.

"You wouldn't have liked it the way it was. So I had it changed." He plunged the cutting blade of the automatic can opener into the tin of salmon and waited for it to revolve.

"It's, uh, a very nice house."

"I know. I knew this was the way you'd like it." He dumped the salmon into a small bowl.

"Bringing me here — "

"Yes?" he said, breaking up chunks of salmon with a fork.

Cassandra managed a smile. "Audacious. It was — audacious."

He put down the fork, staring at her. He placed his hands palm down on the butcher block. "Audacious." He shook his head in wonderment. "Audacious." he hurried to the wheelchair and crouched in front of it, covering Cassandra's bound hands with his own. She saw tears sparkling in his eyes. "You *are* perfect," he whispered. "I knew it. You're the perfect one for me."

She let him slide the side of his face against her cheek. She let his lips touch the edge of her mouth. She felt his warm breath and smelled his aftershave. She made her body relax. And foggily, unsteadily, she began to pray for wisdom.

Chapter
24

On Sunday evening Ronnie parked the grey Toyota outside the pub in Gibsons, the one that looked out over the water. It wasn't late, but the town was quiet except for the pub. The harbor was packed, boats were roped in three abreast, and on some, lights burned and from some, laughter drifted on the night air toward the shore. The breeze stroked music from sailboats at rest, the sound of rigging against masts.

Ronnie walked up the hill, and the noises from the pub and the harbor and the soft slapping of the sea against the pilings retreated, and now he heard the muted crunch of his sneakers in the gravel at the edge of the road, and in the distance a car squealed around a corner.

It wasn't quite nighttime yet. He turned to look down the hill at the town, and the sky was still light behind the land that stretched out and around to form the other side of the harbor. When he turned back, though, he couldn't see for an instant or two, because it was so much darker where he was going than back where he had been.

The sounds of backyard conversations floated through the hot summer evening, and the smells of barbecued dinners. Most of the houses Ronnie passed were dark; sometimes he saw people moving behind their windows, purplish shadows in the dusk, and that was him, of course, moving through their houses, through their lives, with them never knowing he'd been there. Ronnie smiled to himself in the growing darkness, feeling a kinship with all people, related to them through curiosity and a tender, secret regard.

He came to a corner created by a side street and turned at a new cedar fence, walked to the end of it, where it met a garage, and stepped around behind the garage, into darkness. Here he waited for several minutes. A car drove along the side street, stopped at the corner and headed into town. Ronnie heard the jangling of a licence tag against a dog collar and the thudding of footsteps, and peeked out to see a jogger plodding through the light that spilled from the streetlamp on the corner; a German shepherd trotted next to him. The dog glanced over toward Ronnie, and then they were gone, out of the light, behind the trees.

Ronnie slipped out from behind the garage and along the fence to the gate, which he passed through. He was in a large backyard, and although he couldn't see much, he smelled roses. The darkened house next door, Ronnie knew, was for sale and unoccupied. He made his way up the steps and turned on his flashlight to study the lock. But the door, which led, he saw, to a sunporch, wasn't locked. Ronnie was amazed. A surprising number of people did this, left their houses unlocked except when they went to bed at night and sometimes even then, but Ronnie hadn't expected this to be the case at the home of the head of an RCMP detachment. He knew that Alberg himself was away, but he certainly had thought that anybody a Mountie lived with would also make sure their house was locked. Ronnie shook his head. He put on his gloves, opened the door and went inside.

His list of interesting people had a subsection, which was people who were important in the community. He was starting with the police chief (that wasn't what he was called, but it was what he was) because even Ronnie, much as he loved risks and rushes, wasn't arrogant enough to tinker his way into this particular household while the guy was in town.

Also in his subsection were the mayor and the newspaper editor, and maybe the high school principal. He hoped to get to all of them before leaving Sechelt.

Ronnie had decided not to enter Alberg's house while the librarian was in bed asleep. There was something unseemly about that. So he'd opted to come while she was having her usual Sunday dinner with her mother, who lived at Shady Acres.

Ronnie figured he had at least an hour.

He crossed the sunporch, glancing curiously at the enormous wardrobe that loomed there, and slid through the door into the kitchen.

Two cats had appeared, and were meowing.

But Ronnie paid them no mind. He stood stock still in the kitchen and knew that something was terribly wrong.

Ronnie, unmoving, let his eyes move. They caught on a strangeness, studied this, identified it: a knocked-over milk carton on the kitchen counter. He shone his flashlight there and saw that milk had spilled from the counter onto the floor, splashing the cupboard door as it fell. Next to the milk carton were dishes for the cat food. The cats had lapped up some of the milk, maybe most of it, but Ronnie was breathing through his mouth because there was still some lying there where it had spilled, smelling warm and sour and nauseating.

But what was a pushed-over milk carton? he asked himself. What were two cats, plaintively yowling, as if in hunger?

He stretched his hand behind him, fumbling for the doorknob. But no. He didn't understand this fear he had. He wouldn't let it chase him from the house.

"Hang in there, guys," he said out loud to the cats. It made him feel better, to hear the sound of his own voice. "She'll be home in an hour."

231

When he left the kitchen they meowed less loudly, and then they stopped altogether and sat down to clean themselves.

Ronnie moved in the faint light from the streetlamp into the main room of the house, which was a combination dining room and living room. He cast the beam of his flashlight carefully around, turning in a small slow circle. He saw an ottoman, overturned. On a table next to a wing chair, a glass, almost full of a pale yellow liquid; it must have once held ice, for it had sweated, and sat now in a pool of water that had discolored the tabletop. And on the floor, next to the chair, snuggled up against it, a woman's handbag. Ronnie looked at this for several seconds.

He went into the bedroom, which was neat and tidy — although crowded — and smelled of furniture polish, and then into the bathroom, which was very clean, except for the cat's box under the sink. Then he went to the front door. It, too, was unlocked.

Ronnie sat on the edge of the wing chair and tried to think. He had no real reason to believe that anything was wrong. No logical reason. So the milk had been spilled. So the ottoman had been knocked over. So the cats hadn't been fed. So she'd left her purse behind. These things were probably insignificant. She'd gotten upset, maybe had a distressing phone call, and had rushed out of the house forgetting her handbag, maybe tripped on the ottoman on her way out. Ronnie nodded to himself. This made sense.

But there was still this feeling he had, of dreadful strangeness.

He thought a bit longer. Then he went outside, into the backyard.

He waited, in the corner by the gate, the fragrance of roses keeping him company, for a long time. He waited until it was midnight.

Then he went back inside and fed the cats. He thought about locking the doors, front and back, before he left, but decided to leave everything the way he'd found it.

Ronnie went down the hill, unlocked the Toyota and drove home, troubled and uneasy.

Chapter

25

On Sunday, Alberg sailed from Silva Bay to Ganges, on Saltspring Island. He tried again that evening to reach Cassandra. He called Sid Sokolowski, too, but couldn't reach him, either.

He ate, and read, and found himself becoming irritated with Cassandra. He was worrying about her instead of enjoying his boat, and this wouldn't have happened if she'd called him like she'd said she would.

Early Monday morning he turned on the radio, and was putting the coffee on when he heard the Vancouver Coast Guard radio giving out the traffic list: among the boats listed was his. He called them immediately and was intensely disappointed to learn that the message was not from Cassandra but from Isabella.

Alberg didn't want to talk to Isabella.

He wiped off the seats in the cockpit and got the cushions out of a locker. He made himself a cheese sandwich and when the coffee was ready took his breakfast up into the cockpit, and ate sitting in the morning sun.

On the other hand, he thought, he could ask Isabella to have somebody go to his house and find out what the hell was going on. He wasn't seriously worried. But he was somewhat worried.

So he called the Vancouver marine operator and got put through to Isabella.

"We've got trouble over here, Karl," she said. "You're going to have to come home."

"What's going on?"

"It's Sid Sokolowski."

He felt a wave of relief, which he told himself was to be expected; he didn't live with Sid Sokolowski; he wasn't in love with Sid Sokolowski.

"He's gone round the bend," said Isabella. "Just sits there at your desk staring down at it. Whenever anybody tries to talk to him he just says to leave him alone. So I told him to go home."

"Jesus Christ," said Alberg. "Do you know how to reach Elsie?"

"No. Nobody's in charge here, Karl."

"Don't be ridiculous. Who's on duty? Let me talk to him."

"Well the thing is — " He heard her take a breath. "Everybody's down at Winnifred's. She's locked herself in her house with those kids belonging to the waitress at Earl's."

Alberg was looking out through the hatch at the shore, watching a black Jeep winding down the hill toward the village. "I'm not believing you, Isabella. This is a cruel practical joke you're playing on me."

"No, listen, she's in there with the kids and a great big jeezly sword."

"A sword."

"She stabbed somebody with it. He's not hurt bad, but still. . . ."

Alberg looked unhappily around the shadowy cabin of his sailboat.

"I'm awfully sorry, Karl."

"I'll call Tyee Air," he said. "I'll be there in an hour or so."

Cassandra in her dream was standing with a group of people, both male and female but mostly female. Everyone was shaken and horrified, their eyes focussed on a woman in the middle of the group who was quiet and docile, dressed in grey and white. Her head was bent. She was sitting on something — a stool — and all these people, including Cassandra, were surrounding her. She was a woman who periodically went berserk and stabbed people to death, and she was just now recovering from one of these attacks. She was extremely strong at these times, and nobody could stop her.

Cassandra, gazing upon her, realized that the madwoman must be killed, immediately, while she was still in a state of dormancy. She was horrified by the idea but knew that it had to be done, for the good of the community. She spoke this aloud; the others accepted it.

They helped Cassandra take the madwoman by the arms, lead her into an apartment and lay her down in a bathtub. She lay there quietly, unaware of people or place.

Cassandra had a large knife in her hand now. She knelt next to the tub, raised the knife and plunged it into the woman's chest. . . .

She wakened abruptly, gasping, staring unseeing into the corner of the room, and began to sob, wiping her hands over and over again on the front of the T-shirt in which she had slept.

She tried to get out of bed but her legs were shaking, from the dream, from the drugs he gave her, whatever the hell they were. She let herself fall onto the carpeted floor and curled into a ball. She saw herself do this: I am now assuming the fetal position, she remarked in her head.

She tried again to figure out when people would start wondering where she was. She was on holiday from the library. She wasn't expected at Shady Acres for days and days — and when she didn't show up her mother would assume she'd just forgotten. Helen Mitchell would be a martyr for a day or two, expecting an apologetic phone call, and when one didn't come and didn't come, finally she'd bring herself to call Cassandra — but how long would she wait? And then there was Karl — oh god, oh god, tears again... she ached for him, reached for him, spoke to him through the ether: help me, I love you, help me...

The night before he left she'd looked up from her book and recognized the degree of her contentment. Propped up on pillows, her bedside radio playing softly, Karl sleeping beside her, the cats curled up at the foot of the bed, she had acknowledged that she was already missing him, and was deliciously aware of how happy she would be when he came home. This, she had thought, is as good as it gets.

On the floor in Gordon Murphy's guest bedroom, her cheek against the carpet, knees up to her chin, Cassandra felt a tiny dribble of anger, timid and tentative. She pictured herself in some woods somewhere on a cold, cold day, kneeling in front of a pile of dry leaves and twigs, rubbing two stones together. (Would that work? she thought. Don't distract me, she told herself.) She imagined this; imagined that a small spark appeared, and imagined herself breathing upon it, encouraging it to grow... soft puffs of her breath tenderly applied to the spark that was anger... the trick was to get it big enough to make her strong but not so big that she couldn't control it.

The music started, billowing into her room from a speaker in the corner. The music helped the anger grow.

Cassandra clambered to her feet and walked unsteadily into the bathroom to wash, to comb her hair, to prepare for the day. She would keep her anger on a shelf in her mind, folded, like a long velvet skirt. It was deep red in color — an appropriate shade for anger. She folded it, placed it on the shelf, ran her hand lovingly along its length.

Back in the bedroom she dressed and sat in the easy chair waiting for breakfast, her hands flat on the arms of the chair. Gordon Murphy arrived a few minutes later.

He knocked lightly on the door, unlocked it, and entered, carrying a tray. "Porridge today," he said.

Cassandra noticed that his expression was grim and tried to interpret this: was it in her best interests that he be grim? How could she use his being grim to her advantage? Was he preoccupied? With something else? Was he getting tired of her? Ready to let her go? How the hell can he let you go, idiot, you'd charge the bastard with kidnapping and I'm pretty sure he knows that.

It had of course occurred to her that these moments, the breakfast moments, offered her the best opportunity for escape. She would only have to overpower him. Smack him over the head or something. But she'd gone through the bedroom and the bathroom with scrupulous care and had found nothing that could serve as a weapon. Maybe a dresser drawer, she thought, but couldn't see herself keeping such a thing hidden, and the gaping hole in the dresser would be obvious to him the minute he opened the door. There wasn't anything on the food trays, either. The dishes were plastic — maybe not plastic, but something unbreakable, anyway. Even the cutlery. It wasn't fair, Cassandra thought resentfully, watching as he approached her chair. He had had all the time he needed to prepare for this. She had had no time at all.

"And some toast and marmalade," he said.

"I hate marmalade."

His hand moved so quickly she didn't even see it, just felt the slap. She thought for an instant that her head had been dislocated from her neck. I hadn't known that was possible, she thought, amazed, and placed her palm against her cheek, where the pain bloomed like a flower in time-lapse photography.

Gordon Murphy had put the tray down on the desk and was staring at her truculently. Cassandra, with an effort, turned her head to look at him straight on. Her whole head, she thought, must have swollen up like a pumpkin. Pumpkinhead. That's me.

"If you hit me again, you son-of-a-bitch," she said, calmly, clearly, "you can kiss your dreams goodbye."

She and Gordon Murphy stared at each other for a moment. Cassandra wanted desperately to be outside. There wasn't enough air in this room.

"I hate marmalade," she said. "I also hate Wagner. I want you to get rid of the marmalade and turn off the Wagner."

"Oh, you do, do you."

"I do. And then I want you to show me your photograph albums. I presume you have photograph albums?" I'm blithering, she thought. Maybe dithering. Shut up.

His forehead creased. He looked suspicious and perplexed. Taken aback. Good, thought Cassandra. The more aback he's taken, the better off I'll be.

"Why?" he said.

"I want to have a look at your family. Your genes."

"My genes." He smiled a little, as he turned and went to the door. "I might have changed my mind," he said absently. "You might be too old." He looked back over his shoulder. "Too — used."

"Fine," said Cassandra, whose heart was hammering in accompaniment to the throbbing in her head. She tried to sound cheerful and confident. "Then I'll be on my way." She didn't stand up, though. She couldn't have stood up.

"Not yet," he said. "Eat your breakfast. I have to think." He left the room, and she heard him lock the door.

He went directly to his gym. He was wearing dark blue today, navy blue gym shorts, sweatshirt, socks and training shoes.

He got on the treadmill first, warming up, walking, and set the timer for five minutes, when he'd start to jog. He was beginning to feel elated. He had thought when he struck her that it was another no-go, but then that amazing thing happened: she hadn't wept or pleaded, she had looked at him with anger and contempt. So it had turned out to be not an act of violence at all, but a test. And had she passed? *Had* she passed!

He resolved to remain calm, not to let his excitement grow just yet. He had to keep things under control — keep himself and the situation under control. . . .

"Divine loves her man," Jean Genet had written. "She bakes pies for him and butters his roasts. She even dreams of him if he is on the toilet. She worships him in any and all positions."

Gordon Murphy imagined Cassandra sitting over there in the massage chair, smiling indulgently, watching him. She'd be leaning forward a bit, her hands linked around her crossed legs. And she'd be wearing a very short skirt and a top with a low neck that permitted him to see the beginnings of her breasts. And her hair would be long, tied up on the top of her head with a red ribbon.

Her hair was short, though.

But it would grow.

The timer went off. Gordon Murphy set it for ten minutes this time and began a slow jog. He kept on jogging while he pulled off his sweatshirt and tossed it to the floor. From the massage chair he heard Cassandra catch her breath. He glanced at himself in the mirror. God, he looked good. Tanned, strong, healthy. Unlike a lot of men who worked out, he hadn't neglected his legs. His thighs and calves were gratifyingly muscular. His hair was thick. His nose was perhaps slightly too large; he wondered if Cassandra thought so. He'd been giving some thought lately to having surgery. He hated the idea of knives working on his face, but he might go for a consultation, see what the guy had to say for himself and his procedures.

Sweat had broken out on his face and body. He stretched as he jogged, pulling in his stomach muscles, pushing back his shoulders, and thought about Cassandra over there in the massage chair having a hard time keeping away from him. He thought about her getting up and coming over to the tread-mill, slipping off her shoes, and skirt, and top, revealing the

241

leotard beneath, the kind that provides nothing but a thong between the legs, and no leggings with it, either. She'd get up behind him on the treadmill — he could feel her presence there, smell her perfume. And now he felt her breasts against his back, jiggling as she jogged, keeping up with him. Her hands were on his waist, moving around to the front, down into his shorts.... Gordon Murphy, hanging onto the treadmill handles, couldn't keep up with the moving surface beneath his feet. He turned the treadmill off and thrust his hand down there where Cassandra's hand wasn't: "Jerk jerk jerk jerk," he said, and when he was finished he shook his head. "It was only my workout clothes this time," he said to himself.

Ronnie drove slowly past the house Monday morning, expecting to see her car outside, but it wasn't there.

He parked in Gibsons and went into a place across from the bookstore for a coffee. He was supposed to go see a guy who had black Labrador retriever puppies for sale. But Ronnie was rattled not to see the librarian's car in front of her house. Finally he called the guy and told him he'd be later than he'd said, and he walked up the hill and turned down the side street, through the gate and into the staff sergeant's backyard.

He wasn't worried about being seen. If anybody saw him he could pretend to be a guy come to cut the lawn — which could have used it, too, now that he had a look at it in daylight. But nobody would see him. The neighbors' house was empty, there was a vacant lot across the street, and the garage blocked the view of the people who lived in the house behind this one. Ronnie pulled on his gloves, mounted the steps and went in through the sunporch.

He found everything as he had left it, except that the cats' dishes were empty again. They didn't seem interested in the fact that he'd returned. One of them was playing with a ball of aluminium foil, and the other one was lying on the sofa. She opened one eye and gazed at Ronnie for a second, then drifted back into sleep.

Ronnie got down on the floor next to the wing-back chair and pulled the handbag from where it sat between the chair and the table leg. He unclasped it and looked inside. There was a keychain, but when he examined the keys on it he saw that none was for an automobile. Maybe she kept her car keys separate, he thought. He poked around in there: a brush, a wallet, a notebook with a ballpoint pen clipped to it, an envelope, a package of Life Savers, a Day-Timer. He removed this and leafed through the pages. Shit. She'd taken her car to Warren's shop on Friday, that's why there weren't any car keys here. And she'd drawn a line through "Dinner with Mom."

Ronnie sat back on his heels, thinking. Then he went back into the handbag, drew out the envelope and pulled from it a handwritten letter.

"Cassandra," it began. Ronnie knew from hearing it in the library that that was the librarian's first name.

"I think you will agree that you have encouraged my interest. I am not easily dissuaded.

"You deprive yourself of unimaginable joy. Please abandon this quixotic behavior."

And it was signed "Gordon."

Ronnie's face — he could feel it — was all round eyes and open mouth.

"Gordon Murphy," was printed at the top of this extraordinary letter, plus a Vancouver address and phone number. Ronnie read it again. And again.

When one of the cats brushed suddenly against his thigh, he nearly jumped out of his skin.

He was full of confusion and resolve. He read the letter one more time and memorized the address and the telephone number. Then he folded it, put it back in the envelope, put the envelope back in the handbag and pushed the bag carefully back into the space between the chair and the table leg. He got to his feet and looked down at the handbag from several angles. Then he reached down and pulled it out a little bit, so it would be more visible.

There might not be anything wrong. But he was pretty sure there was.

Before he left, he fed the cats again. He put this empty can and the one from yesterday into a plastic grocery bag that he found in a kitchen drawer and took them away with him.

Down the hill in Gibsons he found a trash barrel for the catfood cans.

Whatever was wrong, it might not have anything to do with this guy in Vancouver who'd written her the weird letter.

But it would take only... say, three hours, four hours tops, to check this guy out.

Ronnie got into the Toyota and drove to the Langdale ferry terminal.

Chapter

26

It was late morning when Alberg arrived back in Sechelt.

Winnifred's neighborhood, he thought, looked more like a county fair than a crime scene. Naomi was sitting in a lawn chair, which she told him later she had borrowed from the drug addict next door. She had set it up in the middle of the street, just outside the yellow tape that had been strung around Winnifred's house and yard. Among the crowd that had gathered were people drinking coffee or pop or beer, people taking pictures, people eating potato chips or hot dogs or chewing gum. They sat on lawns or leaned against treetrunks or stood with their weight on one foot, their arms folded. They looked through sunglasses, from under visors and around other people who were closer to the scene than they. They were being warily observed by several police officers, but they weren't an excited crowd — curious, of course, but mostly bemused.

"I want my kids to see me if they look out the window," Alberg heard Naomi tell Jack Duggin. "Why the hell should I move? That's a sword she's got in there, not a gun, for godsake, she can't get at me unless she comes charging outa there, which is what I want her to do anyway." She turned to address the crowd. "That's a crazy woman in there," she said, speaking very loudly. Alberg knew that Winnifred could prob-

245

ably hear her through the open windows in the living room and the kitchen. "A crazy person who's a kidnapper."

"I don't think you should try to make her mad," said Corporal Duggin uneasily.

"Well, I do," said Naomi, furious. "I told you, I want to make her charge outa there at me."

"But what if she turns on your kids instead?" said Duggin. "She already speared your husband, right?" Naomi looked at him. He was crouched next to the lawn chair, speaking softly. "Deranged people are not predictable."

"He's right, Naomi," said Alberg. He looked up the walk at the house. "What's the situation, Jack?"

"This has been going on for almost twenty-four hours now, Staff," said Duggin. He stood up. "The kids' father came to the house, said he was going to take them away. She said no way. He was hollering, banging on the door — so she poked him with this sword, and he falls on her porch, screaming. The next-door neighbor over there called us. Turns out it's this Keith Hellyer guy we've been looking for."

"How bad is he?"

"Oh hell." The constable laughed. "Not bad. It's just a scratch, really. We've got him in custody for twenty-four hours. We'll get busy checking his house and his truck for evidence in the Kijinski thing" — he gestured toward Winnifred's house — "as soon as we can wind things up here."

"The damn druggie," said Naomi with contempt, staring at Winnifred's front door. "Cokehead. Dragged off to jail. Good riddance, I say. She was right not to let him have my damn kids. But now she won't let *me* have them, either."

"Why not?" said Alberg.

"She's turned out to be crazy, that's why," said Naomi, glaring at him. She ooked moodily at the house again. "I should of never come to stay in her damn guest room."

"Did anybody try to get her on the phone?"

246

"Yeah," said Duggin. "She doesn't answer. And she won't let anybody get close to the house."

Alberg sighed and started slowly up the walk.

"Stop right where you are, Karl," Winnifred called out.

Alberg stopped, took his hands from his pockets and held them up, palms out. "What's going on here, Winnifred?"

"Neither of them is a fit parent. So I'm pondering what to do about that."

"Are the children okay?"

"Of course they're okay, for heaven's sake. That's what this is all about."

"I'd like to talk to you, Winnifred."

"Well, I don't want to talk to you."

Ronnie was on the ferry when he decided he had to call the police.

Sure, it could be nothing at all; she could've turned up back home safe and sound while Ronnie was driving to the ferry, or that could be happening this very minute.

On the other hand, she could be in a lot of trouble, and it was Ronnie's responsibility to let the police know about it.

He had to stand in a line-up for the phone and was for a while worried that they'd get to Horseshoe Bay before it was his turn. But soon there were only three people ahead of him, and then two, and then it was Ronnie's turn. Fortunately the person behind him, a teenaged kid, had a bunch of friends with him and they were all talking and laughing together and not interested in Ronnie's phone call.

He had to get the number from information.

He dialled it, and a female voice said, "Sechelt RCMP."

Ronnie talked in a very quiet voice, and made it deeper than his normal one. "I've got some information for you," he said.

"Just a second, I'll get an officer."

"No," said Ronnie quickly. "I don't want an officer. Listen. It's got to do with the staff sergeant. Something funny's happened at his house."

"Who is this?"

"Never mind. You gotta take this seriously, ma'am. Send somebody over there to have a look. Quick." He hesitated, and then hung up.

Ronnie made his way in the middle of a crowd down to car deck "A" — they'd announced that the ferry was nearing the terminal. He found the Toyota, unlocked the door and climbed in.

What the hell did he plan to do when he got to this place? he asked himself, hands on the steering wheel, gazing through the windshield at the tourists trying to remember where they'd left their vehicles.

He flexed his hands, and flexed them again, and a torrent of possibilities flooded his mind: he'd find that no such address existed, or else it had been burned to the ground. Or there'd be an ambulance in front when he got there. And he'd see the librarian lying on a gurney, and he'd see somebody covering her face with a sheet.

Ronnie shuddered. He tried to work out the likely course of events if the police did go to her house, and did get alarmed, like Ronnie had. They would want the guy who wrote the letter checked out, wouldn't they? And they'd probably get the Vancouver police to do it, because that would be faster.

Even so, Ronnie thought, as the ferry eased against the dock, he would probably get there first. But he could hold the fort for a while, he thought staunchly. Sure he could.

"Do you need anything?" Alberg asked Winnifred, about half an hour later. "Food? Anything?"

"I need you to get off my sidewalk."

"Staff Sergeant?"

He turned to see Alistair McNeil waving at him from behind the yellow tape. He walked over to him.

"Would it be all right if I tried?" said McNeil.

With his peripheral vision Alberg saw Isabella slipping rapidly through the crowd toward him. He had a sudden image of Sid Sokolowski sitting alone in a darkened house, lifting his service revolver, blowing himself away.

He stared at Winnifred's front door, painted yellow to match the new siding, and he couldn't get apprehension for Sokolowski out of his head; it had rooted there, pervasive and malevolent.

"Yeah. Go ahead," he said to McNeil, and the man slipped under the tape.

"Stop right there," said Winnifred sharply.

"Call her twins," said Naomi suddenly.

"Let me have my say," said McNeil to Winnifred. "I'll be brief." He glanced behind him, at the crowd, and lowered his voice somewhat. "We got off on the wrong foot, you and me."

Alberg turned and searched the crowd for Isabella, and there she was, emerging from behind a portly man wearing a straw hat and eating an ice cream-cone.

"You looked at me standing there talking about garden services," said Alistair McNeil. "And I was a man of about your husband's age. And I was alive. And he had just died. I think that's what it was, Mrs. Gartner, that got us off on the wrong foot."

"Her damn twins," said Naomi impatiently.

Alberg stared at Isabella, trying to read her face. Then he turned back to watch McNeil.

"Mrs. Gartner, you need somebody to talk to about this situation," said Alistair, "and I'm him."

"Call her damn twins!" said Naomi, tugging at Alberg's sleeve. "In Vancouver! They'll come over, talk some sense into her."

Winnifred's front door slowly opened. She pushed two swords onto her porch. Alistair McNeil mounted the steps and went inside.

"What twins?" said Alberg to Naomi. "Winnifred doesn't have any twins." Isabella, hurrying toward him, was looking into his face. "Is it Sid?"

"No, Karl, it's — it looks like there's something wrong at your house."

"Why did she die?" Cassandra had asked her mother. She was six.

"Old age."

This was incredible. Cassandra knew trees that were older than her grandmother.

This was incredible, too. To be snatched away by a sex-mad crazy person. It was ridiculous.

He hadn't come to her room all day. She didn't have a watch or a clock, but she figured from the way the light entered through the skylight that it was afternoon.

"Good luck!" they had chorused, the friends who'd given her a moving-in-together shower. Wishing her luck. As if she'd been setting out to swim the English Channel.

Cassandra badly wanted to have a plan. So far she had none.

She was feeling somewhat more alert today, which confirmed her suspicion that the madman was mixing some damn drug into her food. She'd been eating as little as possible and drinking a lot of water, in the hope of flushing it out of her system. And this seemed to be working.

"I'll call you!" she'd shouted, waving vigorously as he motored out of the harbor. He waved back, grinning hugely. She thought his sailboat looked perilously small.

She got up from the armchair and did some stretching exercises, and then some sit-ups, but after five sit-ups she was feeling weak and dizzy so she decided that was a bad idea.

He must have wondered why she hadn't phoned. Maybe he thought she'd forgotten how to get the marine operator. He would have called her, finally. Surely he would have. When was it that he left, anyway? How many days ago?

Incarceration was a hell of a life, she thought, wandering through her cramped quarters, touching each wall in turn with the tips of her fingers. You were either scared out of your mind or bored to tears. Nothing to read. No television to watch.

Her only hope was to get him to trust her enough to let her out into the rest of the house. And then to make a break for it. She saw herself pelting down his driveway, the madman at her heels. If she yelled and screamed, would Shaughnessy listen? Would Shaughnessy care? Or would Shaughnessy ignore her unseemly outburst and go about its business as usual?

Her mother wouldn't expect to see her until Friday, but Cassandra usually called her several times a week. Maybe she was even now sitting in Shady Acres, brooding about Cassandra's forgetfulness but too proud to complain. "Complain, Mother," Cassandra said aloud. "*Complain*, for god's sake."

A seagull was scrabbling on the skylight, trying to grab hold. Cassandra was tempted to see it as a messenger from Karl. She resisted this, though; she didn't like to think of herself as a fanciful or a sentimental person; sentimentality had been expunged by the decades of her life.

She wondered how he would react, this madman, if she told him she was menopausal.

What was likely to happen to her, anyway? Her heart rose in her chest, then plummeted, like a wounded elevator.

She was dozing in the chair when she heard the key in the lock. The door flew open and the madman stood there, filling the doorway, holding a tray, which he deposited on the coffee table in front of her. It was hard to judge his mood, even though he was smiling. Not at her. Just smiling. He went back into the hall and picked something up from the floor, then returned, closing the door behind him. With a gesture vaguely theatrical, he tossed a photo album on the table next to the tray. He was wearing jeans and a white sweatshirt and, yet again, sneakers without socks.

Cassandra looked down at the album. "Good. Let's have a look." She opened to the first page, which held an eight-by-ten glossy of Gordon Murphy in graduation robes. So did the next page. A picture for each degree.

"I think you should eat first." He squatted next to the coffee table and took a mug of soup from the tray. "Campbell's tomato. And a piece of cheese bread to go with it."

"That's very kind of you. I'm actually very hungry." She lifted the mug to her mouth. "Ouch. Hot. I'll let it cool for a minute," she said, giving him a smile. "This is an excellent picture of you," she said approvingly, tapping the album, which was an old one, Cassandra now noticed, with black pages thick and fuzzy, almost like heavy blotting paper. She saw gashes where things had been snicked away, and remembered albums belonging to her mother, with tiny triangular pockets designed to contain the photographs' corners.

Cassandra turned the page. The shock of what she saw kept her still and silent, desperate not to move or speak. She felt his eyes on the side of her face. He was still crouched down, level with her. Cassandra's fingers moved hesitantly through the air toward first the left-hand page then the right. "My goodness," she said. "What beautiful women." The one on the left was in her thirties, smiling at the camera, wearing a bronze silk shirt and a pair of lilac silk pants, apparently sewing a pillow. The picture was an irregular shape, the background having been cut out.

"My mother," said Gordon. "And over there," he said, pointing to the opposite page, "my sister." She was about eighteen, with long wavy hair, and she was sitting on a bench in front of a bed of tall pink flowers. This picture was perhaps four inches square. Both had been carefully cut from magazines, and taped into the album. Gordon Murphy reached out and turned the page. "I don't have a separate picture of my brother. But here's the three of us together." This one showed a girl of about six, also with long, wavy hair, standing between two boys who were older, a blond about eight and a taller, dark-haired boy of ten or twelve.

"Goodness," said Cassandra. She was acutely aware of his presence.

She concentrated on the pictures.

He chuckled, pointing. "This is one of my favorites. My dad," he said fondly. A balding man in his fifties, on a bench, surrounded by larkspur. "And here's the family home," he said, turning another page. A chunk had been carefully removed from the middle, where there had probably been type. The picture showed the front of a white house, with lattices covered with roses, a round table on a flagstone patio and hollyhocks growing along a fence. "And finally," he said proudly, flicking another page, "here. You want to see genes? How are these for genes?"

Five black-and-white photos, reproduced in the pages of another magazine. Two oval, two rectangular, one square. All from the last century. A man with wild hair, holding a violin. A grim-faced young woman, full-lipped, with thick hair piled on top of her head. An old woman wearing a shawl over her head and shoulders, and a black dress and black gloves. A family portrait, dour parents and three bored children. And a bearded man whose eyes still blazed. None of them looked happy about having been purloined to serve as Gordon Murphy's ancestors.

He slapped the album shut and stood up. He leaned against the doorjamb and folded his arms. Cassandra was looking at the front of the album and nodding to herself.

"Speak," said Gordon. She looked up. He was expressionless.

"I'm wondering why you did it," she said. He didn't respond. "You must have a real family. Everyone does. So I guess they don't meet your expectations. So you decided to invent another one." She opened her eyes wide. "That is an extremely creative act." He continued to look blank. Vacant. "I approve of your choices, too. Very much. Although if I may — ?" He nodded. "I think that your garden, the one here, is quite a bit more beautiful than the one in the picture. Of the family home."

He continued to study her. She felt very much like a laboratory specimen.

Suddenly he squatted down in front of her, moving swiftly, taking her by surprise so that her heart lurched. He stared intently into her eyes. "I cannot decide," he said slowly, "whether you are bullshitting me. Or not."

Cassandra looked back at him, trying hard to appear direct and honest and dignified. Trustworthy.

Chapter
27

*A*lberg couldn't park directly in front of his house because there was a patrol car there. He pulled in behind it, got out of his Oldsmobile and closed the door. He watched himself do this: saw his hand on the edge of the door, saw it push the door closed, heard the thwacking sound, looked intently at his hand, which was reddish brown from the sun.

Across the street, George Peterson was out in his front yard, leaning on something, a rake, maybe, and he was staring openly at Alberg. George cocked his head, questioningly. Alberg looked back at him and remembered his father's funeral, and how much food there had been. He imagined George and his wife — whose name Alberg had temporarily forgotten — trotting across the street toward his house, laden with casseroles and cakes.

He walked past the patrol car, in which he saw Norman McIntyre talking into the radio. He went through the front gate in his new fence and along the newly repaired walk and into his house. Norah Gibbons stood just inside the door.

"Is McIntyre calling the Gibsons detachment?" said Alberg.

"Yes, he is, Staff."

Alberg stepped along the short hallway and stopped, and looked around. "Have you seen my cats?"

"Yeah, Staff," said the constable. "They went outside when we came in. I hope that's okay."

The caller had said "something funny" had happened. Isabella said he'd sounded concerned.

"Was the door locked when you got here?" said Alberg, looking at the overturned ottoman. He felt frustrated, acutely impatient.

"No, it wasn't, Staff."

He saw the glass, sitting in a puddle on the end table.

Maybe it was a neighbor who'd called, Isabella had suggested. Maybe it was George Peterson who'd called, Alberg thought now. What the hell could he have seen?

He saw Cassandra's handbag.

He strode across the room and reached for it, hesitated — was he in the middle of a fucking crime scene or not? "Get me some gloves, please, Norah," he said, crouching down in front of the chair. The handbag was the one he had given her, a bag with shape and substance to it, not one of those big, limp over-the-shoulder things.

Norah Gibbons handed him a pair of disposable gloves and he put them on, pulled the handbag out and opened it.

Minutes later he dropped the letter and stood, his heart hammering, and saw the world through a haze of pain and fury. He made his way out of the house, stumbling through the kitchen and the sunporch and down the stairs to stand in the middle of his backyard. He stripped the gloves from his hands and let them fall to the ground. He couldn't think. He felt like he was in the middle of a hurricane.

"Karl."

Alberg didn't move. "Jesus, Sid," he said. "I don't know what's going on here."

The sergeant came into his field of vision. "I'll phone the guy. His number's on there."

A jolt went through Alberg, leaving him breathless. "No," he said. "I'll phone him."

He sprinted across the yard and up the steps, consumed with the need to hear Gordon Murphy's voice.

He got an answering machine. Alberg listened intently. He left no message.

"Sid, you call him now. I want you to hear him."

The sergeant placed the call. He listened, looking out the living-room window. "He sounds like a sleazy bastard," he said when he'd hung up. He frowned, thinking. "Murphy. Murphy. That's Irish. He doesn't sound Irish. Not that there aren't Irish sleazebags, I guess." He glanced at the constables. "You two go on back to Sechelt now. I'll stay here and work with the Gibsons crew when they get here."

"You were sent home," said Alberg. He was in a tremendous struggle to remain calm, to get logical. Methodical. In control. "You're on leave."

Sokolowski put an arm around Alberg's shoulder and walked him into the kitchen. "I can handle this, Karl. You can't. Even if you could, you can't, and you know it."

"Jesus Christ, I just can't sit around doing fuck-all. I don't even know what the fuck's going on here." He rubbed his temples and leaned against the counter. "She's gone. She didn't take her car. She didn't take her purse. She didn't take a coat or a jacket. She left in a hurry, and I don't know why or where she was going. She leaves behind this fucking letter, which has been torn up, which suggests she didn't like the tone of the fucking thing, but which has also been stuck together again, which suggests what? Christ." He was shaking.

"This is what we're gonna do," said Sokolowski. "We're gonna talk to everybody who knows her. We're gonna collect evidence throughout the house. We're gonna question the neighbors. And I'm gonna get on the horn to Vancouver and have them send somebody over to talk to this Murphy guy."

Alberg, staring at spilled milk on the kitchen counter, tried again to summon the cold, enigmatic side of him, the side he associated, for convenience sake, with his Scandinavian heritage.

"That sounds good, Sid," he said quietly. Cassandra might not tell him, he thought, if she had become attracted to somebody else. "Yeah. Okay." But she sure as hell wouldn't run off with somebody else without telling him. He pushed himself away from the counter. "I'm going to make myself scarce around here." Besides, he thought, she was using the purse I gave her. He headed for the door to the sunporch. "Thanks, Sid," he said as he left the house.

"I'll keep in touch," Sokolowski called, "over your car phone."

He'd tell them it was a police emergency, Alberg thought, heading for the ferry. They'd move him to the head of the line.

Chapter
28

"I have been considering," said Gordon Murphy, staring into Cassandra's face, "moving on to Phase Two. Or Three or Four or wherever we are. That is to say, I've been thinking that it might be time to offer you more space."

"I'd like that," said Cassandra. She tried to look at him fondly, focussing on the scar near his right eyebrow.

He brushed hair away from her forehead. "You could perhaps roam throughout the house. Becoming acquainted with your new home." He leaned close and laid his lips against her cheek. "Sleeping in my bed." He turned her head and kissed her lips. Cassandra let them open slightly, and made them soft. "Mmmmm," said Gordon Murphy. He pulled away before she did. "I'd have to turn the alarms on, of course." He studied her for a moment. "Just for the first day or so." He kissed her temple. Cassandra tried to persuade her body to relax. "I know," he said suddenly. He stood, and dazzled her with his smile. "We'll have a celebration dinner! I'll cook — and you'll help!"

"Wonderful," said Cassandra, stretching her mouth into a smile.

Jesus, he thought, staring at her, exultation beginning to grow. It was going to work. He pulled her out of the chair and hugged her. With his arms around her he said, "You haven't had a tour of the house, have you. You don't know all the wonderful stuff there is here for you, oh my darlin', my darlin', we're going to be so happy...."

The front-door chime sounded throughout the house. Gordon's smile faded. He tilted his head, quizzical. He could let the machine take his phone calls. But he didn't think he ought to ignore the doorbell, not with his car sitting there in the garage.

He backed out of her room and locked it, and made his way downstairs. Fuck! Why hadn't he locked the damn gate!

Through the peephole he saw that on his doorstep stood two police officers. Their patrol car was in his driveway. Gordon waited until he was filled with calm. Then he opened the door.

"Hello," he said, polite but questioning.

"Are you Gordon Murphy?" said the older cop, who was older than Gordon and had a belly on him that didn't look healthy.

"Yes, I am."

"You know a woman named Cassandra Mitchell?"

Gordon lifted his eyebrows. "Why, yes. Is something wrong, officer?"

"You seen her recently?"

He frowned, thinking. "Not since — oh, late June, I guess it was. We served on a committee together."

"We're just making a routine inquiry, sir," said the other cop, who was tall and young, with cold eyes. "You mind if we take a look around?"

"Where?" said Gordon, amazed.

"Inside," said the young cop, looking behind Gordon into the house.

"Inside my house? Oh no. I don't think so. Why? For what?"

"She's missing, see," said the cop with the big belly. "Her friends are worried about her."

"What the hell makes you think you'll find her here?"

"Well, there was apparently a letter found."

Gordon Murphy looked blank. Then he laughed. "Oh. Oh dear. Oh yes." He glanced down, then up, wearing a shamefaced expression. "I admit, I found her attractive.... Gee, you know? I'd almost forgotten about this." He laughed again. "She spurned my advances, gentlemen. I try to forget such experiences just as quickly as I can."

"Well, we haven't got a warrant," said the older cop. "Not yet, anyway. So we can't make you cooperate."

"I'm cooperating by talking to you," said Gordon with a smile.

"Sure you don't want to change your mind?" said the young cop.

Gordon shook his head, still smiling, and they got in their car and drove away. He watched them crunch down his gravel driveway, stop to pull open the gate, drive through, and stop to close the gate again.

Gordon closed the door and turned the keypad set into the wall. He punched in the code that set the house alarm system and then the one for the gate. Then he took the stairs at a gallop, unlocked Cassandra's door and burst into her room.

"The cops were here. That was the fucking cops." He was looking at the wheelchair in the corner and the scarves that had bound her to it. "They'll be back. I've gotta get rid of that damn thing." Then he looked at her. "Why did you have to keep that letter, you fucking bitch."

"I couldn't possibly *not* keep it," said Cassandra, with an effort. "It was a love letter."

He stared at her for a long moment, his breath coming fast. "I've got to think." He left her room, locking the door behind him.

In his gym, he stripped, put on shorts and a muscle shirt and picked up his leather skipping rope.

Christ those goddamn stupid cops. It was going to *work*, she was going to *love* him, and *live* with him. But now... They hadn't left him enough fucking time. He needed more time with her. Not much; maybe even just another forty-eight hours. He knew she couldn't yet be trusted to say to the cops when they returned, "I am here freely, of my own free will. This is the man I love." No, she would not say that yet. He knew it.

But how could he know that for sure? She had been warm and loving today, hadn't she? Hadn't she demonstrated a depth of feeling and understanding that was staggering in a woman?

He skipped, feverishly. She'd already passed a number of tests. Could he trust her. *Could* he?

Or, goddamn it, was she going to turn into Woman Number Five on him for fuck's sake and end up fertilizing the rose garden with Julia Garcia....

But no. Oh no, there had to be a way.

And Gordon skipped and skipped, until sweat ran from his forehead into his eyes and mouth. He stopped and put on a sweatband, and climbed aboard his exercise bike, and pedalled hard, thinking harder.

The police were looking for her. Cassandra wanted to be jubilant, but this could be the most dangerous time of all. What's he thinking, she wondered; what are his alternatives? How could she persuade him — and of what exactly *should* she persuade him? She walked up and down in her tiny room.

It was getting dark outside. Cassandra had turned on a lamp.

It's been days since I've seen myself in a mirror, she thought, and her mind flitted drunkenly from one thing to another, touching on Gordon and the wheelchair and the drug he'd been giving her; on Karl and the darkening sky and the closeness of the city; on giving up, giving in, remaining brave; on making choices, taking chances, dying.

262

She didn't know where he went when he said he had to think. Did he leave the house? Maybe he sat on the floor in a corner somewhere. Maybe in the hallway right outside her room. Maybe he was there now, right outside her room.

She had been looking absently at the door for several seconds when she saw the handle turn. Oh god. Oh no. Her heart soared, and she felt nauseated.

And angry. Incredibly angry. How humiliating, to be so completely at the mercy of somebody else.

She tried to calm herself, to steel herself for whatever crazy decision he'd come up with.

The door didn't fly open, bouncing against the wall. It didn't open normally, either. It just — slid open, almost soundlessly. Cassandra's gaze was riveted on this three-inch gap. She had to do something about it. She went to the door and pulled it wide open, saying, "Gordon?" almost in a whisper. Not a sound. She stepped into the hall. "Gordon?" Nothing. She felt weak and faint, looking down the stairs that led to the second floor.

She made her way down the steps, her legs trembling, her hand on the banister cold and clammy, and stood in the second-floor hall, looking up and down. All the doors were closed. She still couldn't hear a sound. She called his name more loudly. "Gordon!" No reply. Cassandra went to the top of the next flight of stairs. From here she could see the entrance hall. She could see the front door. It was standing open.

This was a test. She knew it. It was a test, and she mustn't fail it. She had to go down those stairs and across the hall, reach for the door and push it closed, and lock it, lock herself back in here with the madman. She *had* to do this, she thought, moving down the stairs, her footsteps making no sound on the thick carpet. She heard nothing except her own voice, a quick shallow whisper, saying oh god dear god please god, over and over.

She glided down the stairway, thinking, he's watching me from somewhere, I cannot fail, I must not fail. Now she had reached the bottom, now she was walking on shiny black marble, but she still made no sound as she crossed it because she was barefoot. She'd forgotten that, until she felt the shock of cold marble on the soles of her feet.

Through the open door Cassandra saw moths fluttering around the outside light and a sweep of pavement encircling a flower garden and a gravel driveway disappearing into darkness and at the bottom of the driveway, a lighted gate. Standing open.

Cassandra approached the front door expecting at every second to hear his voice. "Aha!" he'd say when she pushed the door closed. Or, "You passed!" Or, "Oh, darlin', you do love me!"

She reached for the doorknob — sobbing, now, knowing she had to do it....

Cassandra bolted through the doorway, down the gravel driveway and through the gate. Weeping and staggering, she propelled herself to the end of the block and around the corner and saw a Mercedes gliding onto the street from a driveway fifty feet away. Cassandra screamed, waving her arms. The Mercedes stopped, then started driving away. Cassandra screamed louder, pelting down the street toward its taillights. And the Mercedes stopped once more. The passenger door opened and a woman got out. Then the driver, another woman. They stood, hesitant, glancing uneasily across the roof of the car at one another, then at Cassandra; they stood firm, though, waiting for Cassandra.

Less than half an hour later, Sid Sokolowski called Alberg.

"I just talked to her, Karl. She's fine." He told Alberg where to find her. Vancouver police, he said, were on their way to pick up Gordon Murphy.

Alberg pulled over. He rested his forehead on the steering wheel. He was weak and trembling, from the relief that flooded through him.

He realized that he was only blocks from the address Sokolowski had given him. Only blocks from Cassandra.

Only blocks, too, from Gordon Murphy.

The son-of-a-bitch might get away, he told himself.

Gordon Murphy got off the bike, his heart pounding, and wiped sweat from his face and body. "You're gonna kill yourself with all this fitness shit," he said out loud, and gulped bottled water from the small refrigerator next to the bathroom.

How much time did he have until he could expect the cops back? How long does it take to get a warrant, anyway? They didn't have much. They had fuck-all, he told himself. Probably not enough to get a fucking warrant. So what should he do?

He tried to think. He positioned himself at the rowing machine and began to pull. Get rid of the wheelchair, probably, he thought, breathless. Though maybe not. He could tell them it was for his aged mother. He sputtered some laughter. His aged mother! Who wasn't aged and probably wasn't his mother — the world was filled with nothing but lies.

But what about the woman, what about the fucking woman, the woman who was supposed to be his life partner, his fucking other half —

Gordon turned. And stared. He stumbled to his feet. His brain must be short-circuiting. "How did you" — he was panting, his voice was harsh, like noises made by broken glass — "get in here?"

"The front door's open," said Alberg.

"Open?" He looked wildly behind Alberg into the basement.

"Yeah," said Alberg. The guy was drenched with sweat, dressed in shorts that offered a good view of his genitals and a T-shirt that practically didn't exist. His black hair dripped sweat, his grey chest hair was matted with it.

Gordon walked unsteadily to a bench that sat against the wall and picked up a towel. He dried himself with it. "You have her, I take it."

"She's gone," said Alberg, "yeah."

Gordon laughed. His laugh sounded as good as ever. He was getting himself back under control. His mind was working sharp and fast, like laser beams. He sat on the bench and looked him over — the Mountie. Pale. Blond. Clearly a man of little emotion. Gordon felt disinterested, gazing at him. "And what did she tell you went on here, between us?"

Alberg didn't reply.

Gordon Murphy tossed the towel onto the bench and walked toward Alberg, who stepped between him and the door. "Are you planning to arrest me?"

Alberg shook his head.

"Then what the fuck are you doing here?"

"I came to get a look at you. Before they take you away."

Gordon Murphy said, "Nobody's taking me anywhere, you idiot. Nobody's going to listen to the ravings of a hysterical middle-aged woman — "

Alberg couldn't take his eyes off the guy's teeth.

He argued with himself, halfheartedly.

Then — what the hell, he thought. I can always take early retirement.

And he nailed him, right in the mouth.

Chapter

29

Once the swords had appeared on Winnifred Gartner's porch, and Alistair McNeil had been admitted into her house, community interest dwindled. The crowd broke apart and began trickling away.

Alistair McNeil remained inside for several hours.

At dusk, lights were turned on, and Alistair and Winnifred and the two children could be seen through the living-room window: the children were sprawled on the carpet watching television, Alistair was on the sofa, and Winnifred sat straight and tall in an easy chair. Alistair was leaning forward, talking, and Winnifred was apparently listening to him.

Naomi, squinting in at them from her lawn chair, roused herself from a sullen silence. "It's time my kids had dinner. I want my damn kids! Just lookit them in there, ignoring us, for god's sake."

Jack Duggin thought it looked like a stage set. And the people looked like actors, too — Winnifred wearing a blue costume covered with a big orange birds, and Alistair in his olive coveralls. The constable was curious about what Alistair might be saying to Winnifred. He looked at the swords lying on the porch, and stared once more through Winnifred's living-room window. Then he went up the walk and pounded on the door.

Winnifred opened it and said, "I'm sorry for all the trouble."

Naomi bounded from the lawn chair, over the yellow tape and up onto the porch.

"You are not actually a bad mother," Winnifred said to her, as Tiffany and Walter ran into the hall. "You can take your kids. Or you can come in, if you want."

"Are you gonna get crazy and violent again?" said Naomi severely, pulling her children close to her. "Because I've had my fill of that in my damn life."

"No, no," said Winnifred, pressing a hand against her forehead. "It was just a — some kind of spasm. It's over now."

"It may be over, Winnifred," said Jack Duggin, "but you're going to have to come down to the detachment with me. There's paperwork from hell waiting for us there."

"I didn't mean to poke him," said Winnifred. "I only meant to threaten him."

"Yeah, well, that's illegal, too."

"Except it turned out that the asshole Keith was a wanted man," said Naomi, stroking Tiffany's hair. "That oughta make a difference."

The constable thought this over. "Maybe," he said, nodding.

Alistair McNeil emerged from around the corner. "I'll come with you."

Winnifred turned and looked at him gravely. "That won't be necessary." She picked up her handbag from the hall table. "I very much appreciate your kindness, and your advice. It's good advice, and I'll take it. But enough is enough. You fix those kids some supper," she said to Naomi, going out the door. "I'll phone you if they put me in jail. Will I be able to do that?" she asked Jack Duggin as they went down the walk toward his patrol car.

"We're not going to put you in jail, Winnifred."

"But if you do. I read that in Canada we don't necessarily get to make a phone call. Is that true?"

"I promise you Winnifred, I personally promise you," said

268

the constable, opening the car door, "that if we put you in jail, we'll let you make a phone call. Get in."

"Don't be silly. I'm not sitting in the front seat. I go in the back, behind the bars, with the doors that don't open from the inside. Because I'm a criminal."

"Winnifred. Get in."

"I don't know what came over me."

"I know, Winnifred. Hey. It's going to be okay."

"I really think you should put me in the back seat."

The constable leaned on the roof of the patrol car. "Earlier today," he said, "I picked up Ray Barfield. He was staggering along the highway, down by Davis Bay. Drunk as a skunk."

"Huh," said Winnifred disapprovingly.

"Put him in the back. I thought he might fall out, if I put him in the front."

Winnifred nodded.

"He threw up. Made a hell of a mess in there. And I haven't had a chance to clean it up real good yet." He grinned at her. "Hop in," he said, holding the front passenger door open wide.

So Winnifred got in.

"You're in trouble, aren't you?" said Cassandra the next day. "Because you hit him."

"What the hell." Alberg shrugged.

Gently, she touched his right hand. They were sitting side by side on the sofa, watching the summer afternoon through the living-room window. The hydrangeas were bursts of blue along the cedar fence. The front door was open, and the cats had arranged themselves across the threshold. "He's a madman, Karl." She prodded her psyche, cautiously. She didn't know yet how damaged it might be.

"I wanted to go in there on a horse," he said. "Or a motorcycle. Wearing the Red Serge." He tried to laugh. "Like Nelson Eddy. To rescue you."

She kissed the swollen knuckles. Hitting wouldn't have been enough for her. She wished she'd been able to wield the axe named Thunder against Gordon Murphy. Or at least shoot him dead with a gun.

"But you were already rescued," he said.

"Yes," said Cassandra, frowning. "That was pretty damn peculiar, wasn't it?"

"Apparently," said Isabella confidentially to Sid Sokolowski, "that old guy Dutton's got a case. You know. About us owing him rent."

"What?"

"Yeah. So I heard. His lawyer — "

"Stop. Don't." He backed toward the door. "I'm not listening to this. Save it for Karl. I'm going home."

"Sergeant — are you okay?"

"No." He rubbed his head and put his service cap on. "But maybe someday."

When he had gone, Isabella turned back to her computer screen.

A few minutes later she heard the door open and looked up. "Is that dog housebroken?" she said.

Ronnie Plankton laughed. "No, not yet. He's only twelve weeks old. But he just went, outside. I was wondering if I could see the person in charge."

"That'll be Corporal Michaelson, just at the moment," said Isabella.

She summoned Mike, who expressed interest in Ronnie's dog, because he was thinking of buying a pet for his five-year-old.

"He's a Labrador retriever," said Ronnie. "His name is Phoenix."

When they'd finished talking about dogs, Mike said, "Now, are you here to report a theft, by any chance?"

Ronnie, startled, said that he was not.

"Oh," said Mike, obviously disappointed. "Okay. What can I do for you, then?"

"I was wondering," said Ronnie, "if you could tell me how I go about applying to join the Mounties."

FOR THE BEST IN PAPERBACKS, LOOK FOR THE

In every corner of the world, on every subject under the sun, Penguin represents quality and variety—the very best in publishing today.

For complete information about books available from Penguin—including Puffins, Penguin Classics, and Arkana—and how to order them, write to us at the appropriate address below. Please note that for copyright reasons the selection of books varies from country to country.

In the United Kingdom: Please write to *Dept. JC, Penguin Books Ltd, FREEPOST, West Drayton, Middlesex UB7 0BR.*

If you have any difficulty in obtaining a title, please send your order with the correct money, plus ten percent for postage and packaging, to *P.O. Box No. 11, West Drayton, Middlesex UB7 0BR*

In the United States: Please write to *Consumer Sales, Penguin USA, P.O. Box 999, Dept. 17109, Bergenfield, New Jersey 07621-0120.* VISA and MasterCard holders call 1-800-253-6476 to order all Penguin titles

In Canada: Please write to *Penguin Books Canada Ltd, 10 Alcorn Avenue, Suite 300, Toronto, Ontario M4V 3B2*

In Australia: Please write to *Penguin Books Australia Ltd, P.O. Box 257, Ringwood, Victoria 3134*

In New Zealand: Please write to *Penguin Books (NZ) Ltd, Private Bag 102902, North Shore Mail Centre, Auckland 10*

In India: Please write to *Penguin Books India Pvt Ltd, 706 Eros Apartments, 56 Nehru Place, New Delhi 110 019*

In the Netherlands: Please write to *Penguin Books Netherlands bv, Postbus 3507, NL-1001 AH Amsterdam*

In Germany: Please write to *Penguin Books Deutschland GmbH, Metzlerstrasse 26, 60594 Frankfurt am Main*

In Spain: Please write to *Penguin Books S. A., Bravo Murillo 19, 1° B, 28015 Madrid*

In Italy: Please write to *Penguin Italia s.r.l., Via Felice Casati 20, I-20124 Milano*

In France: Please write to *Penguin France S. A., 17 rue Lejeune, F–31000 Toulouse*

In Japan: Please write to *Penguin Books Japan, Ishikiribashi Building, 2–5–4, Suido, Bunkyo-ku, Tokyo 112*

In Greece: Please write to *Penguin Hellas Ltd, Dimocritou 3, GR–106 71 Athens*

In South Africa: Please write to *Longman Penguin Southern Africa (Pty) Ltd, Private Bag X08, Bertsham 2013*